# A SUMMER AFFAIR

# A SUMMER AFFAIR
## Ivan Klíma

*Translated from the Czech*
*by Ewald Osers*

Chatto & Windus

LONDON

Published in 1987 by
Chatto & Windus Ltd
30 Bedford Square
London WC1B 3RP

Czech title *Milostné Léto*
Originally published in Czech by Sixty-Eight Publishers, Toronto, in 1979
Revised edition first published in 1985

British Library Cataloguing in Publication Data

Klíma, Ivan
A summer affair
I. Title   II. Osers, Ewald   III. Milostné
léto. *English*
891.8'635[F]      PG5038.K5

ISBN 0 7011 3140 3

Typeset by Wyvern Typesetting Ltd, Bristol
Printed in Great Britain by
Redwood Burn Ltd,
Trowbridge, Wiltshire

[ 1 ]

# CHAPTER ONE

1

He was walking downstairs to the laundry. It was dark there and now and again he had to probe with his foot, and that irritated him because, as usual, he was in a hurry. Then his hand found the switch and he turned on the light. The mice were sitting in their cages and flashing their huge incisors.

'They've grown again, David,' a young man in a white overall informed him. In spite of the young man's dark glasses he recognized him reliably as his assistant Mencl. 'Real monsters they are!' He seemed nervous, as usual.

'That's okay. I don't mind them growing so long as they're alive. Better be huge than not be at all.'

'It's not natural!' his mother spoke up. She was sitting there in a wine-red dress with white lace on what looked like a school bench or perhaps a church pew. 'Can't you see that it is against God's will?'

'Leave the boy alone!' his father shouted at her. 'He's got to start somehow. Let's see what he achieves.'

'David,' his mother insisted, 'why are you doing this when you know that you're hurting me?' She was pale, she had changed so much he scarcely recognized her.

'I'm doing it for you, too, Mother. I don't want to lose you a second time.' He instantly realized that he'd said something he shouldn't have said, but before he could put it right he felt something warm licking the nape of his neck.

'Don't turn round, David!' his mother shouted.

But already he'd seen the animal; it had evidently gnawed through the wire of its cage, he could feel its hot breath on his forehead and he saw its huge front teeth at close range.

'Pray, David!' he heard his mother's voice.

He opened his eyes.

'David,' he recognized his wife's voice; 'you told me to wake you. You said you'd get up a little earlier if I didn't feel like it.'

'That's all right.' He sat up and tried to dispel the unpleasant sensation left in him by his dream. 'Quite all right.' He looked at her pale, eternally tired and now even sallow face and didn't feel the slightest touch of affection, only irritation that she was ill and thereby causing him extra work. 'How are you feeling?'

'I think I'm feeling better. I'll go for my check-up tomorrow.'

'Go back to sleep then!'

He went to the bathroom, did a few knee-bends from force of habit, although he'd make up for the rest of his morning exercises by running down to the cellar for coal (their two north-facing rooms needed heating until mid-May). He dressed, trying not to look at his face in the mirror. His sense of unease persisted. It didn't stem from his dream alone, or even from the fact that his wife had been ill for two weeks now and the whole weight of domestic chores lay on his shoulders. For some time he'd been waking up with a sense of emptiness, he couldn't think of a reason why he should get up, or why it was necessary to live.

As a rule he brushed the feeling aside. He was too busy to afford to indulge in such feelings. His work hadn't been going well lately; maybe that was the source of his depression.

He loved his work, he could spend whole nights at the laboratory, but when he had to push large buttons through those illogically small buttonholes in his daughter's cardigan he felt he was wasting his valuable time. 'Can't you at least brush your own hair?' It sounded so hostile that Margit burst into tears. She was four, and by contrast to her older sister she was quiet, even cowed. Only when he came home from work did she rush up to him with loud cries and demand that he should hug her – something Anna would be too proud to do.

'Mum does her hair,' Anna announced.

'And where the hell is that comb then?'

'Mum uses a hairbrush.'

'Mum can use what she likes,' he snapped, and Anna withdrew to the table, offended.

'You can get up from there and find me the comb at once!'

'Ow, Daddy, that hurts!'

Camilla appeared in the doorway. 'Don't be so rough with her, David.'

'Not my fault she's got such stupid hair. When was it last cut?'

'She's got perfectly normal hair. You're irritable because you haven't had enough sleep.'

'And how can I have enough sleep when I haven't got the time?'

'At least you realize what it's like for me.' She'd put on a yellow dressing gown in the bathroom, one he'd given her shortly after they were married. It was one of the few presents he'd ever given her and it didn't suit her at all.

When he'd bought it for her she was still dyeing her hair black, and he'd liked her then. But once the children were born she no longer had much time to care for her appearance. He realized that he hadn't been able to give her an easy life. But what could he do? If he wanted to earn enough for his wife to stay at home he'd have to change his job: he'd have to become a waiter, a motor mechanic, a bad journalist, a pop singer, a bricklayer or a dishonest

9

supermarket manager. But he was only a biologist and no one had the slightest interest in making life easier for him, let alone for his wife. On the contrary, they made him feel that his work was a kind of tolerated luxury (one graduate assistant, two laboratory assistants and a shared secretary for something as useless as research into ageing almost exceeded the financial means of his institute). It was odd that people were prepared to pay much more for their death, for their oppression, for their stultification than for their lives.

'Leave the washing up,' his wife said. 'I'll do it. Are you taking Margit to kindergarten?'

'Of course.' He looked out of the window. Above the roof of the villa opposite black clouds were scurrying. The little street outside yawned with emptiness, the grey dust-bins stood in their place, and their car, the only luxury in their lives (a red Renault bought second-hand for sixteen months' salary) was parked outside the low fence. The garden gate was swinging open and shut, creaking, in the gusts of wind. He was surprised that their landlady, who so carefully guarded her former property, should have left the gate unlocked, and indeed open, all night, and suddenly he realized that for several days he hadn't heard any shouting from that lonely, embittered and long expropriated member of the propertied class.

'Listen,' he said to Anna who was hanging about in the hall, 'when did you last see Mrs Svobodová?'

'That old witch?'

The moment he uttered her name he regretted the question. She had probably gone away somewhere, and he had enough worries of his own without concerning himself about her.

'I don't know. Why do you want to know, Dad?'

'No particular reason.' He helped her on with her satchel.

10

His wife was waiting in the doorway. 'You've been so good to me; all week you've looked after me and the children.' She watched Margit put on her little coat. 'It's strangely quiet here when you've gone.'

'What do you mean: strangely?'

'I didn't want to bother you with it, but seeing that you've noticed it yourself – for a number of days now there's been no movement at all upstairs.'

'She's probably gone away.' He really didn't have the time or the inclination to bother about it.

'Suppose she's lying there.'

'Who's lying where?'

Silence. She looked at him with anxious, vulnerable eyes. She always looked at him like that when she was ill or tired or afraid of something: a spider, war, the children, or losing her job.

'Stop worrying about it,' he said. 'You can call the police if you think something's happened to her.' He kissed her hurriedly.

'Do you love me?'

'Course I do.'

'But you love your dogs more. Even your mice!'

'For heaven's sake.' He felt like screaming at her. It wasn't his fault she didn't like her job, her depressing and humiliating job teaching school. But he controlled himself. After all, she was ill and he was in a hurry.

'I'll ring you,' he promised, took Margit by the hand and walked out.


2


The board meeting at the institute started at half past eight. Although he regarded all such meetings as a waste of time he invariably attended them because the director wanted to see all his staff once a week, and because he had learned during his student days that the best way to preserve one's inner independence in this society was to forego it in outward matters. Needless to say he was late because Margit had got her shoelaces in a knot and it had taken him ten minutes to disentangle them at the kindergarten, plus another ten minutes for her to stop crying after he had inadvisedly slapped her.

At the secretariat the scene resembled a bar: wine glasses (evidently from the previous evening), a transistor playing soulful music, and Maria, who he had reckoned should have finished typing his report, drinking coffee with the other Maria from the laboratory. A quick glance told him that of the thirty pages of his report a mere eight lines had been typed out. In such conditions and with such people you could have tea parties and political demonstrations but you couldn't get any real work done. But if he criticized her she would be offended and talk behind his back, and he'd get the reputation of being an anti-social person.

'I thought,' his secretary spoke up, 'you'd go straight to the meeting, David.' The radio had been silenced and the second Maria had slipped out behind his back. Anyway, he already had the reputation of being anti-social because he didn't gossip or drink with the others. 'Milan's gone to stand in for you.'

That was what irritated him. Everybody on first-name terms, not because they were friends or had anything in common but because they regarded each other as fellow-conspirators in a common endeavour to fiddle their way through life.

'Of course the mail hasn't come yet.' It was the only criticism he felt like making.

When he opened the door of the conference room he noticed that Dr Strong, the director (everybody called him the Strong Old Man although he was barely forty), was holding forth, and his graduate assistant Mencl really was in David's own place. As they changed places Mencl whispered to him, 'Just spouting off.' It was a trivial piece of information, and really more like a sigh. He observed that nobody was listening (they all had that look of concentration which conceals total absent-mindedness) and he opened his note-pad. Instantly he felt in a different world, in the world he loved above all else, even though its reality was mostly wearingly monotonous and was forever posing the same questions – questions which he at least tried to hear correctly even if he couldn't answer them.

What was the real relation between the body's defensive system and the length of life? Didn't the fact that the thymus survived only until the phase of sexual maturity limit that maturity itself, the life of an animal or human being? Wasn't the predetermined number of cell divisions in the thymus and in related tissues in itself an irrevocable and, for the time being, immovable threshold of death? And wasn't therefore any attempt to prolong life once a person had reached sexual maturity a hopeless endeavour? Surely from the moment that man had fulfilled his task for the preservation of the species he was surviving only artificially, the defences of his tissues were weakening from day to day, until one day, no matter how far it was pushed into the future, he must reach the threshold behind which death was waiting.

On the whole man survived without hope of survival. But if the function of the thymus could be prolonged, if the organism continued to be young, then it would react as a living thing and man's life might be prolonged to a multiple of its present span. That had been his research task for a number of years. And for its solution he had one graduate assistant, two laboratory assistants and a secretary shared with the General Immunology Department, as well as a few dozen mice and the right to order eight or ten foreign-language books (of which they disallowed half) each year, to be paid for in hard currency. The solution, of course, was in the distant future, even though he devoted all his time to it and all his energy, so that lately he'd been feeling depressed, feeling that he was no more than an alchemist dreaming of discovering the elixir of life. That depression he chased away by ever more furious work. At such moments he found it almost unbearable to have to waste time by listening to non-information and vacuous noise.

Camilla had once persuaded him to read a novel. In it the hero was constantly writing letters to his cat. This theme stuck in his mind and became a symbol of a pointless waste of time. But any activity that would permit a person to formulate his thoughts would be more useful than sitting in this conference room, where, no matter how hard one tried, all one's ideas died in the brain. If only he didn't have so much work. But there was a pile of unread journals and research papers on his desk. And they'd be bringing the mice round today to be weighed. Just then he caught sight of Maria in the door of the conference room, beckoning to him urgently to come out into the corridor.

'That letter from London has come,' she announced the moment he shut the door behind him. She typed most of his correspondence and therefore knew that he was waiting for an invitation to give some lectures in London. She passed him the envelope. It was probably not the right thing to open it there in the corridor or in front of her, but he was unable to control his impatience.

In the letter (with the letterhead of University College, London) the Head of the Department informed him that he would be pleased to welcome him among his staff, starting in September of that year. As for the subject of his lectures to the students, he was leaving that entirely to him, but he would like to count on his collaboration with his own team working on ageing. A few polite sentences followed which he didn't bother to take in. Signed: Alex Ford.

He folded the sheet and returned it to its envelope. 'That's all right then,' he said, and his systematic mind was already composing his answer and outlining the subjects for his lectures. He would get his lectures ready before leaving because his time there would be enormously precious. If he left on the last day of August, or better still the last-but-one (they'd need a day to settle in), he'd have 132 days left, and if he gave thirty-five lectures he'd have exactly four days (exactly, without remainder) to get each lecture together – not much, but he'd manage.

Maria was still waiting. It occurred to him that he should now fish out a fifty-crown note and send her off to buy two bottles of wine for them to drink with the others from the department (Mencl and the two girl laboratory assistants) to celebrate his good news. But he didn't like drinking and he didn't like wasting time on any kind of celebration. Besides, he begrudged the fifty crowns which might be spent on something much more sensible. With a slightly embarrassed smile he said, 'This is excellent news,' and returned to the detested conference room – but now with the hope of an early and prolonged escape.

3

That same afternoon he made time to go to the Foreign Department of the Academy and complete half a dozen prescribed forms; he even managed to make the last half hour of a department meeting at the university. At half past five, after he'd twice tried vainly to phone home to keep his promise, he left the university, dog-tired after a nearly twelve-hour day but in exceptionally good spirits. He bought some bread, cheese and a bottle of blackcurrant juice, and as he was leaving the supermarket he noticed to his surprise that right next door was a small florist's shop.

Perhaps it hadn't been there long, or else he'd simply never noticed it – flowers were not one of the things that captured his interest. But today he needed to do something out of the ordinary. (How would Camilla react to the news? He'd promised her that trip so often, a flat in a red-brick detached house in Hampstead, that she'd begun to regard it all as a fairy tale.) From behind a curtain, decorated solely by an aura of heavy though invisible aromas, an assistant appeared. Her bespectacled, almost touchingly plain, features were made hideous by a purplish rash. She smoothed her short hair with a hurried gesture. Almost as if behind that curtain there was a small bed from which she'd just arisen.

He had to overcome his embarrassment. He was seized by the curious idea that only lovers and lunatics ever entered florists' shops: 'I'd like some cut flowers, for my wife.'

'And what is it to be?' She had a deep, almost boyish, voice – assuming that she wasn't actually a boy with feminine features.

His eyes wandered around the patches of colour until they fastened on some narcissi (his mother's favourite flowers). 'How much are they, each?' At once he felt ashamed of his question and, without waiting for an answer, said, 'Let me have four of them.'

She pulled out four blooms. Now that they were lying on her open hand they looked pitifully lonely, and he corrected himself: 'No, let me have seven instead.'

'Would you like me to add some birch twigs or asparagus fern?'

'Perhaps. You know best.'

From another vase she took a few green twigs and quickly arranged a bouquet. 'Your wife will be pleased with these,' she said while she was working on it. 'I've chosen fresh ones for you, to make sure they'll keep.'

It was a girl after all, and the thought struck him that,

16

though she lived among flowers all day long, she had probably never been given flowers by anyone. Who would give flowers to such a plain girl, especially one who worked in a flower shop?

'Thirteen crowns.' She handed him the bouquet wrapped in tissue paper. He only had a fifty-crown note. It wasn't a great deal of money and he might have said to her: And another bunch like that for yourself! He gave her the banknote and watched her rummaging in her till. He'd probably embarrass her.

The girl said, 'Thank you. Come again soon,' and handed him his change. Before disappearing behind her curtain she flashed him a smile.

With his flowers, the bottle of juice, the bread, the cheese and his good news he opened the front door. Children's feet rushed up to meet him. 'Dad, d'you know what's happened?'

'Dad, the police have been here!'

Camilla appeared from the bedroom in the terrible yellow dressing gown he'd condemned her to. 'Why didn't you ring?' she asked reproachfully. 'I needed you so much.'

'I did ring, but it was constantly engaged.'

'That was the cops telephoning,' Anna announced.

'Daddy, the old woman's dead. She's lying there – killed!'

'Not killed, she only died,' Anna corrected her.

'What's been happening here?'

'They found her upstairs. She'd been lying there all this time.' Camilla took the flowers from him. 'You got these? Whatever possessed you? Or did somebody give them to you?'

'They climbed up a ladder,' Anna shouted. 'Come and look, Dad!'

'They're for you,' he said and let his daughter drag him

to the balcony, where a long rickety ladder was still leaning against the sill of the window above. 'So what have they done with her?' he asked in a matter-of-fact way.

'She's still there,' his wife said softly. 'They won't take her away till just before midnight.'

'The ravens!' his daughter exclaimed. 'They said the ravens would come round later!'

'Fly round, I suppose.'

'How can you talk like that,' his wife shouted at him.

'No, no,' his daughter explained to him, 'that's only what they call the funeral people.'

'Just imagine,' Camilla said in a plaintive voice, 'she was lying up there all that time. And down here we laughed, and ate . . .'

'Don't keep thinking about it. When a person's dead he doesn't mind what's happening around him.'

'But the living should mind.'

He glanced up at the top-floor window on which the rays of the setting sun glowed red. He didn't want to talk about the dead woman or reflect on the hopelessness of human destiny; he turned on his heel and went into the kitchen to get the supper.

It was ten o'clock by the time he succeeded in putting Anna to sleep; she was afraid of the ravens and at the same time wanted to stay up till they arrived. Himself, he felt in the grip of a depression which seemed to have settled in that room, and he went into the only other room in their apartment. Camilla was already in bed but she was not asleep. 'Come to me.'

'I thought,' he objected from force of habit, 'that I'd do some reading. I haven't had any time for myself all day and I brought a pile home with me.'

'Today I want you to be with me.' When he lay down beside her she whispered, 'Listen. Sounds like somebody walking.'

He listened in the sudden absolute silence, but he couldn't hear anything. 'I haven't even had time to tell you,' he took the plunge, 'they've invited me. Ford's inviting us to London.'

She made no answer.

'For a year.'

'Oh,' she breathed. 'And you want to go?'

He was so used to her accepting his destiny, his goals and his ambitions as her own that her question dumbfounded him.

'It's a unique opportunity. At long last I'll have the things I need and the peace to work.'

'Yes, I can believe that.'

'Also I'll have five times my present salary.'

'Yes. But don't talk about it now.'

'Why not now?'

She pointed to the ceiling. 'Just imagine, as they were climbing in through the window they stepped on her. Apparently she was covered up to her neck. She has – she had – her bed by the window.'

'Don't keep thinking about it,' he said almost angrily. 'She was a stranger to us who'd never helped us one bit. None of us. Except that she built this house.'

'You oughtn't to talk like this. Everybody does some good.'

Just then a door slammed noisily somewhere below and footsteps came clattering up the stairs.

'They're here.' She pressed herself to him and he could feel her trembling. Footfalls sounded above their heads, then something heavy was set down on the floor. With his ears he followed their invisible work. Now they were lifting the body, a soft rustle, then the coffin lid came down.

She had never allowed them into the garden. The garden was full of fruit trees, the fruit was ripening below his window, then the over-ripe fruit dropped into the grass, and she no longer had the strength to pick the fruit but she was too greedy and too malicious to let anyone else have it. Now the house would probably go to the state, together with the garden, and the garden would be open to the tenants. Upstairs a door slammed again and strange footsteps sounded heavily above their heads. Then the steps moved down the stairs, closer and closer, as if they were making straight for them, as if the men had mistaken their way and were making for their front door and their bed. Just then there were a few frightened and confused steps, someone shouted something, and something heavy crashed to the ground with repeated noisy bumps.

His wife screamed at his side. He jumped out of bed and ran to the front door. But there was nothing to be seen on the landing; on the floor below them the footsteps were fading away. He looked out of the kitchen window and saw a large, dimly lit vehicle outside. Three men were coming out of the villa's front door, three 'ravens' with their heavy oblong burden. Their faces could not be made out from the first-floor window, nor even their clothes. For all he knew their wings were neatly folded away under their black overcoats.

The back of the vehicle was suddenly opened as if by some invisible hand and the three men bent their knees to slide the coffin into the hearse.

'David, where are you? What are you doing?'

The coffin somehow got stuck, the door couldn't be closed. One of the men climbed inside, into the space reserved for the dead and tugged at the coffin.

'David, come here.'

There was the sound of an engine and the hearse disappeared behind the trees.

'David, I'm afraid.'

He lay down close to her and put his arms around her.

'That's better. But those poor children are on their own.'

'The children are asleep.'

'Shouldn't I go in and have a look?'

'No. You settle down.'

'I don't know.' She sighed. 'What was that frightful noise just then?'

'Probably tripped up – I expect the one at the back – and dropped the coffin.'

'That's terrible.'

'Dropping a living person would be much more terrible.'

'How can you talk so cynically?'

He was silent. He didn't like it when she reproached him or mistook him for one of her schoolchildren.

It must be midnight by now, and he hadn't done anything that evening except a lot of housework, including finding a somewhat battered vase at the back of the sideboard, behind a pile of wine-red special-occasion plates. He now turned to look at it: the flowers were slowly wilting in the vase on the window sill, they were a darkish grey in the moonlight, and he felt sorry at the thought of these uselessly picked flowers which nobody was taking any notice of, and for an instant he was overcome by the pointlessness of existence. The old woman who was now being ferried across the Styx in a black sailing boat had been saving for dozens of years to build this house, and over that period she had turned into a vicious hateful creature who'd been denied all joy, even the joy of owning a house. Now the house was standing there, he could almost see it towering in the darkness with two pointless little angels by the entrance. The house was there but she would never again set foot in it, and he was lying in that house, holding his wife in his arms, and with every breath they were both drawing nearer to that same river the old woman was now crossing. Suddenly he remembered something: 'Do you know that when I was a little boy I believed I was immortal?'

She jerked away. 'You've always thought of yourself as a god.'

'No, it's not that; my mother told me. When my grand-father died in Vrchlabí I asked her, the way children do, whether she would die too. She said she would. This troubled me. I couldn't imagine her dying when she was so young and beautiful. And then it occurred to me that if she could die then I could too. I asked her but she said: "No, not you, you'll never die."'

'And you believed it?'

'Yes. I believed it because she said so.'

'Surely,' she whispered, 'she was a goddess to you too.'

'What mother isn't?' He refused to argue with her. 'When you're seven years old?'

He was yearning for the time when he believed in his own immortality

He lay motionless, gazing out through the glass door. The ladder, illumined now by the moonlight, was still standing propped up against the wall. He could only see part of it, a few rungs, and as he was sinking into sleep it struck him that they were leading up to the gallows.

4

Rather than having regarded his mother as a goddess he'd regarded her as a queen. When she wore her red dress with the white lace at the throat, when on her slim wrist she put the gold bangle in the shape of a serpent with a garnet eye (frightening idea that the serpent would come to life, stretch its head to the exact spot where his mother's pulse artery was and bite through it), when she piled her hair on top, emphasizing her high forehead, she seemed to him like Queen Genevieve. (For a long time he'd prided himself on having inherited her hands, her long slender

22

fingers and the colour of her hair.)

His mother had graduated from the conservatoire. In her room, above the polished grand piano, hung two framed posters: the first was of her graduation recital and the other announced a concert at London's Wigmore Hall. But the recital in London had not materialized because just then he'd appeared on the scene, still nameless, confining his mother to her bed.

He felt sure she'd never stopped regretting that her most important engagement had failed to come off. Maybe her life would have taken a different turn altogether, and so, whenever the subject had come up, he had always felt a sense of loss and an illogical feeling of guilt which he knew he ought somehow to redeem.

One day when I'm rich and famous, he used to dream, I'll hire the biggest concert hall for her and she'll sing for the Queen of England, and we'll drive in a carriage through Kensington Gardens. People would be crowding the pavements and throwing her flowers.

At the time he was remembering his mother no longer sang. Except for herself or for the guests who would sometimes come to their house, but less and less frequently because quite soon – he was barely eight at the time – the Occupation began and shortly afterwards the war, and guests stopped coming. He never understood why his mother had given up singing, maybe because his father had wanted her to out of fear for her health, or else because he didn't want her to be away from home so much, and used her health as an excuse.

One of his mother's ancestors, five generations back, had been a leading figure in the National Revival movement and his name could actually be found in all the school textbooks. Even though these Revival figures were mostly poor people and hard-working self-taught men, who made up for their lack of education by a surplus of enthusiasm,

23

the fact that in a nation where nobody had noble ancestors his mother was descended from a universally acknowledged and respected family was a factor in making him see her as a noblewoman among commoners. Moreover, she did not as a rule participate in the activities by which the mothers of his contemporaries shared time with their children: she did not cook for him (his meals were prepared by a maid), nor did she even sit at table with him. In the morning, when he left for school, she would still be asleep, at midday she wouldn't be at home but out lunching somewhere with his father, and in the evening she would always have her meal later than he did. She did not take him out for walks – that, too, was left to the maid – and for his holidays he'd usually go to his father's father, who was a doctor in the foothills of the Giant Mountains, in a small town that was practically all German. Even when on one occasion he'd been really ill, with pneumonia, he was looked after by a hurriedly hired nurse.

On Sundays his mother would sometimes take him along to church. Probably because she had no one else to go with; his father was far removed from anything transcendental and considered any concern with anything not of this earth, with anything that could not be grasped and put to use, as a waste of time. When he was still small he got a lot of pleasure out of being there by her side, substituting for his father as it were; and time and again, whenever the organ notes swelled and she began to sing, the knowledge that he belonged to that glorious voice, to the woman whom others turned their heads to see, filled him with satisfaction and pride. But as he grew up – he was barely sixteen then but he'd read most of his father's books and he thought he knew all that was necessary about the universe and the human body and heredity and the composition of matter – he realized, without any horror or shock, that there was no immortality and no redemption

24

and no damnation. (How could individuals be saved if they'd died at the epicentre of an atomic explosion, how could the human soul or anything human survive the heat that melted rocks?) Nor was there any God in the shape in which he was being invoked. Was it conceivable that he who, on the Cross, had so painfully and desperately called upon his father, had created the nebula of the Hounds, the Milky Way, that vast amount of matter, was it possible that he could bridge those distances of time and space which humans could not even imagine? That was when he began to dislike his Sunday mornings. Yet he dared not turn his displeasure against his mother (in his mind he made excuses for her: church was the last place where she could still sing in front of other people); he turned it against everybody and everything else in church. He took a violent dislike to the fat little baroque angels, the upturned eyes of the saints in the pictures, the insinuating voice of the priest, the smell of incense. But his strongest dislike was focused on a fat old woman who somehow always managed to be close to him: smelly, with bare swollen feet stuck in black, usually dirty, lace-up boots. Although crippled by rheumatism, so that any unnecessary violent movement must have given her pain, she would fling herself to the floor in unbelievable ecstasy so that her forehead touched the stone, and in so doing she revealed a pair of pale fat calves. His mother, on his other side, would merely hint at a genuflection, reluctantly touching the floor with one knee and slightly and gently bowing her head to show a little of her magnificent nape. One day he had determined on action and had taken a white mouse with him in his pocket (he kept mice in a small room in the cellar, next to the laundry, to the displeasure of all the women in the house but with the approval of his father), and when everybody knelt down for the benediction he'd slipped the mouse, with an inconspicuous but careful gesture, into the gap between the calves which stuck in those dirty old boots.

That was the last time his father had boxed his ears (he didn't understand why he'd done this, why he'd been so angry since he didn't believe in God himself and should therefore have sided with him) and his mother had not spoken to him for several weeks. But after that he didn't have to, or wasn't allowed to, accompany her ever again to church on Sundays, and he never again watched her delicate hint of a genuflection, so perfect and so noble.

When he was a little boy – he remembered that too – and he would lie in his darkened room in the evening, with his eyes open, his mother would sometimes come in. She'd sit on a chair by his bed and ask him if he'd said his prayers. He would answer that he had. Then she'd ask him whom he'd prayed for and he'd answer that he'd prayed for all good people, also for her and for Father, and for those who were suffering and for those who didn't believe, and for those who were dying. His mother would approve and sometimes add a few sentences or reproofs: she'd heard that he was eating badly, that he hadn't done his homework well, that he hadn't been washing his hands, that he hadn't tidied his satchel, that he hadn't said good morning to the neighbour. Then she'd talk in her beautiful contralto voice about what he should be like so that she could love him and so that others would love him, that they would respect him as they now respected his father, and though he was happy to have her near him, he didn't take in the meaning of her words which demanded that he should be truthful, God-fearing, self-sacrificing, hard-working, honourable, that he should think not of himself but of others – he only took in the colour of her voice and her perfume, the artificial violet or lilac of those exquisite scents that enveloped her body, and he wished that the moments when she stayed by him and talked to him would continue as long as possible, he wished for her to remain near him so he could be sure she loved him. He would try to detain her by haltingly telling her something about school or about his mice, even though he realized that his classmates did not interest her and his mice revolted her, and that all his stories would merely accelerate her departure. But although he continued for a long time to believe in her perfection, and even though later on he still tried to gain her favour – with the first money that he earned, while still a student, he had bought her flowers – he realized at the same time that they were passing each other by, that they had never felt any real love for each other.

Maybe he'd fallen in love with his wife for the very reason that she did not remind him in any way of his mother. There was nothing exceptional in her appearance and no militancy in her mental make-up. The world of the arts had, happily, never touched her at all.

# CHAPTER TWO

1

On his way to the institute David stopped at the hospital. There, as a white board by the entrance announced, his father had reigned over the surgical department for the past twenty-five years. The son had no special reason to visit his father. But both of them preferred to see each other like this, at their work and during the day, whereas mutual visiting would take up an entire evening each time, and the two would not have any more to say to each other. (Moreover, David didn't feel too happy in his father's flat, where, shortly after his mother's death, young women, or even girls, began to appear and act as if they were at home.)

His father was sitting in his study, surrounded on all sides by a multitude of books, papers and flowers. (The flowers came from grateful patients, male and female, alongside other more substantial presents which, to David's discomfiture, his father accepted.) His large head still had a good thatch of hair and his broad bearded face had remained virtually unchanged throughout the years he could remember, just as if time could not touch it.

'So at last they've delivered that X-ray machine I told you about,' his father announced as soon as they'd greeted each other, just as if they'd last talked about it at breakfast. 'A marvellous machine – want to see it?'

They stepped out of the building and walked between lawns.

'Camilla's told me,' his father remembered, 'that you want to go abroad at the end of August. Why wait till then?'

'I need time to get my lectures together.'

'I don't know,' his father said doubtfully, 'if I were in your place I'd leave as soon as possible. That kind of opportunity should never be postponed.'

'I've no intention of postponing it.'

'You know, I was supposed to go there too. Before the war that was, I was barely forty then. At that age you can still make a fresh start, but I postponed it because of Mother, until eventually I got stuck here – for good. You're just about the age when one can start afresh.'

'But surely I don't want to stay there,' he said in surprise.

'You never know,' his father declared categorically. 'Maybe you'll get better offers once you're there. It's your duty to go wherever you can achieve most. To tell the truth,' he reverted to one of the unanswered questions of his life, 'I don't know why Mother was so reluctant to go – after all she was such an Anglophile and always wanted to visit England.'

'Maybe she didn't want to leave her country because of her ancestors.'

'No, ancestors are no reason for a woman. More likely to have hesitated because of her dressmaker, who she wouldn't be able to see there, or because we couldn't take the grand piano with us. But I think it was from spite. Because she hadn't been able to go there that time when she wanted to, when she was to give her recital. Maybe she was afraid to go there seeing how the first time went wrong. You know yourself how superstitious she was.' He liked talking to David about his mother, probably because he was the only person with whom he could talk about her.

'Camilla will come with me wherever we may have to go.'

'I'm pleased this has come off for you. I think you'll achieve something there. How old are you actually?'

'Nearly thirty-six,' he said in surprise.

'High time you did something. Otherwise you'll be dissatisfied. A man's got to achieve something. It's because he can't bear children.'

Yes, thought David, but why is he telling me? All my life he's been giving me this sort of pep-talk, just as if I were shirking work or had made up my mind to accomplish nothing in my life.

They entered a low building, where everything still smelled of chemical paint and rubber. 'Nowadays everything's a race against time,' his father pronounced. 'Here they haven't cottoned on to it yet, they've still not caught the rhythm of our age because they're prisoners of their hundred-year-old ideas. If you miss your moment too then you'll remain outside – just like them.'

They walked through a door marked DO NOT ENTER. 'Just look,' his father urged him. 'Isn't she a beauty?'

They entered the control room, where David saw the familiar panel. His father began to explain the instrument's various functions; he belonged to a generation that was still fascinated by technology. He still took a delight in comparing modern equipment with its primitive ancestors, the ones he'd used in his younger years, and that comparison gave him pleasure and convinced him of the (basically) rational development of the world.

'How about me taking a picture of you?' Though his father's suggestion was made as a joke he was at the same time ready and willing to take a picture of his son's insides. It was one of those small services he was always ready to perform for him. From childhood on he'd always made sure his son's body was receiving a regular supply of vitamins, the necessary amount of exercise, fresh air and sleep. David could not remember his father devoting himself to him in any other way, ever playing with him, let alone telling him stories; he'd been too remote, most of his day had been spent at the hospital or in the lecture theatre, in the evenings he'd sit in his study and often, as David remembered, the telephone would ring at night and his father would get up hurriedly and drive off. In spite of all this he had accepted his father's view of life. That view was essentially simple or at least simplifiable into a few straightforward principles: it was man's duty to work, and it was work that lent meaning to all activities. Success in work set the crown upon a man's life. The world and mankind were steadily moving towards a higher degree of perfection, and this was attained by deeper understanding, and that in turn was getting more difficult from year to year, demanding ever greater efforts and self-sacrifice. His father assessed people according to their readiness to make that effort.

'No, thank you,' he said to his father. 'I had an X-ray not so long ago.'

At that moment, in the emptiness of a room where so far no one held sway, where no one had yet made coffee and where there was still not even a notice on the door saying BACK SHORTLY, the telephone started to ring. He looked about himself in alarm, trying to discover the source of the sound, but his father swiftly picked up the receiver. 'It's for you. It's Camilla.'

Although he was not easily frightened, the fact that the telephone had rung for him in a room where presumably no telephone had rung before, seemed to him so fatefully urgent that his fingers shook as he took the receiver from his father. 'It's me. What's happened?'

'I'm sorry, David,' her voice sounded neither desperate nor plaintive, and that calmed him, 'I thought you might be at Dad's and so I . . .'

'What is it?' With an effort he suppressed his annoyance at having been so frightened a moment before.

'David, I've just found out, can you imagine, that her

funeral is today. Mrs Svobodová,' she hurriedly added. 'At
2 pm, at our cemetery, and it's our day for seeing parents.'

'So what?'

'I can't go, David. I wanted to go but I can't. Lots of
parents are coming to see me.'

'Okay, so you aren't going. There's no need for you to
go anyway. It's not as if she was a relation or something so
you had an obligation to go to her funeral.'

'But we lived in the same house. She built that house.'

'Those rooms are like an ice-box,' he snapped angrily.
'I'm living for the day when we can get out of them.'

'But we live there, Margit was born there, and she is . . .
she was all alone. Just imagine, maybe no one's going to
her funeral.'

'For one thing, she won't care now. For another, if she
hadn't been so vicious and rude to everybody who crossed
her path, including us . . .'

'David,' she interrupted him, 'I wanted to ask you, I
know you don't like funerals and you've got a lot of work,
but you should make an exception for once . . .'

'Listen, if you're so set on going to that funeral then go
yourself. The parents won't throw tantrums.'

'I can't, David! Please. If you won't do it for her sake do
it at least for mine. Do it for me.'

'But I've got work to do too.'

'But you can manage it, David. After all, it's an exception
and you don't have to get anybody's permission.'

'For God's sake, what's got into you?'

'Please, I'm asking you to do it for me.'

'What time did you say it was?' He surrendered.

'At two. I knew you'd understand. And please, if you
could get some flowers, it doesn't have to be a wreath or
anything.' She was talking rapidly. 'Just so she has at least
one little flower.'

'You're so sentimental it makes me sick,' he said angrily.

'If she were still alive she'd laugh at you and that little flower.'

'That's beside the point, we won't hear from her again. It's right to say goodbye to a person . . . who . . . when it's for the last time. Whatever they were like.' She seemed to be waiting for him to say something. Now that she'd got her way she was worried that she'd irritated him, but he hung up without a word.

2

It was just beginning to rain when, a few minutes after two, he hastened up to the cemetery gate, clutching a bunch of carnations (his second lot of flowers within a few days). He was aware of the totally nonsensical nature of what he was doing. Since his mother's death he had managed to avoid funerals of relations and colleagues, and now, because of an incomprehensible whim of his wife, he was hurrying to attend the burial of a strange vicious old woman who, while she was alive, had never aroused any sympathy in him, only dislike.

The ceremony had already started and of course there were some people there, a few people invariably turned up at any funeral, maybe the priest or the sexton arranged it, or maybe this was simply the statistical probability in a city of over a million. There was really no need now for him to go through with it – in fact he needn't have come at all, he could have lied to Camilla, told her he'd been here, described the few people who had turned up without even looking at their faces, but he didn't like lying and he especially didn't like lying to his wife. He was still clutching the bunch of flowers and he'd have to put it down somewhere, so he made for the little crowd which surrounded the grave.

The coffin had already been lowered, the sexton nearby

was leaning on his spade, and the priest, standing on a stone step, was giving an address whose amiable phrases made it obvious that he had never known the deceased.

He took up a position behind a young couple and tried to take in the details of the ceremony, so that he might at least describe it to his wife, seeing that she'd made him come here, but he found it impossible to concentrate on the priest's words and the faces of the people were getting blurred in his mind. A biting dusty wind was blowing into his face so he edged his way inconspicuously round the people until he had the wind at his back. What a waste of time. He should be finishing off his first lecture. He could have been working on it now but instead he was standing here like a ninny. Of no use to anybody. Suddenly he became aware that the girl he'd been standing behind a little earlier, who was now separated from him by the freshly dug grave, was looking at him. In her glance there was something improper, something that almost disconcerted him.

She was with a young man, to whom she evidently belonged (how, he wondered, had the two belonged to the dead woman?), the only young creatures there, but it was not so much her youth that distinguished her from the others as the total absence of even a feigned expression of grief on her face. She was regarding him with the same kind of unabashed glance as if they'd just met on the beach or in the foyer of a theatre, but maybe he was doing her an injustice and her gaze was resting on him only because she had to look somewhere if she didn't want to stare at the ground or at the wizened face of the old priest, and the whole impression of impropriety was produced merely by her appearance, her eye shadow and her dark hair brushed over her forehead, and by her brilliant red clothes, the short skirt and short sleeves which didn't seem right for the occasion.

The priest at last uttered 'Amen,' bent down and, with the spade passed to him by the sexton, flung a few clods of earth on to the coffin and stepped back. At that moment David felt the wet touch of raindrops, but he didn't move and waited for the few old women around him to stoop, groaning, and pick up handfuls of earth. The small stones rattled on the coffin lid. Then the young man who was with her also bent down and she too made a movement as if to stoop and David caught sight of her long magnificent neck and noticed that her hair was piled up at the back and held in place by a long pin. He watched her fingers cautiously, almost repugnantly, picking up a clump of earth, yet it really was nothing in her appearance, nothing in her physical shape, but the movement with which she half-knelt and again straightened herself which produced in him an unexpected excitement.

The girl straightened up, once more glanced at him, and at that moment he nodded his head as if in greeting. Almost imperceptibly she smiled at him and then walked off with the young man to whom she belonged.

Someone turned to him to say something, he realized that it was a neighbour from their street, he hurriedly muttered some greeting, then bent down to lay his flowers by the pile of freshly dug-up earth. The rain was now coming down heavily and the drops were noisily smacking against marble and granite headstones and the fat faces of sculptured angels.

He caught up with them by the cemetery gate. 'If you'd allow me,' and he was himself surprised at his action, 'I've got my car here. May I give you a lift?'

They got into the back seat without protestation (their shoes were all muddy and their hair dripping, he was only making extra work for himself what with having to clean up the car) and the young man said: 'As a matter of fact, I live quite near here but Iva's got to get all the way to Liben.

So if you'd be good enough to drop us somewhere at a tram stop.'

He caught sight of her face in his rear mirror. She was licking her lips, then she pulled out a tiny handkerchief from her bag and with slow careful movements dried her face.

'You two are relations?' he asked.

'Not me,' the girl replied, as if realizing that he was mainly addressing her. 'She was a distant aunt of Tom's. Sister of the husband of his uncle's cousin or something of the sort.'

'No, no,' he said. 'I've told you she was the aunt of my stepmother.'

'He lives just round the corner here,' the girl pointed, 'if you'd be so kind, seeing how it's pouring.'

He turned the corner; they were treating him like a taxi driver. He pulled up by the kerb and the two said something to each other in nearly a whisper and then he saw, or rather surmised, the girl leaning over to the young man and quickly kissing him.

'So long then,' he heard. 'Ciao, Tom! You'll ring tomorrow, won't you?'

'About nine?'

'You must be crazy. You know I'm still asleep at nine.'

'I'll ring at ten,' and the young man got out.

She leaned forward to David. 'I'd better sit in the front, hadn't I?'

'As you wish.'

So she got out and got in again and sat next to him and he moved off once more.

'Whereabouts in Libeň do you live?'

'Right at the top,' she said, 'almost in Kobylisy. You want to take me all the way?'

'In view of the rain.'

She sat bolt upright next to him; her face, on which he

could now at closer quarters detect a fine layer of make-up, was as immovable as a statue's. Her wet hair had a black sheen but he wasn't sure if that was its real colour.

'Maybe I can repay your kindness,' she said after a while, 'when I have a car of my own.'

'You're getting a car?'

'I've been promised one by several fellows. In fact, one Italian architect promised me a Bugatti. Have I got the name right?'

'Yes. You've been to Italy?'

'You haven't been there?'

'No.'

'I love Venice,' she declared. 'When I drive down the road from Treviso and suddenly smell the canals I feel I'm going crazy. You should go and see it some time.' She fell silent and he didn't know what to talk about. He knew nothing about her, he didn't know what any of her interests were except that she loved Venice.

'That was your boyfriend?' he asked.

'Husband,' she said indifferently.

He felt a sense of disappointment, as if he'd just discovered he'd been cheated.

'We wouldn't have got married,' she said, 'except for Bert. Bert's the one that Tom lives with. He invited him into his tiny flat when Tom was kicked out of the student hostel. Fact is, they play in the same group. Bert's a wizard on the drums and a good sort, he's odd in one way though: he's a dyed-in-the-wool Catholic.'

He recalled his mother who had a similar inclination but he kept silent.

'So we had to get spliced. He just couldn't bear the thought of Tom and me living in sin. He felt it was his fault whenever we did it in his flat. At the registry office we had to sign that we'd love each other until death and all that and we'd bring up our delightful children for society. All that for Bert's sake. Anyway, we can always get a divorce when we get tired of it, can't we?'

'When you get tired of what?'

'Loving each other,' she said. 'And giving children to society. Bound to get tired of it some day, don't you think?'

Her words, her questions, which reminded him of his daughter, were perplexing him. 'I don't know,' he said because she seemed to be waiting for an answer. 'Can't say I've ever given it much thought.'

'That's odd,' she said.

'Why?'

'I thought gentlemen like yourself always gave a lot of thought to everything. A lot of thought to everything serious in life,' she rephrased her words more precisely. 'They lecture about it and write books.'

They had got as far as the abattoir, the rain was coming down even harder and torrents of muddy water rushed down the gutters. A few pedestrians were sprinting to the tram stops; from outside came the stench of wet road and old bones, but he was far more aware of the faint, barely perceptible, fragrance of violets (Camilla never used scent, powder or make-up) that emanated from her body. He looked at her sideways again. She was undoubtedly beautiful, or at least she resembled those girls whose photographs he'd now and again seen on the covers of illustrated magazines. It occurred to him that no woman who in the least resembled her had ever sat in the passenger seat. This time she noticed his glance, half-turned towards him and gave him a smile which didn't even pretend to be natural or cordial.

'Did you go anywhere for your honeymoon?' he asked in order to say something.

'No,' she seemed surprised. 'Should we have done?' Then she added, 'Thomas didn't have the time. They were just going on tour. That's what it's like all the time. He plays in a touring group. If you'd be so kind,' she said in a voice that was so gentle that he felt it was embracing him, enveloping him and disturbing him, 'turn left here.'

He turned into a side street (it was called Pivovarská or Brewery Street) and clearly they were inexorably approaching her place. Unexpectedly he was seized by sadness – the forgotten sadness of parting. He didn't even know her name, he knew nothing about her just as she knew nothing about him, and he would open the door and she'd get out and vanish for ever. And so he said resolutely, just as if he'd learned it from a conversation guide for tourists, 'I really should get back to the institute, but if you feel like it we might have a cup of coffee somewhere first.' And he felt a wave of shame engulf him at this miserable and crude proposition.

'I don't mind,' she said. 'I don't have an institute where anyone's waiting for me.'


3


She sipped her wine slowly. Her fingers (delicate, slender fingers with unpainted but beautiful nails) were playing with the glass. Across her wrist, as he now noticed, ran a pale, long-since healed scar.

He hadn't chosen a good place; it was a suburban restaurant lacking character, a dive with smoke-stained walls and the kind of run-of-the-mill furniture that suggested a factory canteen. The other tables were occupied by men drinking beer, and every now and again they looked across to their table and this embarrassed him. What was he doing here anyway? The woman they were ogling didn't belong to him, she belonged to that nonsensical funeral and chiefly to another man, and here he was pointlessly wasting his time and money on a coffee (weak

39

and smelling of soup flavouring) and on the wine she had chosen.

'Pure accident I met you,' he was saying. 'As a matter of fact, I never go to funerals.' He was about to add that his wife had sent him there but some inner guardian in his subconscious intervened just in time with a raised finger and he stopped himself. 'Did you know that woman?'

She shook her head. 'Thomas has a terrible lot of relations,' she explained. 'He'd had several mothers and his dad was one of something like thirty children.'

'We lived in the same house,' he continued. 'She built it forty years ago. A frightful building with windows facing north. But she clung to it so much she couldn't bring herself to think of anything else.'

'You don't have to tell me about her,' she said indifferently, 'I really didn't know her.'

This struck him as impolite and he fell silent, but she appeared oblivious. She slowly raised her glass, just as slowly drank from it, and said, 'In Italy the wine's so light you can drink a whole bottle and you're still okay. This stuff here, if you were to drink two glasses you'd be blotto.'

'Were you there with your husband?'

'Where?'

'In Italy.'

'But I wasn't married then.'

'I thought maybe you'd known each other before.' He was startled by her logic.

'But surely you wouldn't go to Italy with someone you've known for five years. The good Lord invented Italy for relaxation and love-making. You can't relax or make love with someone you're doing it with all year round. Might as well stay at home!'

'You have some interesting views on travel.'

She turned her made-up eyes on him. Her irises were

the colour of the bluish-grey argillaceous clay which turns slimy after a heavy rain and gets baked by the sun to this strange shade.

'I don't know a single girl who'd take her regular fellow there with her,' she said decisively. 'You probably can't picture it if you've never been there. People there aren't like they are here. Here, if you walk down the street you feel like a fish, you're swimming like a carp in a pond and all round you there are masses of other fat carp. And now and again they'll open their mouths at you or they'll touch you in a crush with their repulsive bodies, but down there, before you can cross the road some boy will always turn up and ask you out to dinner or at least for an ice cream. And then you're sitting somewhere under one of those big parasols and other boys turn up and sit down on all the empty chairs at your table and ask you out dancing or to listen to records, or they promise to drive you from Rome to Cortina and from Venice to Naples, and if you say okay they'll put you into their sports car and drive off with you and all the time they talk, all the time they explain something, gesticulating with their hands, and then suddenly they tell you they love you and wouldn't you like to marry them – good Lord,' she sighed, 'it makes me feel like crying even talking about it.'

He still had not managed to discover any real information about her nor had he managed to tell her anything about himself, so he jumped into her momentary silence with another phrase from that conversation guide: 'I'm sorry, it's just occurred to me that I haven't even introduced myself.'

'That doesn't matter,' she said quickly, just as if she were afraid she might have to burden her memory with another unnecessary name. 'To me you are the gentleman who gave me a lift when it was raining and even invited me to a glass of wine.'

'Dr David Krempa,' he announced. But she, instead of telling him her name, said, 'David – he was a prophet or something, wasn't he?'

'He was a king.'

'A king,' she repeated, 'but he probably wasn't an ancestor of yours, or was he?'

'I shouldn't think so.' With amazement he realized that he'd allowed this undignified kind of conversation to be imposed on him. 'I'm not aware of having any Jewish ancestors.'

'That king was a Jew? I thought Jews couldn't be kings.'

'Why shouldn't Jews be kings?'

'I don't know, I just had that idea. Probably because they've nowhere to be kings of.'

'They did then; it was their own kingdom.'

'I didn't know they ever had a kingdom. You probably deal a lot with this kind of thing, right?'

'No, I don't. I'm a biologist,' but he doubted that this word meant anything to her.

'Ah yes, you work in an institute. You should be there now and instead you're sitting here with me. No doubt they've been waiting for you and by now they'll all be in a tizzy. Not knowing what to do because you hadn't left them any instructions.'

Maybe she wasn't so stupid. She was pulling his leg while he was seriously and intently listening to her babbling.

'What do you do?' he asked. 'What do you do for a living?'

'But I don't have to do anything for a living, now I'm married. That's a good occupation, being married, don't you think? Or aren't you married?'

He didn't reply.

'Now you're angry,' she said. 'You'd really like to know what I do for a living. But I don't do anything for a living. I haven't gra-du-ated yet. If that's what you call it. Thomas says I'm an absolute idiot with foreign words.'

'What sort of school?'

'One that'll fit me for the theatre provided I stick it out. The puppet theatre,' she explained. 'And once a week I sing. If you know the little Lantern Theatre in Spálená Street.'

He nodded although he didn't know it. 'You like puppets?'

'You think I should like them?' Her astonishment sounded genuine.

'But didn't you say . . . So why are you studying puppetry?'

'I don't really remember. I think I wanted to be an actress but the course was overcrowded, I had a bad school report and then I didn't know the right people.'

'But some day you'll have to practise what you're studying.'

'You think I'll have to? I can never visualize what will happen some day. Or maybe it won't happen at all. I may go to Italy or to Australia. Bob's always promising us that we'll visit Australia some day. I might even stay there. It's so far away that I might even want to live there.'

Her answers came from another world, a strange world. She astonished him just as if he'd seen a live and kicking kangaroo under his microscope. 'On the whole I've mostly enjoyed what I've been doing,' he said. 'And do you enjoy singing?'

'How could anyone enjoy having to sing the same silly little songs every Wednesday? But they're a decent crowd. Tom used to play there but that was three years ago. Sometimes after the show we party into the small hours. Bob plays the banjo, the guitar, the mandolin, the piano, the organ and, if he feels like it, even the glasses, and he's a good director – incredibly thin, looks as if he'd just descended from the Cross, everybody's bound to be in love with him.'

She finished her wine, put down her glass, dabbed her mouth and said, 'By now they're bound to be in despair at your institute.'

He called the waiter, paid the bill and gave him such a tip that he actually bowed, but she didn't notice it.

She disappeared 'for a second' and left him alone at the mercy of that dreary room. Whenever he had a few spare minutes between two activities he would try to think of his work. He had a knack of rapidly concentrating, of returning days later to some shelved idea, but now he felt unable to think of anything except what to do, what to say to her, whether he should try to see her again at least once more. He must be out of his mind, he shouldn't have invited her even to this place, she was a stranger, what's more a married stranger, whether she was crazy or stupid he had nothing to talk to her about. He'd drive her home, he had to do that, he'd already lost a whole half day and there was no sense in losing another. Just then he caught sight of her returning, walking towards him, slim and graceful, at least by comparison with his wife; she wound her way between the tables so perfectly that all eyes were on her, and he, though he was looking at her, was aware of them approaching, along with her, and he felt their envy and that envy flattered him.

They were once more out in the car. She lived in an old four-storey tenement block at the very end of the street. Beyond the building lay some lumberyards and further still was the railway track.

'Well, thank you very much,' she said. 'I think it's stopped raining.'

'Listen,' he said without looking at her, 'may I see you again some time?'

'You'd like to see me again some time?'

44

He got out as well. In the road some boys were playing football and chasing round the car. He was clearly in their way: with his car and with his presence. 'Do you think you might . . .' He had got totally out of the habit of thinking up dates and places to meet, besides he was a married man, Camilla might suddenly take it into her head, after six months or so, to buy tickets for the cinema, and in the evenings he'd have to be at home. If he had to stay late at the institute Camilla knew about it. He was unable, even though he'd thought about it all the way, to think of anything, to make any useful suggestion, and so he said, '. . . how about a week from today, the same time?'

'But won't they be waiting for you at the institute?'

He glanced at his watch; it was a quarter to five. 'No, not at this time any more. I'll drive here to see you. If you don't mind.'

'Why should I mind you driving here to see me?'

Without even offering him her hand she just walked off. She hadn't actually promised to come, maybe she wouldn't come, she'd be watching him from the window, she'd be inviting her husband Thomas and a few friends and they'd have a laugh watching him waiting at the corner.

It was high time for him to hurry back home. At least he could grudgingly describe to his wife the funeral she had insisted he attend. But he stopped in Spálená Street and in the passageway found a small display box. A number of different groups performed in the hall, and the Lantern was clearly the smallest. Its Roneoed little poster was all but lost among the photographs of semi-nude dancers.

Someone stopped beside him and he, as though caught in some improper act, quickly stepped back from the box. He now knew her full name and that seemed important to him then.

When he was not quite fourteen he had spent a holiday with his parents at a hotel not far from Trebon in southern Bohemia. A stream called Zlata Stoka ran past the place, dividing into two narrow arms which embraced a small island, its banks overgrown with bushes and stunted willows. One day a couple of khaki-coloured army tents appeared at the lower end of the island.

He took no particular notice of them until one evening he overheard his mother, in an outraged voice, telling his father about those youngsters in the tents. They were holding orgies there at night, she said, especially that blonde, the daughter of Professor – his mother said a name which didn't mean anything to him but which was clearly familiar to his father – she was a slut, having it off with all the men in the camping party.

He didn't know where his mother had got her information from, nor whether it was even partially true, but it so excited his imagination that early next morning he went down to the river, found himself a spot with a good view of the tents opposite, hid in the tall grass and waited. Thus he lay there, like a patient angler awaiting a bite. Brightly painted boats floated lazily down the dark water and a flock of moorhens sailed past, but the tents remained motionless. It was nearly midday when he finally caught sight of her. He immediately recognized her as she stepped out of her tent, she did have long fair hair, almost white, certainly lighter than the colour of her skin. She wore only a swimsuit, whose black colour for some reason seemed sinful to him, and she stepped down to the water's edge so that only the narrow stream separated him from her. He lay there, pressed to the ground, motionless, as if asleep, and because he'd been waiting for her and she had really appeared he indulged in the illusion that she'd come over to him, that she'd dive into the water and swim across, and then, wet as she was, would lie down close to him. But she only bent forward, dropped her shoulder straps, pulled down her swimsuit to her waist and quickly washed herself.

For the first time in his life he was seeing live bare breasts, and even though they were unattainably far away he experienced such delight that he had to clench his teeth in order not to cry out. He was totally unable to leave, and so he watched the campers (they were two men and two girls) sunbathing, swimming, and cooking their lunch on an open fire. In the afternoon she went off with the other girl (there was a wooden footbridge at the far end of the island, linking it to the riverbank); they were evidently making for the village to do some shopping and he loitered about behind them. When they entered the shop he decided to go in too, and so it was that he first heard her voice and saw her face and sun-tanned neck close to, and as he lowered his glance he realized that he'd seen those breasts which were now resting hidden behind a barrier of bright material, and that thought so aroused him that he had to thrust his clenched fist quickly into his pocket so the people in the shop shouldn't notice anything, and he felt a burning and exciting ecstasy run through his whole body.

Surprisingly it did not occur to him to address her. He let her go off and again followed her at a distance, and in the evening, as he was lying in his hot room under that hot, all-covering duvet, he kept visualizing that single move-ment down by the river, and he visualized even more: he imagined her taking her swimsuit off altogether and stand-ing naked on the bank and returning naked to the tent where he would be waiting for her. He buried his mouth in his pillow so that his quickened breathing shouldn't be heard. His mind, washed over by waves of pleasure and waves of longing, was now totally enslaved, he couldn't tear it away or turn it to anything else, and in the morning, so early that the sun was scarcely above the horizon, he stole out of his room to take up a position by the river again, and lying in the grass he kept watch over that entirely motionless tent whose canvas, covered by a fine net of dew, was glistening, and he pictured her lying in the tent naked, waking up, and running out into the reddish morning while the river and the banks were still deserted.

But that day she only splashed her face – and then she went off, this time with one of the young men from her camping party. Maybe that was why he dared not follow her and so his whole day suddenly turned into a pointless expanse of time.

Luckily his father went to bed early on holiday, and so he managed to leave his room, through the window, in time to catch the campers still sitting round a dying fire, singing. There were more than just the four of them, maybe eight or ten, and he didn't have the protection of the fire, only the cover of darkness. The midges were biting him mercilessly, and he couldn't even move in case he attracted attention. He tried, across the width of the little stream, to make out her voice in that medley of voices and guitars and he thought he really could make it out, and he also tried to detect her face but in vain; the dull red light of the fire had wiped all the features from each individual face.

At last they stopped singing, the fire died down and most of those who had been sitting there got up and moved off in the direction of the footbridge; only the four who belonged to the tents stayed behind, and he could just see the men walking down to the water's edge for a wash on one side of the island, and the women on the opposite side, and he could see them after a while climbing up again and splitting up, one man with one girl, and now he thought he could make out her light hair and her slimmer figure, and as quietly as he knew how he ran to the foot-bridge and over to the island and then stole up to the two tents. In the absolute silence of that summer night (except for the distant rush of the weir and the occasional splashing of a fish in the river) he carefully tiptoed closer, his breath held in expectation and in the fear of discovery, until he was quite close to her tent. And so, a lonely uninvited listener, he entered the auditorium, and in between the chirping of the crickets he could now hear the barely audible whisper of their voices and then the quiet rustle of the grass, and the gaps between whispers were getting longer, and then he made out a soft moaning and noisy panting and the moans grew into cries and female sobs. He desperately longed to see at least part of her body, he longed to touch her, but his wide-open eyes saw nothing but the grey shape of the tent and his fingers were clutching crumbs of dry clay.

He spent two more days in this activity, so overcome by his passion that he felt no sense of the disgracefulness or even impropriety of what he was doing. Around noon on the third day they began to fold up their tents. She was leaving. He was lying at his spot on the far bank, the grass now was flattened like in the lair of some wild animal, he watched her walk off with a rucksack, it seemed unbelievable that she was leaving, that he should be staying while she left – and only in that moment did he begin to realize that he'd been but an onlooker, but a thief of the whispers and lovers' moans of others. He had not entered into the action and he shouldn't now enter into it, unless he ran after her and shouted: I love you!

When they reached the footbridge he rose to his feet and slowly followed her. He didn't even know her name, except if she really was the daughter of the professor he might somehow find her again, but he knew he wouldn't try.

# CHAPTER THREE

1

On Saturday morning he didn't wake up until half past eight; it was the only day when he could lie in a little. (On Sunday he would get up at seven again, turn back his duvet so that it got aired while he had his breakfast. He'd gulp down his breakfast almost on his feet and hasten back to fold up the couch and thus turn his bedroom back into his study.) From next door came the clamour of his daughters and from the bathroom came the rattle of the scrubbing board. He took a deep breath and caught the smell of boiling soapy water. He felt sorry for his wife who got up early even on Saturday to do her chores; he should buy her a washing machine even if it ate into the savings they'd put by for a small house of their own, but now, if they went to England, he'd save enough money for a house and a washing machine. But why should he buy a washing machine if they were leaving in four months, they wouldn't get the full benefit of the warranty. His eyes were still shut, he was rocking in that pleasant state of half-sleep in which he could dream of eventually getting a house of their own, where he'd have his own study with his own large library, or of being offered a chair at Cambridge, or even of one day receiving the supreme honour, a Nobel Prize for outstanding work in the field of the ageing of organisms. Suddenly there dawned on him an awareness that something wasn't right, that something had changed in the familiar rhythm of his life and his thoughts. It was as if he could hear from a distance the strange insinuating voice, and four days later he realized he'd hear it again, and with that realization he became fully awake.

He got up, bowed a few times towards Darwin (it was an old and worthless print, showing the famous naturalist on board the Beagle) whose picture, his only work of art, he'd hung up over his desk, rotated his arms, did a few knee-bends and went to the bathroom, where, not because he enjoyed it but because he regarded it as good for his health, he stepped under a cold shower.

Camilla was doing the drying up in the kitchen. On the cooker, under a lid, stood the hot milk she'd prepared for him. He fished off the skin and flicked it into the sink, then he leaned over to his wife and kissed her on the cheek. She had dark rings under her eyes. She put a plate back on the table, waiting for him to embrace her from behind, and so he embraced her from behind.

'Why don't you have a little lie-in?' he asked.

'I wouldn't get through my work, you can see what there is to do. You won't do it for me.' Her appearance and the way she held her body betrayed permanent fatigue.

He took a roll from the bread-bin and moved sideways to the kitchen table. He realized that he had placed the whole burden of the household and the children on her shoulders and that, moreover, he sent her out to work because they needed her salary as well, otherwise they couldn't have bought even that second-hand car and would be condemned for ever to living in that tiny flat with its two north-facing rooms. Now they'd already saved one-quarter of the cost of a little house, he already had one-quarter of his study with one-quarter of an ideal window and the whole of an ideal view (they'd already found the spot, a quiet spot on the Točná hill with a view over a wooded valley). As soon as the house was built Camilla would stay at home or she'd take on some help; a year abroad would certainly make all this possible. This conclusion so appeased his conscience that he didn't even feel irritated by his wife's dishevelled look in the morning. He expected from those around him the same unflagging vitality that he had himself. She didn't have it. Their love-making had almost stopped, not because they had totally stopped loving each other but because Camilla would fall asleep as soon as she lay down and it was impossible to arouse her either with kisses or violence. Maybe she was suffering herself, at times she was seized by a mood of dejection which, towards the evening, turned into fits of silent weeping. She'd sit in her rocking chair between the couch and the ficus plant which he'd have got rid of long ago if he'd had any say in it, it was only taking up a lot of space (and space was something they were short of), or else she'd be mending or reading, and a continuous stream of tears would run from her reddened eyes. Sometimes her despair moved him so much that he'd get up from his work, sit down by her feet, kiss her hands, rock her chair and try to extract from his memory some amusing or at least epic event to divert her, or else he'd try to say something tender to her and as a rule he actually succeeded in staunching the flow of tears, and she'd either close her eyes and fall asleep in her chair or she'd let him carry her to the bed, curl up in his arms and instantly sink into oblivion.

'Some fairground swings have arrived up on the housing estate,' she spoke up. 'I saw them yesterday.'

He reacted defensively; he knew what would follow that information.

'You might take the girls there.'

'What, now?'

'Now would be best, I've got a lot to do.' She was ready to remind him that he too should have obligations towards his children other than just to feed them. However, quite exceptionally, he made no objection.

It was a gloomy day outside, so he put on an ancient grey windcheater (he had a dislike of new things, or rather he was reluctant to throw old things away if they might still come in useful some time) and a blue beret which since his student days had covered his shock of hair.

In the next room he heard the bossy voice of Anna and the whingeing of the little one. Then the door burst open. 'Margit won't put on her sweater,' the elder complained. 'Nana's hitting me,' came a plaintive voice from within.

He took the little one on his lap and dressed her. She resembled his wife, both in appearance and temperament: she tired quickly; it didn't look as if she'd be particularly good at anything; she was a little awkward in her movements, her speech and her dealings with other people; she was living in the shadow of her older sister. That one had inherited his determination, ambition and stubborn perseverance – she'd begun to read at four and about the same time had shown an interest in dogs, and in an odd and unchildlike systematic manner had begun to collect information on them, cutting out and pasting up pictures of various breeds, of dogs in films and at dog shows, and of police dogs which had distinguished themselves in some operation or other, and she collected articles about them which she could scarcely read with all their difficult words.

The houses in the street (it was two days before May Day) had flags out, the school windows had been decorated by the young children – under the guidance of their zealous teachers (including Camilla) – with masses of white doves and above the entrance a red streamer proclaimed one of the previously published and approved slogans.

He pictured himself, the day after next at six in the morning, parading under the banners and portraits of the statesmen, while a brass band played at the bus stop and the loudspeakers, with professional enthusiasm and ad nauseam, blared out the previously published and approved slogans, and he felt a sense of revulsion.

53

He hated all ceremony and he felt ill at ease in a crowd. He was depressed by his inability to do anything sensible or useful. At the moment he approached the red-cloth-covered platform on which he saw the same faces as the one carried aloft over his head he was seized by a wish to escape from this world of gestures, slogans, portraits and loudspeakers. Yet each time he turned up conscientiously and punctually at the rallying point. He participated in processions just as he did in harvest brigades, political instruction courses, departmental meetings or elections, to make sure no enemies could possibly accuse him of disloyalty and so prevent him from carrying on with his work. And although during these activities he felt distaste, he had no pangs of conscience. These demonstrations, after all, were so superficial and obligatory, and simultaneously so generally accepted, that they had ceased to have any meaning, apart from being a nuisance to him. Sometimes, when several such events occurred close together the thought struck him that it would be better for his work if he could live in some other country, somewhere where he'd be left alone and where the yardstick of his loyalty (if there really was a need to worry about the loyalty of an ordinary citizen) would be solely his work and his civic honesty. And it astonished him that his father, with his superb skill in solving situations logically and rationally, had yielded to his mother's dislike of leaving her native country and that he hadn't at the time gone to England or to some other quieter land. (On one occasion, when he'd complained about his father's decision to Camilla, she'd said: But then we wouldn't have met at all, and that would have been dreadful! And he'd been amazed at that feminine logic because surely everybody meets somebody and they would have lived just as happily or unhappily.)

It was still early and the merry-go-rounds and swings were deserted. He placed his two daughters in a couple of boat swings and walked over to where, by a miserable patch of grass, further dishonoured by countless pieces of rubbish, stood a solitary bench.

He looked at the beflagged housing estate. He realized that he now had an opportunity to do what his father had failed to do, but until that moment he'd shied away from the thought not because he was scared of the idea of losing his homeland – he was convinced that he could find a home anywhere and indeed that he had the right to make his home in any place he chose – but because it had seemed to him that such reflections were premature. But now, as he shut his eyes, he imagined that he was sitting on a park bench near his own detached house in Hampstead. He saw a thick and perfect lawn, a hedge and a creeper-covered red brick building. The children were playing on a swing behind him and in the quiet of the suburban morning he could hear the rope rubbing against the branch of a tree. From the kitchen window came the smell of lunch. Camilla was coming out of the door, and she was no longer the tired woman with the haunted look of a creature ceaselessly rushing from one duty to another; her hair was dark, just as it had been when they first met, and her features were relaxed and happy.

You haven't even noticed I'm wearing eye shadow, she pointed out to him.

Yes, you haven't looked so pretty for a long time.

See! You don't have to chase after that girl, she said, if you think I'm pretty.

All of a sudden his action seemed utterly foolish – that he'd arranged to meet that weird, crazy creature, that he'd even tried to fit a strange person into his essentially closed life.

'Dad,' he heard his elder daughter's voice behind him, 'Margit wants to go home already.' He turned and saw the younger one, head on her knees, sitting in a motionless swing. He walked over. 'What's the matter? Don't you want to swing any more?'

'She'd want to all right,' the elder one announced, 'but she's stupid, she doesn't know how to do it and she won't listen to what I tell her.'

It hadn't occurred to him that she might not know how to work it, he had so little time left that he didn't even keep track of her abilities. 'Come on, little one, I'll give you a push.' He stepped up to the swing and with his handkerchief dried her tears. She extended her arms to him.

'What's the matter?'

'I want to go home,' she whined. 'I don't like it here.'

He took her in his arms. She put her head on his shoulder and her cheek touched his.

'Wait,' he suggested, 'I'll teach you how to swing, but first we'll have a ride on the roundabout.'

'You're going to ride with me?' she asked incredulously.

He stepped up with her on the worn platform of the merry-go-round and sat her on the back of a greyish-blue or maybe just a rather dirty blue elephant. An old man, operating the motor and the tape recorder from a little cabin, seemed only to be waiting for their arrival and struck a brass bell with an iron bar and the merry-go-round, squeaking and moaning, went into motion.

He leaned forward to see her face, and when he saw her smiling he said, 'There you are then.' And it seemed to him that he was also talking to himself.

He always carried a small note-pad with him, and he now pulled it out and wrote:

*Dear Madam,*
*Unfortunately, an unforeseen . . .*

He realized that the form of address wasn't right, so he tore off the sheet, crushed it into a small ball and threw it into the inside of the merry-go-round.

'Daddy,' said the little one in front of him. 'That was great. Can we have another go?'

He gave the old man another two crowns, waited for the mighty sound of the bell and started writing again:

*Dear Miss,*
*Unfortunately an unexpected visitor has turned up, all the way from Britain . . .*

He checked himself. He didn't like lying or making excuses. But to explain why he had decided to cancel their date seemed to him too complicated.

*I am afraid I shall have to devote myself to my guest and would therefore ask you to excuse me on the day when I myself wished to see you.*

He signed it and read it through again. Maybe it was even good that his fiction was of the same order as she herself. There was no visitor from England just as she herself didn't exist; he'd just expunged her from the world of hard fact or at least from his life.

And because he naturally always felt compelled to act with the least delay he set out immediately after lunch (he told his wife he was collecting a book he'd forgotten – yet another but fortunately the last lie), and set out for the opposite side of the city in order to drop his message into her letter box.

As he was standing in the dingy passage, which was flooded with the strong smell of roast pork and sauerkraut, with the sound of a door slamming and a child calling out upstairs, his assurance began to leave him. Suppose she were to emerge just then from her flat and see him with the envelope in his hand? He wasn't sure whether he wished to see her or not, he wasn't even sure whether he wanted to deliver his note. He opened the envelope and read the letter again, and now it didn't seem to him quite as perfect.

It was curt, wooden and too final. He pressed the letter against the tin side of the bank of letter boxes and added:

*P.S. I'll be in touch some other time if I may.*

This wouldn't commit him to anything, nor would it rule out the possibility of his contacting her again if he should decide to do so. He found the letter box with her name – under her card someone had painted a running horse in white oil paint – dropped the envelope in and with a sudden feeling of guilt or perhaps embarrassment (as if he'd just looked through a keyhole into someone else's flat) he ran out of the building.

2

*From the dawn of history, ever since he emerged from the darkness of the animal kingdom, man has been accompanied through life by deities, demons, spirits and gods. Have you ever reflected, ladies and gentlemen, on what it is that some unimportant local deity from, say, Tasmania has in common with the famous, universally recognized gods like Vishnu, Allah or the Lord? You may say: omnipotence. Yet the gods of good are often powerless against the gods of evil and are often outwitted even by humans. You may say: invisibility. But surely all deities have sometimes manifested themselves, either in some embodiment, human or animal, or at least in the shape of a cloud or a burning bush. Nor do the gods share any moral qualities; there are benign gods and malignant ones, and still others stand above good and evil. What in fact unites them all is their independence of human time, their endurance beyond birth and death. Their eternal existence. Gods do not die. That, from the earliest times on, has been a highly significant fact to man. If gods were immortal then there was the possibility of immortality. But does man too have the possibility of escaping his animal heritage, can he slip out of human time and enter into another time, the time in which the gods move? It did not seem possible in this world, and that is why man tried to extend his existence beyond the visible world. But did this uncertain vision satisfy him? From time immemorial, ladies and gentlemen, man has longed for real immortality, dreamed of life-giving water, the elixir of life, the fountain of eternal youth. Man dreams of eternal life because without it his existence would lose its meaning.*

*Man has been ready to believe that one day in the distant future, when the angels sound the trumpet, he will return to this world again in corporeal form. He does not care that the world will be changed beyond recognition, that his cities will have crumbled to dust and the nation he belonged to will have been forgotten. He wants to return to the human world, because he suspects that the farther world, from which he will be raised, is shrouded in the horror of the unknown.*

*Ladies and gentlemen, we are on the threshold of discoveries which may perhaps lead man out of his ancient anxieties, his ancient time frame, and transport him into the time which hitherto has been the prerogative of the gods. Maybe it will be one of you, or possibly all of you, who will jointly light the lantern of life where hitherto there has been only the flickering flame of vain and illusory dreams. It will be you who will proclaim to mankind: The elixir of life has been discovered!*

He was sitting at his desk – next door, or maybe in the bathroom, his elder daughter was holding forth in a loud voice, Darwin, leaning over the ship's rail, was gently smiling, and Camilla's muted voice was telling Margit to do something or other.

From his desk drawer he produced his diary and under the 2nd of May he entered a big figure 1. He was a little behind schedule with his first lecture, even though he'd allowed twice as much time for it as for the rest. He was never at his best when he had to step out of the world of experiments, numbers and formulae – philosophy and the gods were not his field.

He put the diary away, fastened his first lecture (ten sheets) together with a paper clip and also put it away in his drawer. A festive mood came over him.

'You've finished already?' Camilla observed, alarmed. 'I'm nowhere near ready myself. The girls have been very trying today.'

They were both invited to dinner at his graduate assistant's. They didn't often go out. They had no friends, or at least not the kind for mutual socializing; they just didn't have the time to cultivate such friendships.

He had only accepted the invitation because the director of the institute was also expected (he urgently needed to talk to him about the details of his departure and how his department was to be run in his absence) and also a young American from Princeton who was working on *corpora alata* in silkworms – meeting him might be useful.

'I've still got Margit's hair to wash before I start dressing.'

Margit was whining in the bathroom beside the half-filled bath. The time was nearly half past seven. Whenever they were going out somewhere it was always the same scene: the children were crying, Camilla was rushed, irritable and not ready because it was not in her power to be ready on time.

'Do you have to wash her hair today?'

'It hasn't been washed for a week.'

'That's just the point. Why does it have to be washed today when we are going out?'

'I don't feel like going anyway,' she said with feminine logic. 'I've got a lot of work here – and I don't know the people. And they'll probably all speak English.'

'Precisely. At least you'll have an opportunity to practise your English.'

'I have no wish to practise my English.'

'Oh? And how do you expect to communicate when we're there?'

'Who said I want to communicate? Or even to go there?'

'You don't want to go to England?'

'I don't see why I should want to go there!' She turned her back on him and started to shampoo the child's hair. The fact that she was absorbed in a meaningless activity, thereby indicating to him that she considered it more important than continuing their conversation, infuriated him.

'I thought you were looking forward to it. It's your chance to see a foreign country.'

'The chance,' she repeated sarcastically, 'is yours. You perhaps will learn something there. Do you think I can't imagine what it will be like there? I'll be sitting in the kitchen of some little house from morning till night while you're hanging about the university. I'll be cooking and looking after the girls, who will be desperate without friends. I don't care whether I'm sitting at home here or over there. Here at least I have my school.'

'Fancy, suddenly you care about your school.'

'I've got people here I can talk to. How do you think I would manage otherwise? I'd go round the bend. As for you, I can't say a single word to you all day.' She pulled Margit out of the bathtub and wrapped her in a towel. A quarter to eight: he should either go back to his work or leave the house now, but instead he was in the way in the bathroom and conducting a quarrel that wouldn't and couldn't solve anything.

'Leave me at home,' she said, 'and go on your own.'

'Now or later?'

'Now – and maybe later too.'

He knew of course that this utterance was of no significance at all, that it was the expression of a momentary mood, of her momentary rebellion. Of course they'd leave

61

together, for England, and even that evening if he'd only wait for her for twenty minutes. But at least for that evening he was willing to take her statement at face value (and punish her for all other blasphemous statements) and so he walked out of the bathroom without another word.


3

His doctoral assistant lived not far away, on the eleventh floor of a high-rise block which, according to its architects, was to provide the central feature of the housing estate. As David stepped into the dirty corridor with its battered and flaking walls he was overcome with distaste, as if he were visiting his dentist. He had long read all there was to know about *corpora alata*, and silkworms had too little in common with humans to be of any real interest to him.

On the door to the lift, as might have been expected, hung a notice: OUT OF ORDER. Some Americans, he reflected, especially the younger ones, were fond of going in for 'fancy' subjects; he remembered one, as he was climbing the stairs, who had spent several years researching into differences in impotence and probable life expectancy between mice living in dirty and clean environments. In the end, needless to say, he'd proved that there was no difference. That was because they had plenty of money and were living in a totally enclosed world, he thought, and hardened his mind against the American before he even met him.

As for the Strong Man, he could have seen him at any other time and discussed his problems more profitably. Just as he convinced himself of the utter pointlessness of what he was about to do, he pressed the doorbell on the eleventh floor and found himself in the company he'd rather do without. He immediately spotted the two Americans. The man was lean and everything about him was long: his hands, his legs, his neck and his hair; on his wrist he wore some shiny wire (probably some health thing), and on his bespectacled face an expression of interest in everything about him was firmly established. The woman was slim and bony, her loose hair came down to her waist, her dress was periwinkle-coloured with red toadstools printed on it, round her wrist she wore the continuation of the wire which adorned her husband's wrist, and at the spot where her cleavage would be, if her breasts had been such as to give it a chance of developing into a cleavage, a black-and-white enamel button asked for love (Love me!). They were introduced to him (he was John and she was Charlotte), and, sitting in a rocking chair, the only untypical piece of furniture, was their Strong Man boss.

He sat down next to the American woman and asked her politely if this was her first visit to Europe (Oh no) and if she also studied science (she had studied literature). He hoped that he had thereby discharged his social duties and that he could now indulge in his thoughts.

By his side, however, John (undoubtedly a left-wing sympathizer like the majority of young people in the other hemisphere) was shouting, 'So what do you actually mean by your socialism? What human elements have you brought in? From what have you liberated man? Do you have even a single really new community?'

'What kind of community?' The boss in the rocking chair didn't understand.

'Like in Israel, like in China, or like our hippies created – a communist community in which alone informal relationships can develop.'

'We haven't got communism yet,' replied the Strong Man.

He could never understand how otherwise intelligent and even educated people could make such monstrous statements, and with such conviction, on matters they didn't understand and to which they could have no answers. He tried not to listen, but they were talking too loudly for that. As a rule people arguing about politics or about the future of the world raised their voices.

'He's terrible.' The American woman leaned over to David. 'Wherever he goes he holds forth about new communities. He also used to talk about his scientific work but I've forbidden him to do that. It's really quite insufferable. They nearly kicked him out of the university because in some demonstration he smashed the window of a bank. He wanted to drop everything and join a commune in Taos.'

'And you refused?'

'I had a girl friend there, a schoolmate, and I went to look at it. They were all living in a house they'd built themselves from mud, like the Indians. And they didn't have a cooker, or a washing machine, and they were always eating maize porridge. It was so cold there all the children developed horrible diseases.'

She rose and opened the balcony door. 'Oh,' she exclaimed. 'What a fantastic view!'

He followed her – to escape from the room rather than from a desire to converse with her.

Below them shone a multitude of lights. The headlights of cars were moving down invisible roads outlined by strings of lamps.

'A fabulous city,' she exclaimed, 'I fell in love with it the moment I set eyes on it.'

'Do you love many cities?'

'No. Maybe just Paris, Venice and Rio. Have you been to Rio?'

'Never,' and he realized that this was the second time in a few days that he'd heard the praises of Venice sung, and he thought of the girl student whom he was to have met the day before, but he immediately drove the thought away.

'He's got no sense of reality,' she returned to the subject of her husband, 'but he's fantastically gifted. When he finished school he had offers from five universities but in the end he went to Princeton. Everybody thinks he'll go a long way but he says it doesn't matter, he doesn't recognize the category of "going a long way". He says the most important thing of all is to win love and to give love. What do you think about that?'

'I believe that everybody has a duty to achieve whatever is in his capability to achieve,' he said, 'and regardless of reward or success.'

'Yes, you've put that beautifully,' she exclaimed, just as though he'd said something very profound. 'What, actually, is your field of work?'

For an instant he forgot that this was just some ordinary conversation, one in which it wasn't done to take any question too seriously, and he began to hold forth about his work.

'Oh dear,' she said with sudden relief at being able to interpose a few words, 'so you're also one of those who want humans to live to a hundred and fifty.'

'Why stop at a hundred and fifty?'

'Goodness gracious,' she cried. 'A hundred and fifty years – what a terrible thought!'

'Death is a terrible thought,' he said. 'Or don't you enjoy living?'

'Sure I do, life's a terrific thing, but it would be terrible to live that long. Just imagine the Beatles at a hundred and fifty! Singing the same songs for a hundred and fifty years, or listening to them. Wouldn't that be depressing? Or not sleeping for a hundred and fifty years. Do you suffer from insomnia too?'

'No, on the contrary, I think that if there was a chance of living another hundred years I might finally get a good night's rest.'

'No, not you,' she said with conviction. 'You wouldn't find the time even if you lived a thousand years, any more than Johnny. But what about those poor ordinary mortals? It's horrible just lying there in total silence and desperately wanting to go to sleep and instead being slowly gripped by anxiety.'

'Anxiety?' he asked. And at that moment he felt anxiety himself, it would attack him from time to time: a terrible fear that he might be wrong in everything he was doing, that he had taken a wrong turn, that he was sacrificing his life span to a false god. What would he leave behind? A few articles and a youthful – by now unnecessary – book.

'Such . . . well, just anxiety. Mystical maybe. My heart starts pounding and I feel like screaming.'

When he was overcome with anxiety he didn't scream. He would sit down at his desk and one by one pull out from his files his research reports, ancient and less ancient, and reprints of his articles, he would rummage in his card index for the notes he'd been collecting for his lectures or for his planned (and continually postponed) book, he would turn over his ideas and sentences, in order to convince himself, at least by the quantity of his words, by the weight of all that paper, that he'd accomplished something.

'Besides, you'd have nothing left to look forward to, you'd already have everything you ever desired.' She returned to the idea of longevity.

But here he didn't have any of his publications to hand, unless one had found its way into Mencl's study and was buried there under a pile of journals.

He could have written several books in his life – except that writing a book meant too long a break in his actual work, and that he'd never been willing to consider.

'I, for instance, always believed that I would love to have a horse,' she continued, 'because I didn't like driving a car all the time. So Johnny gave me one as a Christmas present the year before last. Because of it we moved from Brunswick to Lambertville. Right on the edge of town we found a farmhouse with stables. It was a lovely horse. White, with a black mane and a black tail. Everybody said it was the most beautiful horse they'd ever seen. And then I found it wasn't all joy. There was an awful lot of work involved, and you still had to have the car if you wanted to get anywhere. A horse is too big – you can't pet it properly.' And this was her final and absolute full stop to the conversation on longevity.

He was aware of the cool wind on his forehead and in the sudden silence he thought he could hear time itself flowing quietly across his face, his life's unrepeatable time. How had he filled it?

He was one more night nearer to the day when it would all be too late for him, and that would be his goal, the only goal he'd attain, his life had already come to an end, been extinguished, and it was now only continuing through inertia. At that moment he caught sight of them, flying above the grey valley dotted with countless lights, lights which would soon be extinguished for him, soundlessly flying towards him on supple black wings, their yellow beaks half-open to swallow him up – three ravens.

He left her on the balcony and walked over to the telephone. He dialled a number and listened to the telephone ringing in his own flat, again and again, he heard it filling their one room, their combined bedroom, study and dining room, perhaps she'd gone out from spite, but he instantly dismissed the idea because she wouldn't have left the children on their own, she was simply asleep. He could see her, lying on the couch, her head buried in the pillow, fast asleep. He felt a sense of disappointment. The others were already at table, and it suddenly occurred to him that he could turn the lectures he was writing for England into a book. He realized that before him lay a year full of hope. For the first time in his life he'd be part of a real research team, he'd have an excellent library at his disposal and he'd meet people from whom he'd learn something or with whom, at least, he'd be able to talk about his problems. That thought gradually calmed him. He joined the others at the table.

They were already a little tipsy, and Charlotte, who was his neighbour, was talking incessantly about a hippie festival in California, about a cheese festival in Holland, about the launch of spacecraft at Cape Kennedy, about the Boston Strangler and about her white horse. He swallowed his food without interest. His unease had still not left him, even though his anxiety had: all he wanted now was to leave, to return to his desk or at least to think about his problem quietly somewhere else.

Soon after dinner he therefore announced (without trying to pretend regrets at his premature departure) that he had to finish an article, thanked everybody for an enjoyable evening and left the high-rise block.

Outside absolute, silent darkness engulfed him. The street lamps were out and most of the windows were dark. He looked up at the sky, having long lost the habit of looking up at it, not expecting either God or anything else, and saw a countless multitude of shining heavenly cells.

From nearby gardens came a mixture of sweet smells. It was just quarter past ten, by the time he got home it would be too late to start working and too early to go to bed.

If Camilla were up, or if she'd been at the party with him, they might have walked a little among the gardens. He climbed into his car and drove down the deserted street which wound between monstrous tower blocks. It was Wednesday evening, so the little Lantern Theatre would be performing – that item of information had stuck in his mind all day long, even though he'd pretended to be unaware of it. But the performance was probably over; if he'd wanted to go he should have forgone his useless visit.

Nevertheless he didn't turn towards the residential neighbourhood where he lived but, a little undecided about what to do, made for the city centre.

4

Slightly embarrassed, he descended the stairs to the basement. The black-painted walls were covered with strident posters which, however, he registered merely as large coloured patches. He walked past the closed ticket office and eventually heard some muted sounds from below. There was no one at the door into the theatre. He opened it far enough to see inside; the spectators were sitting at tables, their eyes turned to a point he could not see. The tables at the back were not occupied. He slipped inside and quickly sat down on an empty chair.

His friend was at that instant on stage. He just caught a few bars of her song, but he was too unsettled by his presence in these unfamiliar surroundings to take it in.

She came to an end, bowed, and there was applause from the room – but he hardly took that in either, the only thing he perceived was the movement with which she bowed, and it struck him that he'd never seen a more seductive woman or a woman who'd captivated him so completely.

Next to appear on stage were two young men, dressed as clowns, one of them tall and slim and the other stocky, who performed a scene which was probably of a comical nature because the people in front of him laughed noisily, but he didn't manage to catch a single coherent sentence nor the meaning of their crazy movements. There was more applause, the two clowns ran off stage, and the stage was immediately taken by a group of four musicians (two stringed instruments, organ and drums) who played a flourish and the house lights came on.

He sat motionless, he didn't applaud (it would have been hypocritical to applaud when he hadn't seen anything of the programme) and just looked at her bowing, running off, returning (her neighbour on stage was now putting his arm around her shoulders), smiling and bowing again. Then the shabby curtain came down, a few spectators got up and left, others stayed behind to finish their wine. It was, to him, an unfamiliar audience. Long-haired and noisy young men with almost girlish hips and in girls' blouses and girls with long loose hair in boyish jeans or in short skirts. Someone jostled him without apologizing, and just then the music started up again, intolerably amplified, and, as if obedient to its call, he stepped up to the bar, albeit a little hesitantly, to ask how one would get hold of an actress who was expecting one. He sat down on the only empty stool. Immediately facing him, like a big sun above a landscape of bottles, hung a clock; although he couldn't hear it he watched the rapidly moving second hand which was counting the seconds of his senseless presence there. He ought to get out of this noisy underworld and get back home as quickly as possible, but he sat there, strangely rigid, as if in some dead field, he didn't want to leave and he didn't want to stay, and so he remained from inertia. Then he felt the light touch of someone's hand on his shoulder, and when he turned the girl student was standing before him, still with her stage make-up on, with long false eyelashes, in a red velvet dress.

'So you've come to have a look. And what have you done with that Briton of yours?'

'With whom?' He felt himself blush. 'Ah yes,' he remembered, 'I left him at a party at the house of some friends.'

'So you left him at a party at the house of some friends,' she repeated.

'I wanted to see you,' he said in embarrassment, 'so I thought I'd drive over for a while.'

'You drove over for a while. And now you'll be hurrying back to those friends or off to your institute?'

'I'm not hurrying off anywhere.' He was surprised by his own statement.

'Well, then you can sit down with us,' she suggested and led him across the hall to the best table, where, immediately below the band, three long-haired young men were sitting (two of them he recognized as the clowns), as well as a girl whose face he was almost unable to see because her eyes, nose, and the major part of her round face were hidden by dark glasses. She reminded him of a civet cat he'd recently seen in an illustrated magazine.

'This is our table,' she said to him and to the others she announced, 'This is the gentleman who was at the funeral of one of Thomas's aunts.' And he supplemented this rather vague introduction by giving his name, he learned that the girl was Paula, that the clowns' names were Alois and Peter, and that the third man at the table, who seemed a little older than his two friends and really did look like Christ just descended from the Cross, was the producer of the show, Bob.

He sat down on the empty chair between Bob and the civet cat (Iva sat facing him) and a moment of awkward silence fell upon them, clearly caused by his arrival. 'I'm sorry,' he said, 'I didn't want to disturb you.'

'That's all right, you're not disturbing us, how would you be disturbing us,' said the producer. 'But a bottle might be a good idea.'

'Your turn today,' one of the clowns reminded him. They argued for a while about whose turn it was to order a bottle, and although they were not looking at him during

71

the argument it was clear to him that it was really his turn even though he'd never drunk with them before and even though he had no intention of drinking with them now. So he got up and asked what kind they'd like and he addressed the question to her and she smiled at him (she could smile in a way that made her smile touch him physically, as if she were kissing him in front of all these people) and she said: red. He walked across to the bar and discovered that in this joint a bottle of wine cost nearly twice as much as in the shops, but maybe one bottle would suffice or if it didn't maybe they'd buy the next one themselves, and he returned to their table with the bottle and some glasses.

'Iva's saying you only got here at the end of the performance.'

'Unfortunately I couldn't manage it earlier.'

'Maybe you'll make time for it some other day,' the producer suggested. 'I'd be interested in hearing your views on what we're doing here.'

He had no idea why the producer should be particularly interested in his views, but evidently this was part of the conversational custom of this company.

'You know,' the producer said, 'I'm trying something quite new here. Even though, needless to say, this isn't what we'd be doing if they'd allow us to do what we really want to do. But we were trying at least to get a piece of real life onto the stage.' He picked up a glass and David observed that he had unusually short and thick fingers, with long dirty fingernails. He averted his head.

Although she was sitting opposite him she was too far away in the frightful din made by the band for him to talk to her about anything. She noticed his glances and again smiled at him in the way that made him almost feel the touch of her lips.

'To make myself clear,' the hairy producer continued,

72

'we want to do the kind of theatre that would be a reaction to today's mechanized world. No doubt you've felt it yourself, but we feel it as something fundamental that there is a great struggle going on in the world between science and the arts about the concept of the human being. In this century it looks as if science is winning. It's paralysed man into believing that everything will be worked out by computers and pharmaceuticals against insects and against sore throats and against sorrow. I suppose you know that utopia by Huxley, where people are bred in artificial incubators in order to produce a suitable superior breed. A perfect human being, except that he ceases to be human, everything in him is mechanized and automated like in a washing machine.'

'Don't be an ass, Bob,' one of the clowns intervened. 'You can't start boring a man the moment he arrives.'

'What we're after, quite simply,' the producer said, 'is to create a totally de-automated theatre. On stage we have simply life itself, in its most basic instinctive manifestations. Have you heard of *Hair*?'

'No.'

'Are you familiar with Grotowski or Schechner?'

He shook his head: 'There are subjects I know something about, but the theatre isn't one of them.'

'Schechner has love-making performed on the open stage,' the civet cat joined in.

The taller clown leaned over to him behind the producer's back and asked, 'Are you connected with the theatre?'

'No, not at all.'

'Oh,' the clown understood. 'You've come only because of Iva. And what do you actually . . . do, if it's not an impertinent question?'

'I do research into ageing.'

'Wait a minute,' the clown exclaimed, 'didn't you say

73

David Krempa? Surely – didn't you write a little book . . . What the hell was its title, something about . . . ageing.'

'You mean *The Ageing of Cells*?'

'That's it,' the clown exclaimed joyously, 'that's it! That was a most interesting book. Most instructive.'

'You've read it?' he asked in astonishment. He was about to say that the book was just his re-written doctoral thesis and therefore still beholden to the views and especially the conditions prevailing at the time, but suddenly he perceived in the clown's expression something cunning and he realized that the young man of course hadn't read his book. He was an actor – and slightly drunk – and he was pulling his leg in front of everybody and especially in front of her.

He turned to her (in the hope that she hadn't been listening) and he saw the short stocky clown put his arm round her shoulders and whisper something to her and that she was smiling at him with exactly the same smile that had taken his breath away because it seemed to be promising everything, and at that instant he was overcome by the hideousness of it all and by a sense of shame. As if he'd been seeing himself through their eyes: a ridiculous old gent in an old-fashioned double-breasted suit, with a tie and short hair, just like their dads, ogling a girl who was married to one of their chums and who, if she were just a few years younger, could be his daughter. He got up. He did so with such vehemence and determination that he knocked over his chair.

She looked up at him. Her stone-coloured eyes, the colour of those granite blocks with which, in his childhood, the pavements were paved, were gazing at him in surprise. He'd made a fool of himself in front of her, but he didn't care because he wouldn't be seeing her again.

'You're leaving already?' she asked. 'Won't you stay for another bottle?'

'What are you talking about?' the stocky clown of hers cut in. 'Poor chap's been sitting here all evening over a soda water.'

'And I haven't looked after you at all,' she said, 'but then you had such an interesting conversation with Bob. Could I make up for it somehow, d'you think?'

He was still feeling embarrassed, a misfit, and he could almost hear the silent laughter with which they were seeing him off.

'Thank you for asking me to join you,' and he bowed a little, realizing that this must produce another outburst of their silent laughter.

She caught up with him on the stairs. 'Something offended you?' she asked.

'No. But it's time for me to go home. I've got to go to work in the morning.'

'You're right. I should be leaving too. But I'm always terrified that the trams might have stopped running. Towards morning they start to run more frequently again. Sometimes I take a taxi, if I'm flush enough.'

'I would of course give you a lift if . . .'

'Would you really? And won't they be waiting for you at home? That would be terribly nice of you. In return I'll tell you a story about Bob.' She was hopping around him on the narrow landing. 'I'll just pop down to get my things,' she said. 'Sure you don't want to come down again?'

He remained standing on the shabby landing. Looking straight down on him from a poster were the features of an outlandish Christ holding a naked infant on his palm. Underneath, in art-nouveau lettering, were the words: GO AND DO THOU LIKEWISE.

The quiet was almost crushing after the din he'd just left and it made him wonder for an instant if he'd gone deaf or if he'd even moved right out of the human sphere.

He was suspended in unreality, waiting, and although

he knew that he should leave now and return to his own sphere, where after all life wasn't too bad, he stood there waiting until he heard the tap of quietly hurrying footsteps from below.

5

Perhaps it was the wine she'd drunk or maybe it was her true nature, but she talked almost ceaselessly while they were driving, and she was still talking when he had left the built-up area and artificial lights behind them and went down a field track to a cinder-covered area in front of the wrought-iron gates to the park of a chateau.

She told him about her father who'd been a head shorter than her mother but nevertheless had found a mistress with whom he'd run away, and about Bob who loved her, and about the short clown who also loved her, and about Paula who'd just had her second divorce and with whom she'd made her first trip to Italy, and about a professor who'd tried to seduce her in a hotel room in Pilsen, and about Venice and a young architect called Mario who lived in a magnificent house with frescoes and had offered her his hand, and about a boy called Carlo and a guitarist called Giuseppe from a little house in a suburb of Turin, and about her husband whom she'd known since she was fourteen, when she was still a silly, ugly, fat goose, happy to have found a boy who loved her, and about the aunt of the boy Carlo, who had a huge house in Sicily that was full of cats, and about her childhood, when she'd longed to win the favour of a certain man who lived in the house next door and owned a tame little monkey and she'd allowed him to kiss her on the forehead because she'd wanted to play with the little monkey, and he'd promised he'd marry her when she grew up but then they came and arrested him and she'd never seen him again. The flow of her communication, however confused and lacking in ideas or useful information, swept him into a strange and unfamiliar sphere full of people whose aims differed from his aims and whose behaviour differed so much from his own behaviour that they struck him as exotic (how would he strike them?); he was also fascinated or perhaps even touched by the fact that in her life there was clearly nothing solid or certain: not one person who'd remained in her mind to such an extent that she'd long to return to him, no emotion that would especially move her, and no thought that would inspire her – everything was just flowing on in one big featureless stream.

It occurred to him that he should be doing what she was plainly expecting him to do since she let him drive her, instead of home, down this deserted blind alley – but he was unable to make that single necessary movement with which he'd now, for the first time and maybe lastingly, bridge the distance between himself and her, overcome his shyness or lack of experience or sense of impropriety, and so he just sat there, motionless and rigid, behind the steering wheel, looking into her darkness-veiled face.

It was getting on for four in the morning, the space around them was beginning to fill with objects, the wall was rapidly peeling and rust was spreading over the wrought-iron gate; it was time, high time, for him to return home – he was amazed at himself, at the fact that he was where he was at that hour, in the company of a strange woman, when he had a perfectly good home – i.e. his own wife and children and an obligation to work.

'Look,' she said, 'it's getting light, the trams will be running again.' And she fell silent, put her head against the headrest of her seat and half closed her eyes; she seemed to be waiting, and he, but only in his thoughts and with his fingertips, touched the carefully pencilled arches of her eyebrows, drew a circle on her cheeks and started the engine. They returned along an equally deserted track, mist was rising from the adjoining meadows, she curled up in her seat but still (with a conspicuous effort) opened her eyes wide and said, 'That's marvellous, not having to take the tram.'

It occurred to him that, while this hour of the day might be unusual for him, she probably returned home at this time quite often, either from drinking parties or from her lovers, just as she was now (from this so unerotic excursion). He pictured her light-boned little figure crouching on a red seat in the tram, and then running down the deserted twilight road, and he felt a tenderness for her such as he sometimes felt for his daughters. 'If you like, you won't have to take the tram.'

'I won't have to take the tram?' she asked without opening her eyes. 'Why won't I have to take the tram?'

'I might drive you.' It was an extravagant promise and he quickly tried to turn it into a joke. 'Suppose it would be my greatest joy to drive you wherever you'd like? At least until I leave for England. The fact is I'm leaving in four months.'

'Yes,' she said. 'I always have singing at eight o'clock on Friday morning. At last I'd get there on time for a change.'

He was approaching her street now, there were only two or three minutes left for him to do or say anything. He looked at her, she noticed his glance and attempted a tired smile, then she produced a mirror from her handbag and tidied her hair. 'You seem to be a rather strange person,' she said.

'What do you mean by that?'

'I don't know; one doesn't have to mean something with everything one says.'

They had arrived.

'Well, thanks a lot,' she said.

'Wait.' He fished his visiting card out of his wallet and

wrote his telephone number on it. His name and the string of figures looked cold and official. He wrote underneath: I like you.

It was too embarrassing. He felt like tearing up the card but she was already extending her hand for it. She read the numbers and undoubtedly also his attempt at a declaration and asked: 'This is your number at the institute?'

'Yes.'

'Must be an important institute, with such a long number.'

'Just in case you should need a lift somewhere, as you said.'

She put the card, or rather flung it, into her handbag: 'I'm bound to lose it.'

'Then I'll bring you another. I'll be waiting for you to call me. Today, when you wake up.'

It was daylight when he got home. As he climbed the stairs he realized that he could still smell the violet fragrance of her perfume. This alarmed him. He opened his front door very quietly and crept into the hall. He took off his trousers and put them away in the wardrobe, then he took off his shirt and, having sniffed it like a good police dog, he stuffed it into the laundry basket, right underneath everything else, and quickly went to the bathroom. He could still smell the perfume, maybe it was clinging to his nostrils or the pores of his skin. He tried to wash it off with soap and a plentiful stream of water.

When he eventually found himself by his wife's side there was barely an hour and a half's sleeping time left to him and it didn't seem worth making the effort, even if he'd been able to, to fall asleep. Nevertheless he closed his eyes; instantly he was overcome by a sense of vertigo. With a rocking motion he was falling into something and during that fall he heard her voice, the unceasing rhythmical cadence of her voice which intoxicated him.

79

His wife moved at his side.

He opened his eyes and looked at her.

Her eyes were open too. 'You're not asleep?' she asked.

'I woke up. It's getting light early.'

'When did you get home?'

'Long time ago.'

'I must have been fast asleep,' she said apologetically. 'I was terribly tired. And I was sorry I didn't go with you. I didn't mean it like that. I was just terribly tired.'

'I know. It didn't matter at all, your not coming along.'

'Did you have a good time?'

'So-so.' He shut his eyes again and continued his free fall.


6


It was during his second year at university that his mother developed cancer of the throat. That magnificent voice he'd admired so now uttered only uncertain croaky sounds. Her sufferings, her transformation from a royally exalted creature into a moaning, pitiful, mortal being affected him far more than he could have imagined. That was when he last tried to pray, to turn to a superior power with a plea for his mother's recovery.

She didn't of course recover, neither God nor his father could help her, the only thing his father was able to do for her was to arrange for a private room at the hospital so she didn't have to die like the rest of the patients behind a curtain. They took turns at her bedside, and it was he who heard the last, by then unconscious, moan from her diseased throat – the sound penetrated to the very core of his being. He was the last to see her already rigid eyes whose colour had always reminded him of wood ash – dust and ashes. And he was the first to bend over the dead body and with his lips touch her high, still moist forehead.

Even before then he'd been convinced that man came into the world to work rather than to enjoy himself. Now he came to believe that apart from work nothing in life had any meaning. He was successful in his studies. In his third year he became an assistant scientific worker, and in the fourth he was entrusted with running a seminar. But the more successful he was in his work the more awkward he was in the rest of his life. He had never had a close friend and he was nearly twenty-three when he was first seduced by a woman. She was a colleague from the university, her name was Alice, she was three years older than him, divorced with a seven-year-old boy, unattractively thin with short crooked legs and unfeminine large hands. Nothing about her was attractive, but a single night spent together made him think her attractive and caused him to fall in love with her, or at least convinced him that he loved her. Her fate filled him with sympathy (she was all alone) and he was attracted by his physical pleasure which he associated, erroneously, exclusively with her person. He didn't mind her age or her status, what worried him more was her frivolousness. She loved entertainment, amusing company, drinking with friends. She dragged him to cinemas, dance halls and operettas which bored him, and the only reaction they produced in him was despair over the time he was wasting. When at times he objected, she would make him sit with her and if nothing else watch television (she had bought a set even though she had only one duvet cover and whenever she washed it they had to sleep under the uncovered duvet).

He couldn't really picture himself living with her because any such life together would clearly mean the end of everything he was striving for. Nevertheless he was prepared to marry her. They were even looking for a bigger flat, in exchange for her bachelor flatlet, and he, in order to please her, pretended to be interested in the

81

furniture she was choosing, and they agreed to get married immediately after his degree, which was then only eight weeks away.

He was saved by sheer accident. The head of the department fell ill and a meeting was cancelled. He decided to use the unexpectedly saved time to visit her. He had a key to her flat, although he always rang the bell. So he also rang this time, and he was surprised no one came to the door because he thought he'd heard her voice inside a moment before (who could she have been talking to when the boy was at school?). So he took the key from his pocket, but when he tried to insert it he found that there was a key in the lock on the inside. So he rang again, he became alarmed that something might have happened to her; he even pressed his nose to the letter-box slit and sniffed in case there was a smell of gas about. Now he couldn't hear any sound at all, and that silence alarmed him even more, surely she must be inside if her key was in the door, but he still refused to consider the most likely explanation: that she was at home all right but didn't want to open the door to him. Strange visions passed through his head, she might be lying there in a pool of blood and he should do something immediately to get inside the locked door. But he couldn't think of anything else but to lean on the bell, continuously and unyieldingly, and then, when he'd still not had any kind of response, he went out into the road (she lived in an old three-storey apartment house on the Smichov embankment) and looked up to her one and only window on the second floor. The blind was pulled down and he felt certain that at the moment he'd glanced up a face had briefly appeared in the gap between it and the window frame. That should have been sufficient for certainty about what was happening but he felt a self-torturing need to stare into the face of betrayal. He remembered the little courtyard of the house had recently been linked up with neighbouring courtyards and turned into a children's playground. So he entered the house next door, walked past a battery of dustbins and between lines of freshly planted young poplars and birches, then re-entered the staircase he'd just left by the back door. He silently walked past her door and only stopped when he reached the attic level and there, overcoming his embarrassment, shame and excitement, leaned against the wall and waited. At least thirty minutes passed (he kept postponing the moment of his departure) before the door below creaked. He descended a few steps and, himself unseen, actually saw her leave the flat. She was alone and maybe he'd wronged her, unless the other man had managed to sprint away at the moment when he himself was circling the building, besides he might question her, he was ready to accept her explanation and he almost rushed off after her to get that explanation as soon as possible.

But he waited for her footsteps to die away and then just a little longer to make sure she'd gone far enough from the house. Just as he decided to abandon his undignified watch the door of her flat opened again and he saw one of his colleagues step out. He might have received the dénouement with a sense of relief but instead he experienced only the incomprehensible betrayal by a person to whom he'd done no harm and whom he'd never wished to betray.

He descended those few steps to her front door, hesitated whether to enter, but eventually unlocked the door and went in. Inside everything was unusually tidy, even the couch which she always left made up had been folded away. He sat down at the table, found a piece of paper and started on a reproachful and hurt letter. He covered all of two pages, mentioning his resolution never to betray her or lie to her, his faith in her, which she'd so shamefully betrayed even while she'd been pretending to love him and while she was about to seal that love by marrying him within a few days. No doubt she'd understand that, having been prepared to give up a great deal out of his love for her, and to adopt her son as his own, he now considered himself released from all obligations. He wasn't exactly an outstanding letter-writer but it seemed to him that he'd expressed his sentiments perfectly and he also felt that with each sentence a new layer of pity for her was peeling off him. After signing it and adding the date (and the time) he had a sense of satisfaction. He folded the letter under the pillow on the couch and tried to picture what she'd do when she found it that evening.

Then it crossed his mind that the whole business might seem ridiculous to her. Surely by what she'd done she'd revealed clearly enough what she thought of his feelings and his love. He therefore walked back from the door, pulled out the note again, thrust it into his pocket, tore off a fresh sheet from his note-pad and wrote on it: 'I was here. I shan't come again. Goodbye.' He left the note on the table and walked out.

# CHAPTER FOUR

1

By 10 am he couldn't bear the quiet of his office any longer. He told Marie to put any calls for him through to the lab downstairs (but she wouldn't be calling yet anyway, she was probably still sleeping, it was only five and a half hours since they parted) and went to his laboratory, where his assistant was just dissecting an experimental male mouse.

He should have been interested in the result (a thymus transplant) but he was unable to concentrate. He still felt her presence which, strangely enough, persisted even in her absence. He felt like talking about her if he couldn't talk to her, or at least talking about anything if he couldn't talk about her.

He sat on the window sill.

Mencl was cutting the tissue with scissors, the girl lab assistant passed him a piece of foreign tissue with forceps, the motionless mouse was pinned down to a wooden base, everything was proceeding as it should, Mencl's hand did not shake in the least even though he'd got drunk the night before, in that respect he was like David's father, he'd never understood how his father could drink when he knew he might be summoned within an hour to perform an operation, he really should ask him what time he'd got to bed.

The doctoral assistant looked up in surprise. 'At about two. We were very sorry you left us so soon.'

'I really had to.'

'The American had a splendid argument with the Strong Man.'

In the kennel under the window the dogs were howling. He looked out. Across the cloudless sky ran the snowy trail of condensed exhaust gases.

Abruptly, totally out of context, except perhaps a connection between the invisible and inaudible aircraft and the invisible and inaudible state of his mind, he began to tell a story from his childhood.

It was in the final year of the war, in bright daylight, when one of those numerous air raid alerts occurred. His mother was afraid of the roar of the engines and the rattle of flak and at the first note of the siren she would run down to the cellar and make him and his father follow her. But his father, if he was at home, never allowed himself to be interrupted in what he was doing. If he was sleeping he continued to sleep, and if he was reading he continued to read his book, and also allowed his son to remain in the flat and look out of the windows for the planes which as a rule didn't show up at all.

But that day they did. He saw them approaching and he even felt a paralyzing fear of the roar of the approaching formation. He glanced back at his father who was calmly sitting in his armchair, reading, and again looked out into the street which was now deserted – except for one woman with a Red Cross armband on her sleeve. The woman was standing in the doorway of the house opposite and, like himself, was staring at the sky. Everything happened so unexpectedly and so quickly that he wasn't aware of the sequence of events. He only realized with horror that the house opposite shook (an unbelievable and terrifying movement of matter which until then he'd regarded as immovable) and in a cloud of dust began to collapse into itself. The sight of it was so unusual, so terrifying and so fascinating that he failed to take in any of the deafening sounds which accompanied it. Everything was expunged from his memory up to the moment when, together with

86

his father, he was kneeling over the prostrate woman (her Red Cross armband still on her sleeve), when he passed his father bandages and scissors and wooden splints from his bag and when he felt neither horror nor revulsion, but only satisfaction in the awareness of his own importance. Then his mother appeared and with a lot of shouting dragged him into the cellar, where she demanded that he should promise her never again to run out into the street in such circumstances and never to become a doctor who had to go out into the street even when the bombs were falling. And he really hadn't become a doctor, even though the bombs had long ceased falling.

He stopped, suddenly embarrassed; surely there was no reason for him to tell them about this incident then. He uttered a few meaningless sentences and left hurriedly.

Surprisingly, however, the fact that he had spoken about something so remote and almost intimate had calmed him and he returned to his office and found himself able to resume his daily work with full concentration. Yet all day long there remained in him a slight excitement, which arose from his knowledge that at any moment the telephone might ring and he'd hear her voice. Why, he asked himself, was he longing to hear that voice, what did he want to hear, what could she tell him? Or had he really lost his senses and fallen in love?

Naturally she did not phone.

2

On Friday morning at five minutes past seven he was waiting in his car outside her house (on Friday mornings I have singing at eight o'clock, at last I'll be on time for a change).

She appeared in the doorway just before eight, just as he was beginning to feel certain she wouldn't come any more.

87

She spotted his car and in a matter-of-fact manner, as if he waited for her every day, she approached him. 'You've come? That's very nice of you. You can see for yourself how late I'd have been.'

Again she sat next to him – in a well-worn dress of light grey corduroy she was looking less elegant and less dazzling than that evening at the theatre when he'd last seen her. An ordinary girl with a snub nose and rather too wide cheekbones, only her perfect make-up and hair lent her that film-star appearance. Why had he come out to meet her, why had he come, he asked himself in amazement, what did he want from her, what was it that attracted him to her, why was he so idiotically, so pointlessly, wasting his time? 'How did you sleep the night before last?' he asked.

'The night before last?' she asked. 'What happened the night before last? Oh yes,' she remembered. 'I think I slept till two thirty. I slept like a log. Then Thomas came and woke me. Thomas says I'm like an owl, I only come to life in the evening.'

'I was waiting for you to phone me.'

'I should have phoned you?' she asked in amazement. 'But I don't even know your name. Or do you think I know your name?'

'I gave you my card. It's all on there, in black and white.'

'You gave me your card,' she repeated. She opened her handbag and rummaged about in it for a while, then she produced the card with the embarrassing message. 'So you did,' she confirmed, 'but I didn't promise I'd phone. Or did I?'

'No, no. That's quite all right.'

'Sometimes I really promise something and then I forget. I've got a terribly stupid memory, especially in the morning.'

'Where do you have that lesson?' he asked.

'In Karlova Street. If you know where that is. You can drop me by the Baths. I had promised Tom I'd follow him to Třeboň and I completely forgot about it. He was waiting for me in his tent for a couple of days, getting terribly wet because it was pouring all the time.'

It was only a few minutes past eight when they stopped by the Baths. He was fond of that spot, he'd walked there with Alice in the old days, they used to sit on the little seat which projected almost above the weir. Now streams of cars were rushing past and sitting there wouldn't be so pleasant. 'I'd like to see you for a little longer,' he said. 'How long does your singing lesson last?'

'Till ten. Except that I have acting afterwards.'

'And lunchtime? Are you going anywhere for lunch?'

'Lunchtime? You think I should be going somewhere for lunch?' Then she said, 'That won't be possible, Tom's collecting me at lunchtime.'

She half-opened the door. 'It was nice of you to come out, this is the first time I'll be on time.'

'But I wanted . . .' he tried to object.

'I'll phone you,' she said quickly. 'After all, you've given me your number, so I can phone you.'

He watched her run across the narrow little street. She disappeared without looking back. He felt, if anything, relieved. He wasn't sure whether this was because for the first time she'd given him at least a slight hint of an interest or, on the other hand, because nothing had happened yet and he'd therefore remained faithful to his wife.


3

Beyond the vast plate-glass window the soundless city looked like a painting. They were in a luxury restaurant, one patronized chiefly by foreigners, but he'd invited the girl student there, it was their first lunch together and he felt it would have been wrong to take her to some low dive.

Strangely enough, although he'd waited for her call all week, he felt no satisfaction now she was sitting opposite him. Perhaps it was because she'd rung on an awkward day (Margit was sick and he'd promised he'd get home as early as possible), or because he'd still not been able to shake off a feeling that his actions lacked all sense. Why was he sitting in this expensive restaurant, listening to idle prattle? Why was he wasting time, of which he was so short? Why was he spending money on feeding and entertaining a woman who was, and should remain, a stranger to him?

She ordered a diplomat pudding and said, 'The last one I had was in Turin with Giuseppe, at a little confectioner's, near the autostrada. They had a shelf running along the entire wall with little motorcars on it. They were all made of chocolate and stuff like that.'

He didn't know what attracted him to her, nor what she expected of him. He was seized by impatience. She was eating too lackadaisically. The whole atmosphere repelled him: the hum of conversation from the neighbouring tables, the obsequious waiters, the strange women in eccentric clothes, the tailors' dummies accompanying them, the delicate fragrance of the exquisite food and expensive scents.

The waiter brought a cup with a yellowish mass in it.

'Would you mind if I also had a coffee?'

He ordered coffee for her (that meal, clearly, was going on for ever) and excused himself to make a telephone call.

'Where are you speaking from?' asked Camilla. 'I've been trying to track you down. Margit isn't at all well. A moment ago she seemed to be delirious. She declared there was a blue elephant crawling up the wall, clicking its teeth. Couldn't you come home?'

'Yes, of course – that's why I phoned. I had to go and

have lunch with those Americans I told you about. This is their last day here. It's possible I may be a little late.'

'For heaven's sake, David. Make some excuse – they'll understand when your daughter's ill. I thought that if she got worse and you were here you could take her to hospital.'

'I'll come as soon as . . .'

'Hang on,' she called out, 'someone at the door.'

He stood motionless in the glass booth, a few foreigners walked past outside and behind their backs, on wisps of cigarette smoke, floated the spires and roofs of the city, and when he looked out sideways, through the glass door, he could see her, her head with the piled-up hair, her bare arms, almost white against the bloody line of the red material of her sleeves, and he was here with her – it seemed unbelievable to him that he was here with her, that he was here with a strange, seductive creature.

'That was Anna,' his wife said. 'She'd popped round to the chemist's for me. So when will you be back?'

'I'll be back as soon as possible. In about an hour or an hour and a half.'

'Please, do come as soon as you can.'

'I'll come as soon as I can.'

'Hang on, Anna wants to say something to you.'

'Hallo, is that you, Dad?'

'What do you want?'

'Dad, when will you be home?'

'Soon.'

'Do come soon, Dad, I bought Margit a little frog which jumps, Dad, I bought it myself, with my own money, seeing she's ill.'

'That was nice of you, Anna.'

'Mum wants to say something to you.'

'David, something else, please. The doctor said she should eat oranges, so if you see any on your way . . .'

'You know perfectly well there aren't any.'

'But they do have them sometimes in town.'

'All right, I'll look out but you know yourself that there aren't any.'

'And phone again if you're held up.'

'Yes,' he promised, 'I'll phone.'

Although it seemed incredible, she was still eating that pudding. Clearly she hadn't missed him, she hadn't even once glanced over to the door by which he would return. Perhaps he was attracted by the total indifference with which she accepted him. She'd go and have lunch with him and she'd sit with him in a car at a lonely spot into the small hours, but she'd never displayed the slightest interest in who he was (she wasn't even interested in his name), she'd never shown him any hint of liking or feeling. She accepted his kindness as a matter of course and as if it were outside the normal order of interrelated events.

He sat down facing her and it crossed his mind that her indifference was directed not only at him but evidently at most people and things that surrounded her: at her own husband just as at her studies or her colleagues at the theatre, maybe she was indifferent even to the food which she was swallowing so slowly, she was indifferent to everything except Venice and possibly those few Italians she'd told him about.

At long last she finished eating. She wiped her mouth with her napkin, lit a cigarette and said, 'Thank you for the lunch. That was a kind of birthday present.'

'Today's your birthday?'

'No, I think tomorrow is. But I don't observe it anyway. Maybe I would have observed it,' she added, 'but no one around me ever observed it. When I was a little girl and my parents were living together I used to have a cake, and one time, I must have been seven or eight, they gave me a big doll. But nothing since. Thomas doesn't hold with such things. All I ever had from him were a few letters and, on one occasion, *Mysterious Palms*, but that's a long time ago.'

'And you'd have a wish?'

'No, why should I have a wish?'

'Everybody has a wish.'

'You think everybody has a wish?' She seemed to be reflecting for a while and then she said, 'I like tinned apricots. And shoes. I could have new shoes all the time. When I bought this pair,' she was pointing to her foot which he couldn't see just then, 'they were so gorgeous I took them out of their box in the evening and went to bed with them on.'

The thought of her slipping between the sheets with her new shoes on reminded him of his daughters' habit of taking soft animal toys to bed with them: teddy-bears, a donkey and a monkey, without which they refused to go to sleep. There was something unexpectedly childish in her remark and he was touched by it.

'I also sometimes think I'd like to have a villa on the road from Merano to Venice – not one of those modern little boxes, the kind they build nowadays, but an old villa with Renaissance windows and with a garden behind a high wall.'

'Who would look after the garden?'

'Gardeners,' she answered without hesitation. 'And inside I'd have a huge Renaissance chest and a four-poster bed, and on the walls frescoes by Giotto and paintings by Giorgione. And Venetian mirrors.'

'Perhaps your wish will come true and you'll have a villa like that.'

'You think my wish will come true?'

'If you wish for something hard enough it can sometimes come true.'

'But I don't want it that badly. I'm sure to die before that wish comes true.'

93

'Why should you die?'

'Maybe because I'm not all that keen on living.'

'If I could I'd buy you that villa. Complete with frescoes by Giotto.' Immediately he felt ashamed of his babbling. He called the head waiter and paid the bill (they had just eaten one window frame of his own as yet non-existent villa).

'There's no need to drive me home,' she said. 'I'm staying in town.'

Of course, she had a date with someone, either with her husband or with some other man, and he suddenly felt angry that she'd allowed him to feed her and now she'd be going off with somebody else. However, he stopped in the little street by the university, told her to wait in the car, and walked into the now familiar florist's shop. The plain assistant was standing behind the counter, maybe she recognized him because she was smiling at him. This time (daffodils were out of the question) he decided on roses.

'How many?' the girl asked.

He looked at the vase before him, unable to guess whether it contained thirty or fifty blooms, and said, startling himself with his decision: 'The lot.' And he watched her counting the individual stems, carefully touching them with her large boyish fingers.

He paid with another window frame of his as yet nonexistent family house (there were forty-seven, at five crowns each), got back into the car and handed her the flowers. 'These are for your birthday.'

For an instant she gazed at the bouquet which he was still clutching. 'These are for me?' she asked.

He put them down on her lap.

'Well really,' she said. 'Well, really.'

They were driving on again and when he stole a sideways glance at her a moment later he noticed she was crying. 'What's the matter?' he asked. 'What's wrong?'

She made no reply, hid her face behind the bunch of roses, pulled out a little handkerchief from her handbag and dabbed her face.

'Is anything wrong?'

'Just let me be for a moment,' she shouted at him. 'Don't keep asking questions.'

He was silent, slightly hurt by her fierceness.

'No,' she said suddenly, 'I won't think about it any more, I won't think about it.' And she smiled at him with the happiest and most carefree smile she could muster. She smiled at him as if she were kissing him. 'Maybe you'd better drive me home after all, what with these flowers.'

He pulled up outside her house. 'You haven't got a telephone?' he asked.

'No, but I can phone you again.'

'Make it soon, we have so little time.'

'We have so little time?'

'I've told you I'm leaving. I'm going to England for a year.'

'Yes, I'll phone you, seeing you're leaving for England.' And he understood that this statement held not the slightest meaning for her. He might be leaving for Klatovy or for Greenland, for a year or for the rest of his life, it was all the same to her, he was of no importance to her.

She was already standing outside the car, the bunch was really huge. She leaned in again (if only she did it so he could kiss her, if only she said: You're so nice!): 'Tomorrow, just in case you felt like collecting me, like that other Friday, please don't come, I shan't be here tomorrow morning.' With that she turned on her heel and walked away. Only then did he notice that the shoes she'd talked about, the ones she'd worn to bed, were crimson red with very solid but now somewhat worn heels.

He stopped at the nearest telephone box. 'Kind of you,

David, to phone,' Camilla said. 'Margit's a little better. When will you be home?'

'I'm on my way.'

'That's good. Did you get any oranges?'

'No hope. But I thought I might get her some juice instead.'

'Oh I don't know,' she said, 'won't that be very expensive? You always say . . .'

'But if Margit's ill!'

'All right then, get a tin of juice.'


4

The year after he'd joined the Institute of Experimental Biology he was sent on a two months' attachment to the research department of a Bucharest hospital. Presumably no one took that trip very seriously, it was simply to comply with some article in a treaty of cultural and scientific cooperation, which was why they sent him there in the middle of the summer when anybody with any sense at all, both at the hospital and elsewhere, had gone off to the seaside or at least disappeared immediately after lunch in order to spend the hot months in the cool of some wine cellar or other.

He'd probably been the only person there who was conscientious about work. He worked because that was what he'd been sent there for, and besides he had no idea what else to do with his time. He didn't know a soul, he was not interested in amusement (of which there wasn't a lot available anyway), he didn't drink and he hated idleness.

Not until three weeks after his arrival did he decide to go to the seaside for a weekend. He stuffed his swimming trunks into his briefcase, alongside his books and a spare shirt, and got onto a stuffy train which carried him to Mamaia.

Yet neither the resort facilities nor the crowded beaches appealed to him. He went down to the harbour, where he discovered that a steamer was leaving in twenty minutes' time for Mangalia, down the coast, and because travelling anywhere was more in line with his active and restless mind than remaining in the same place he went and bought a ticket.

It was a small boat, named Horia (which, as he gathered from a Russian notice on board, was the name of some rebel) and mainly served the local population for travelling to and from the town.

He watched the flat shore receding and all around him was the noise of an incomprehensible language in which sunburned villagers in white trousers and large black or coloured hats were shouting at each other. He climbed a ladder to a deserted deck piled high with ropes, sails, nets and oil drums. There, immediately in front of the deck-house, he leaned against a lifebelt and gazed at the snowy crests of the waves, at the cloudless sky and at distant ships vanishing slowly below the horizon. He felt an unaccustomed delight in his inactivity and half closed his eyes, so that everything dissolved into a multitude of rainbow-coloured circles, and he was able to indulge in the illusion that the things around him, and life generally, fitted into a system, into a direction that he might comprehend some day, and he realized with certainty that the only meaning of everything was life and its duration. Again – as once before in his childhood – it seemed unbelievable and unimaginable that he himself might one day not exist, that his body, his as yet perfectly functioning senses and his precisely and logically assessing brain should perish. What sense would the sea have then, and the sky above, and the air, what sense would the continuance of air have if he was no longer breathing it?

In that state, which was closer to dreaming than to

wakefulness, he became aware of a female voice quite near to him, a voice singing a song in his own language. He looked up, and a little distance above him he saw a girl in a colourful light summer dress, the wind lifting her skirt and revealing a pair of tanned legs. (Somebody had advised her, as he was to discover later, that singing prevented seasickness.) She was not beautiful: her legs were too solid and her face too featureless, though it looked good-natured, and what encouraged him to address her was not so much her singing as the circumstances of their encounter.

That was how he'd met Camilla – on a little steamer named Horia. (She was there with two girl friends; they had all just graduated.)

They had a lot of time, the little steamer moved more slowly than a stagecoach, and so he learned that she had studied natural sciences and history and was fond of flowers, back home in Litomyšl her folks had a big garden with a greenhouse and in her room at the student hostel she had cactuses all along one wall, including a giant Erio-cerus Martinii, so that there wasn't room for even a single visitor, and she'd chosen history as a subject because she loved classical antiquity and the origins of Christianity, even though she wasn't a believer herself, but now she was afraid she'd have to learn some modern history which she couldn't stand, those new legends and half-truths about democracy which was no democracy and about dictatorship which was the highest form of democracy, and also that she loved music, especially folk songs, and that she would sing at home with her father and mother. Her father was a vet and was fond of animals, so their house was always full of lame dogs and stray cats, and when she was still a little girl they'd actually owned a horse which she'd learned to ride; and she didn't smoke or drink, she didn't go out to any entertainments because in the evening she preferred to read, except that now and again she might go to a concert with some girl friends.

He too, as the steamer slowly advanced along the shore, told her about himself, mostly about his work. He bragged a little, so that she must have got the impression she was talking to a man of whom the world would be talking before long. He also mentioned his childhood and his mother (she had actually heard of his famous ancestor and that raised him even further in her eyes) and he informed her that he too didn't smoke and that he disapproved of drinking, and of course he also liked music even though lately he hadn't found any time for it.

They went ashore and he invited her and her friends to a small tavern and treated them to a meal of crab, tomatoes and fermented fruit juice.

He spent the return trip with her as well. It was evening by then, they were standing in the ship's bows, so close together that at each slight shudder of the ship their arms and hips touched. The sea was calm, the surface glistened in the moonlight, the air was mild and fragrant with the strange and to them unfamiliar smell of salt water; she said it was a marvellous evening, she'd never seen so many stars, and he agreed that he hadn't either, and then they held hands, and kept holding hands for the rest of the journey, but they didn't kiss, they didn't even call each other by first names, and indeed when she wrote a letter to him in Bucharest (she had to leave a couple of days after their sea trip together) she addressed him as Dear Doctor Krempa.

He replied at once, he described his work, the hot city which kept forcing upon him the memory of 'that lovely time by the sea', he told her he'd been to a concert, 'music is the only diversion I treat myself to here,' he mentioned that he had a major article coming out in *Nature* ('I am particularly pleased about it because England is a country I am very fond of, I'm an Anglophile, I could take you all the way from Hyde Park to the Tower or to Westminster even though I haven't been there yet but I hope I'll get the chance one day. Would you consider coming there with me?') and he also informed her of his probable date of return.

She was waiting for him at the railway station. It didn't occur to him that she must have met at least two trains before his because he'd only told her the day and not the time of his arrival. That was her last week in Prague, after that she was due to start work at a school in a small town near Litomyšl. Which meant they had just one week and they met every evening. On the final Sunday he invited her on an excursion.

They met outside the station in the morning; she was wearing a pair of well-worn and scuffed shoes and a blouse of translucent nylon which didn't go with her khaki skirt or military haversack. She'd got four meticulously made gigantic sandwiches for him which would have been enough for several days. (He felt touched that in her eyes he was such a ravenous he-man.)

They got off two stops beyond Benešov, he didn't know the place (he never went on excursions) and he set off at random towards a wooded slope while she tripped along by his side. She was talking all the time, she swamped him with information on people he didn't know, on books he hadn't read and on films he hadn't seen because he rarely went to the cinema. Now and again she looked up at him with a calm, trustful glance.

And then suddenly – he had no special reason to do it just then or just there – it was a quiet deserted path all the way, with short grass growing along both sides of it, shielded by tall spruces, and she was continually talking about something remote while he was silently listening or maybe not listening to her – he embraced her and kissed her. 'I'm not sure,' she breathed, 'I'm not sure.'

They were lying in the grass in a little meadow in the middle of an unknown forest (they never saw the place again afterwards, nor did they ever search for it) and because he was kissing her wordlessly she asked him: Do you love me a little? And he answered he did.

In the evening they discovered at the station that their next train wouldn't be for another two hours. He didn't feel like sitting in the crowded station waiting room, so he took her by the hand and they set out along the track. On a siding he noticed an uncoupled goods wagon with its door half open.

On the floor of the wagon there was some straw left and there was a smell of horses, and in the corner, like some gigantic snake, lay a coiled rusty chain.

They kissed again on that straw and then they made love; their first love-making was on the floor of that wagon while trains noisily hurtled past them.

As they returned together by an empty night train it occurred to him that he had just found a woman for his whole life.

[ 2 ]

## CHAPTER FIVE

### 1

'Hello, this is Iva. I've been wanting to give you a ring for some time but I had a sore throat. I've just come back from the health centre and the doctor said I must stay in bed for another three days and he gave me penicillin. Have you ever taken penicillin?'

'And what did the doctor say was wrong with you?'

'An infected sore throat he said, and I have to take that medicine every six hours to the point of total exhaustion. Do you think it'll take a long time to reach that point?'

'Is your temperature up?'

'I've no idea, I don't think my temperature's ever up or maybe it's up all the time. Last time I took it I was about five years old. I'm sure I caught this bug the night after I had lunch with you. I went out dancing with Tom and then there was this downpour and we didn't have the money for a taxi.'

'If I'd known I'd have picked you up.'

'You'd have come all that way? I told Tom, I said to him I know a gentleman who'd be sure to come and pick us up if I phoned him but Tom said I must be out of my mind and to shut up about my gentlemen. Can you hear how thick my throat still is?'

'So how can I see you when you're sick?'

'I don't know how you can see me when I'm sick.'

'Suppose I . . . Are you ever alone?'

'I'm never alone here, there's always a crowd of people. Grandmother and two grandfathers. Sometimes even more if they all come together. That's why I had to get married, because they were always here. They're at my place even now when I'm not there for the moment. Have you any idea how I can take my tablets every six hours at night when I'm asleep?'

'You haven't got an alarm clock?'

'Tom's borrowed it, he takes it with him on his tours. I thought you might perhaps ring me during the night.'

'But you said you weren't on the phone.'

'That's right, I'd have to sleep at Tom's place. There's a gentleman knocking at the phone box now, can you hear him? And there's a chimney sweep walking past. That means good luck. Hang on, I've got to find a button to rub. Those flowers of yours are still in my vase, they're terribly pretty. And now a lady has come with a dog. She's acting sort of important. Maybe she wants to teach the dog how to use the phone. Suppose I ring you when I've swallowed all those tablets.'

Such ramblings and they make me feel happy. Simply because she phoned, because I know why I haven't heard from her for so long. Because she called from some box even though she wasn't feeling too good. Maybe she does feel something for me, or why would she have phoned? Those flowers touched her – except that I still don't know if I really want her to feel anything for me. I don't know what I want and I shouldn't be thinking about it now, I should be concentrating. Otherwise I'll never finish those lectures. How much time have I left? One hundred and five days. I mustn't let myself be distracted. When I gave them to her she cried, that was the first time I'd seen her upset by anything. Maybe it is just a pose, the way she acts, that flood of meaningless conversation, intended perhaps to conceal her feelings – but why should she have any feelings for me when she got married six months ago and that fellow of hers is at least fifteen years younger then me?

I might have asked her where she was speaking from and offered to drive her home. Why didn't I think of that?

Maybe I do have some attraction for her, just because I am fifteen years older. And maybe it isn't fifteen years anyway but only fourteen. In the West that's quite a normal age gap.

What am I thinking about? Surely I can't marry her. I don't want to marry her. I only want her to love me. No, I don't want her to love me. I only want to break her indifference. I want to look forward to her phoning again. That's all.

2

'Could you tell me – this striped one here, what is it?'

'That's an orchid. Paphiopedillum.'

'You only have the one?'

'Just this one. We don't carry a stock of them – they're not much in demand. Because of the price. People, you know, would nowadays rather buy a Hungarian salami than flowers. And when they do buy flowers what they'd like best is dandelions.'

*In view of your sore throat I'm sending you this flower in the biggest envelope I could find. Maybe one of your grandfathers will clear your letter box before it fades. Get well soon.*

*Yours, D.*

*P.S. Do you think you'll be well by next Monday? I could come round to pick you up about five pm.*

3

A quarter to six. Shouldn't wait any longer. Maybe she's still sick or her husband's come back. But she obviously won't come now. Surely she realizes I am waiting for her here. Assuming she got my note. Perhaps they didn't give it to her. Why shouldn't they give it to her? She isn't a

107

child, she's a married woman. I'm going to wait another ten minutes. The final ten minutes. At six I'm driving off. I can do some reading until then.

'Mental difficulties, of course, cover a vast range, including acute brain disorders resulting from toxic reactions . . .' What would happen if I went up and rang her bell? Why shouldn't I be visiting her? But suppose her husband's there just then? That would be embarrassing for me, for her and for him too. So what shall I do? If she doesn't turn up? I should write her another note. Another five minutes. I'll write that note in five minutes from now. I should be reading. I mustn't waste my time so stupidly. I am wasting my time. 'Mental difficulties, of course, cover a vast range . . .' I ought to buy her some flowers and attach my note. What's the time? Three minutes to six. The florists will all be shut now. I shouldn't write another note. I'll regard it as the decree of fate that she hasn't come, that we haven't met. Actually I'm glad she hasn't come because today something might have happened that couldn't be undone. Six o'clock. I'll drive home now and I won't go after her again. Maybe she'll phone, but if she doesn't it will be a shame but it will probably be for the best; why should I complicate my life, I don't want to hurt anyone, I'm fond of Camilla even if I'm not crazy about her, but that's quite normal seeing we've been together for eight years. I'm glad she hasn't come, I shan't go out with her again, I won't wait for her to ring, I won't make a date with her even if she calls. It's five past six now, I'm off or she might come after all, I'm glad she hasn't come. At home I'll get down to work on my lectures, I won't think of her any more.

But suppose she's really ill and can't come? I could write her a few words, so she knows I've been here. Unless she's seen me from her window. I don't even know which are her windows. Bound to be on to the street, it 's got to be a biggish flat if there are so many of them. But maybe they aren't all at home anyway. She's fond of exaggerating, I've discovered that, in fact I don't know half the truth of anything she's told me.

'You're waiting here?'

'I was on the point of leaving.'

'I couldn't come any sooner. On Mondays we have lectures till six.'

'Never mind. The main thing is, you're here. Shall we have something to eat somewhere?'

'You want to have something to eat again? We do nothing but eat together, do we?'


4


Night.

'Where are we actually going?'

'I don't know but I thought you liked driving.'

'I do. I like going fast.'

'We'll go fast then.'

She loves me. Maybe she loves me if she drives out with me, if she lets me hold her hand or put my arm round her shoulders. I've never before driven with one hand, or at least I've never had my arm round anyone while driving, but I have my arm round her, I can feel the warmth of her neck, the touch of her hair, while driving. And where am I going? I've never yet driven anywhere without knowing where I was going. But now I'm driving just for the drive. For a drive together with her. Am I in love with her? No – I mustn't use that word lightly. I feel good with her. We'll have to stop somewhere. And what then? Do I look for a place to spend the night? Maybe she'd refuse to come along with me even if I found somewhere. But probably she'd come. It's what she must expect if we keep going like this. She doesn't have to realize anything, she's riding with me because she enjoys it, she certainly isn't thinking about what happens next, she only thinks about what is now. That's where she is different from me. I think of what will be and that's why I'm now reflecting on whether I actually wish to spend the night with her, though maybe the situation won't even arise. But if I spent the night with her, if she spent the night with me, what would I tell Camilla? What will I tell her when I get back in the morning? Surely I can't stay out all night.

'Now you're driving well. Can I open the window a little? Can you feel the wind? I love the wind.'

We're driving like lunatics. The headlights are carving a narrow and terrifying strip of the world out of the night. Mournful, pale tree trunks rush up to meet us. Maybe we'll kill ourselves. I shouldn't be going so fast, this road isn't wide enough. I'm behaving like a teenager. I'm bragging with an engine I didn't build. But there's some delight in dicing with death. I've always been afraid of death, but now I feel a touch of ecstasy. Camilla would never allow me to go fast. 'Aren't you afraid we might have an accident?'

'Why should I be afraid?'

'If we got carried off the road and hit one of these trees – at this speed we'd be cut to pieces.'

'I'm not thinking of that.'

'You're not afraid we might get killed?'

'No, I don't think about it. And if I did think about it I wouldn't care.'

'Wouldn't care about what?'

'Whether I'm alive or dead. Do you care?'

There is lightning ahead of us, the trees are waving, where on earth are we going? We're going straight into a storm. But that isn't possible – that she doesn't care whether she is alive or not, that's just talk to make her seem interesting. Even though I don't really understand her. She's a bit like a child, at least that's the impression I have, and children aren't afraid of death either. Got to slow down a bit now because the wind's springing up, I can feel the car being lifted. Forest left and right, it's starting to rain, we're in a room made of rain, we're in the shelter of darkness and rain, we are alone, we are together, I must embrace her now, I must embrace her because I love her, there's a track.

FOR FORESTRY ADMINISTRATION VEHICLES ONLY

'Is this where you wanted to get to?'
'Iva, I've been wanting to tell you: I love you.'
'You love me?'
'Do you remember the first time we met, at the cemetery, well, something happened at that moment, I chased after you, I knew I mustn't lose you.'
'So you love me. I'm always pleased when somebody loves me.'
And maybe she loves me too if she lets me kiss her, I'm kissing you now, at last I am touching you, oh my darling, I had no idea it would be such bliss. I am kissing you, your tongue is in my mouth, your mouth is in my mouth, it's ages since I kissed anyone, say something, please say something!
'So you kiss too?'
'What do you mean?'
'I thought gentlemen like you didn't kiss any more.'

5

The light's on in the kitchen. That's bad. Camilla must have woken up, or perhaps she merely forgot to switch it off. I must be very quiet, even if she's asleep she won't be sleeping very soundly now.

'Is that you, David?'

'Yes, it's me. Why aren't you asleep?'

'I've been waiting up for you. I thought you'd be home before now. Where have you been for so long?'

'I got terribly engrossed in my work, I didn't realize it was so late.'

'You're all pale. You shouldn't overdo things.'

'I am not overdoing things, the work went well, that's why I didn't realize . . .'

'What work went well?'

'What's all this questioning? You know I'm working on those lectures.'

'You've never been home this late. Aren't you hungry?'

'No, I'd rather go to bed.'

'And what were you writing about?'

'Why do you keep asking questions?'

'I thought you liked talking to me about your work.'

'Yes, but not at three in the morning! Why did you wait up for me so long?'

'You asked this one before. I couldn't have known it would be so long. Normally you phone when you're going to be late.'

'I didn't want to phone in case I woke you up. I thought you'd be asleep.'

'I was afraid something might have happened to you.'

'I'm not a child.'

'I know you aren't.'

'What's the meaning of this tone?'

'No particular tone. It's you who's touchy. Has anything happened to you?'

'Nothing. I'm sorry. I'm rather tired. Let's go to bed, okay?'

'All right, if that's all you're going to tell me.'

'What else should I tell you? What's the matter with you?'

'Nothing's the matter with me.'

'You have tears in your eyes.'

'That's nothing. So you've nothing else to tell me?'

'What else should I tell you?'

'Where you were all evening.'

Oh Lord, she knows something, maybe she followed me, but she wouldn't have left the children at home alone, she probably just suspects something, or else I have something on my face, maybe a smudge of rouge or a hair of hers, I should have inspected myself more carefully. Or should I tell her everything? Actually, why don't I tell her everything? 'I don't understand, I've just told you.'

'David . . . I did something I shouldn't have done.'

'What did you do?'

'I know you don't like me disturbing you in your work in the evening and that's why you disconnect the telephone, but I got panicky by the time it was midnight and you still weren't home, and you hadn't phoned, so I asked the night porter to pop upstairs and make sure nothing had happened to you.'

Silence.

'I've noticed that something's been wrong with you these past few weeks, I thought . . . I'd always believed that you wouldn't lie to me, David. I beg you – at least don't lie to me.'

'Very well. But let's leave it for some other time. It's late. It's nearly morning. And you have your school tomorrow.'

'You think I can lie down now and go to sleep?'

Silence.

'So you want to talk about it now?' How shall I tell her. To make matters worse, I'm dog-tired. It's getting light outside. She's following me round, waiting. I want to go to bed. I don't want to talk about anything. I don't want to think about anything. 'I think I've fallen in love.'

Silence.

'Do I know her?'

'No. Quite certainly you don't know her.'

'From the institute?'

'No, not from the institute.'

'Unmarried?'

'No, she's not unmarried.'

'How long have you been going out with her?'

'I'm not going out with her at all.'

'So where have you been?'

'We've been out.'

'Where?'

'I don't know. We had dinner first and then somewhere in the woods. I don't know the neighbourhood but surely that makes no difference.'

'Is she pretty?'

'I don't know. Probably.'

Silence. I am falling asleep. No, I'm not falling asleep, I merely want to sleep. Get away from this moment and from this situation. But she is waiting. 'I find myself thinking of her all the time. There isn't anything at all special about her, we actually have nothing to say to each other, and yet I find myself thinking of her all the time.'

'Did you . . . were you unfaithful to me?'

Silence.

'I wasn't unfaithful to you.'

'Why not? Didn't she want to?'

'It wasn't that. For heaven's sake, let it be. Don't you understand that there's no point in these questions. I don't want to love her. I don't want to be unfaithful to you.'

'But you will be, won't you?'

Silence. This is my wife. Crying. We've been together for eight years and we have children. A daughter and a daughter, and I'm fond of them. I'm fond of her too. I know her. I know how she breathes at night, I know her face and her body so that I don't have to see them any more. Now, without opening my eyes, I know how she is crying. I know the way her tears run down and how her upper lip trembles. I know that she's waiting for me to tell her I love her. I know that she is desperately lonely. I know she is lonely now. I know she is waiting for some word or some caress, but I just can't manage it because under my fingers I can still feel the warmth of another woman's skin. I am still full of her warmth and her fragrance, I'm still sitting in the car with her face leaning against mine.

It's terrible, I'm lying by your side and I'm thinking of her.

It's terrible, I'm thinking of you and I'm lying by her side.

# CHAPTER SIX

## 1

I am waiting outside her house, even though I don't know whether or not she's there, let alone whether she'll come out at just this moment. I am waiting here merely because I have an hour to spare and I want to see her. I sound my horn and strange faces appear in strange windows. Camilla recently asked me how I would define the difference between the words foolish and stupid – I've no idea what she wanted it for. I told her the difference was in the quality of the negation. Stupid meant a lack of intelligence, while foolish meant a lack of scepticism. Not a bad definition, yet I can't define myself.

'You've come to see me? But I have so little time.'

It's impossible for her to be that beautiful. It must be the clothes she's wearing. Bound to be from abroad. I'm feeling like a native from Togo. The brighter the colour the better I like a dress. The pattern looks like some proto-beetles or proto-birds in crazy colours.

'I'm sitting history next Monday, and I don't know a thing yet. And to make matters worse, Igor has arrived.'

'Who's Igor?'

'No one you'd know. He's a producer from Bratislava. You know, all women puppeteers are really unrecognized actresses. But he's not a famous producer, he's just a boy.'

'You love him?'

'Where were you thinking of going?'

'I thought we might go to the cinema.'

'That's nice of you, wanting to take me to the cinema, but I can't today. I've got to get something done and then at four I'm meeting Tom. Life's terribly strenuous when you're married.'

'All right. At least I can give you a lift. Where do you have to go?'

'You're very sweet, wanting to take me there. Fact is I spotted some marvellously ugly little shoes on St Wenceslas Square. Just imagine, imported from Italy. My Italy.'

She's sitting on a little stool, trying on her shoes. I've never seen such concentration on her face before. The shoes are blue, shiny, with a massive heel and a gilt buckle. They cost four hundred crowns. I had no idea you could buy such expensive shoes. If I bought her the shoes maybe she'd be happy. But maybe she'd be offended and wouldn't accept them.

'Do you like them?'

'I think they suit you.'

'Tom will be furious. But I've got to have them. So he'll have to give up smoking for a month. Anyway, it's bad for him.'

'Let me see the bill.'

'What do you want to see it for? Watch me walking in them. Aren't they just perfect?'

Camilla's shoes cost a hundred. Camilla never buys anything expensive or fashionable. She's afraid I might get angry. We saved for our car and now we're saving for our little house. Surely there's no point in throwing money about on a pair of expensive shoes. Shoes are utilitarian articles. 'Here's your bill.'

'You've paid it?'

'Now you have a pair of Italian shoes from me.'

'You bought me a pair of shoes. I don't think I can accept them.'

'Why shouldn't you?'

'I don't think anyone's ever bought me shoes before. At least such beautiful shoes.'

'And I've never bought such shoes for anyone either.'

'Maybe I'll end up by beginning to love you. Because you're so kind and you've bought me these shoes. Hold the box a moment for me. I must kiss you.'

She kisses me. We kiss in the middle of the department store. We kiss while people are pushing all round us.

'I'm terribly sorry I haven't got more time. I'd like to be nice to you. At least I'll phone you. But when can I phone you? In the morning I'm sure to be still asleep and then I'll be sitting in the library and there isn't a single pay-phone there. Couldn't I ring you at night? Where are you usually at night?'

'At night I'm usually at home.'

'A pity I can't phone you at night. That's when I'm most alive. I could, for instance, ring you at midnight and you could come out and meet me somewhere.'

At midnight Camilla is always fast asleep. If I carried the telephone to the kitchen she wouldn't even know anybody had rung.

'All right then, ring me at midnight.'

2

As if to spite him, Camilla took a book to bed with her. 'I'll wait up for you.'

'No, don't do that. I'll be working late.'

'You don't care about me any more, now you've got someone else.'

'I haven't got anyone else. I told you there was nothing between us.'

'But there will be.'

'Do stop it. There's no point in talking about it.'

'But you aren't denying that there will be something between you. You don't want to disappoint her.'

'There won't be anything between us.'

118

'But you're still in love with her.'

'Stop it, please. I'd like to do some work.'

'What's her hair like?'

'For heaven's sake, what about her hair?'

'Is it prettier than mine?'

'Go to sleep now, please. You'll be tired out all day tomorrow.'

'What would happen if you went to bed early too, for a change? You have rings under your eyes.'

'You know perfectly well I've got those lectures to finish. I can't arrive there without them. Once I'm there I won't have the time to prepare them.'

'You always have some excuse.'

'Get some sleep. You need it more than I do. You've often said so yourself.'

I am sitting in the kitchen with my files. Tables. Folders with experimental data. Dozens of experiments, innumerable days. I always used to enjoy going through my papers. Just as if they still carried the smell of the laboratory and that of my experimental animals, as well as my hope that one day I'll manage to accomplish something that will give meaning to my life.

I ought to concentrate. It's only half past ten.

The theory of auto-intoxication. We ought to mention this for the sake of completeness, even though we do not consider . . . Suppose she'd want me to come out and meet her somewhere? Surely I can't leave now. If Camilla woke up and found me gone – she'd never forgive me.

Come and meet me, darling. I'll be waiting for you.

But I can't go out and meet you now, dearest.

Do come. I want you to come. Now.

Very well.

There's someone under my window. She's transformed my life. I should now be sitting here, writing. Drawing structural formulae. Seeing matter in its unreal, symbolical shape. It would never occur to me to get up and walk to the window in order to stare out into the night and watch some strange walker. I wouldn't even be aware of this night or of its dimension. I'd have nothing to look forward to except finishing another page and another lecture. I'd have nothing to look forward to. Whereas now I'm waiting for midnight and, with my whole body, am aware of time moving towards that moment.

It's half past eleven – the light's out now in the bedroom. My wife has at last switched off.

Suppose she took it into her head to visit me here.

Darling, I've come to see you, look, I'm wearing the shoes you gave me. Do you mind me coming? I just wanted to see you.

Come in, come on in!

But I can't come in. Your wife's there.

Yes, but my wife's asleep.

Are you sure your wife will sleep right through the night?

We'll only be a little while. I'd like you to sit here by the window. I want to look at you. I want to kiss you.

Suppose Camilla wakes up when the telephone rings? I should hide it away somewhere. I'll put it in the cupboard among my pullovers.

Midnight. I am trembling like a student before an exam. I am afraid Camilla will suddenly appear in the doorway. I'll sit as close to the instrument as possible, to make sure it doesn't ring long.

If anyone were to see me here they'd die of laughter. But maybe a lot of people spend their nights like this, imagine thousands of people spending their nights waiting – pressed into wardrobes, hidden under beds, their hands on the receiver, waiting, often waiting in vain? Perhaps she won't ring after all, her husband may not have fallen asleep or she may have gone to sleep, I should be either working or sleeping. This is embarrassing and humiliating and silly: sitting here, waiting, while next door my children and my wife are sleeping in the same flat. Suddenly the pullovers seemed to swell up, as if trembling, and emitted a sound which rang through the silence like the gritting of teeth.

'It's me. I hope I haven't woken you up?'

'No. I've been waiting for you to ring. Where are you speaking from?' I can hear something on top of her voice.

'I'm terribly pissed. I'm in a wine cellar with Igor. But I've no idea where. Maybe it's in Bratislava, hang on, I'll go and ask.'

Silence. Only a medley of distant sounds. Perhaps she won't come back. She's there with someone while I'm here on my own. Not so, I'm here with my wife. No, right here I am alone and I'm shaking like a student before an exam.

'Well no, I'm not in Bratislava. I'm at Lob . . . at Lob . . . I can't get it out. Looks like some old palace stablings. And I'm drinking red wine. I think we've drunk a whole barrel.'

'So where are you actually?'

'Where am I? Haven't I told where I am? I don't know any more, I've forgotten the name again. Shall I go and ask?'

She's asking someone. I can hear her voice in the distance.

'At Lob-ko-wit-zes. I'm in the Lobkowitz cellar and I'm wearing those marvellous shoes you gave me.'

'Does he like them?'

'Who?'

'Igor. Or whatever his name is.'

'I don't know. He hasn't said anything. Shall I go and ask him?'

'No, don't.'

'He's terrific. If only you could see him – that sweet face of his and his nose. Same as Jean-Paul Belmondo. The shape I love.'

'Do you really love him?'

'Of course. I wouldn't say I loved him if I didn't love him. You'd love him too if you saw him.'

'I don't think I'd love him. I can't manage to love so many people at the same time.'

'I know you can't. You're a bit of a walrus. May I call you that? Walrus?'

'When are you going home?'

'I don't know, I really don't. I don't even know where I am. When he wants to go.'

And she'll go with him, she'll go to his flat or to his hotel room and there she'll make love to him because he's sure to be young and unattached, while I'm sitting here in the cupboard, shaking with fear in case Camilla should open the door.

'Lord, I'm so terribly pissed. You're probably angry with me now for calling you Walrus. And he's looking at me now, wondering why I'm on the phone to a man. I'd better ring you some other time. Go to bed now – okay? Hang on, hang on a minute. Can I send you a little kiss over the phone? So, here it is, that's for being so sweet and buying me those wonderfully ugly things I have on my feet, and now you're sitting by the telephone listening to me rambling on. I love you for that, my Walrus!'

3

The children come pouring out of school, some of them greet me, how do they know I am the husband of their teacher when they've never seen me? I don't remember when I last waited here, I am not in the habit of waiting for my wife, in fact I'm only waiting for her out of spite, because the other one has let me down, if you can call it letting me down seeing she never promised anything in the first place. Now my wife is coming out, a few children swarming around her, she seems to me a little unreal in this role of hers. Now she has spotted me and I can tell even at this distance that she is smiling.

'You're waiting for me?'

'I got here a little while ago. I was at the library but they didn't have the books I needed.'

'That's a bore. What will you do?'

'I'll just have to manage without. And what were you doing?'

'What do you mean: what was I doing?'

'What were you doing in school?'

'Practical lessons today. I took the children out, we collected some blossoms: hawthorn, blackthorn and such like.'

'That sounds useful.'

'They like it, and we talk the while.'

'What do you talk about?'

She is confused. I never ask her about school, in fact I tend to complain if she talks about it. She talks about it chiefly if something unpleasant has happened.

'We talk about different animals. Or about what they're growing in their flowerpots at home. They're city kids, I want to teach them to notice what's alive around them. That'll help them understand themselves better. And other people.' Her face, that tired un-made-up face, has come to life. Perhaps she wanted to say something more but she's silent now. We're getting near home.

'That was nice of you, waiting for me.'

In front of the house the children are making a row. Anna, of course, is chasing the neighbour's dog and Margit is playing in a heap of sand which the workmen left behind after repairing a fence. She's seen me now, she's already wiping her dirty hands on my trousers.

'Pick me up, Daddy!'

'You can play a little longer.'

'No, wait, Daddy, feel my legs!'

'What for?'

'To see how big I am!'

The flat is empty, I don't know why sadness grips me, I don't feel like going in, I don't feel like locking myself up within those four walls, in the silence that I've always longed for.

'Have you noticed, David, how pale Margit is?'

'Is she? Yes, you're right.'

'She doesn't seem to be picking up after that throat infection she had.'

'Shall I mention it to Father?'

'No, she doesn't need a doctor, what she needs is getting out into the fresh air. I phoned my parents, they'll have her for a week or a fortnight.'

'That would be ideal.'

'I thought perhaps this Saturday or Sunday. Could you drive us there? We'd just hand her over and we'd be back by evening.'

Yes, of course. Admittedly, it will eat up a whole day but I've got to do it. It's been part of my duties since I've owned a car.

But if I didn't do it she'd go with her herself, she would have to go by train and I'd stay behind on my own, a day and a night, because they can't get there and back in a day. I feel myself going rigid at the thought. A day and a night, would you be free on Saturday night, my dear? God knows where she is or if I can even get hold of her to tell her.

'What are you thinking about, David?'

'Merely that it would be a lost day, or rather two days. You know what your mother's like. We'd have to stay.'

'If we arrived on Sunday? She knows you've got to be at the institute on Monday. And you can take your work along.'

'You know very well I couldn't get any work done there. And that we wouldn't get away before midnight. And then one's no use the whole of the following day.'

'So what are you suggesting?'

'If I took you to the station on Friday afternoon – there's that fast train around three o'clock, you'd be there just as fast as by car. And on Saturday or Sunday you come back by the express and I'll meet you at the station.'

'I just thought it might do you good, too, to get out of town for a while.'

'Quite so – if I didn't have such a pile of work. You know yourself how much each day means to me.'

She is looking at me, all joy drained from her face. 'You always have a reason for everything. But I know quite well why you don't want to come.'

'What do you know?'

'That it would suit you if I was away from home. It would suit you, wouldn't it?'

'What do you mean? It was you who suggested the trip.'

'But it would suit you if we went without you.'

'Well, don't go then. It wasn't my idea.'

'Margit needs it. All right, I'll take her there – but you'll have to look after Anna then.'

She doesn't quite manage to conceal a triumphant smile. But I must remain calm. 'She'll be disappointed, being left behind.'

'She enjoys being with you. I'll tell her to look after you.'

'Whatever you say.'

'She won't be in your way. She plays quite happily on her own and during the day you can let her run about outside. I'll get your meals ready before I leave.'

'Whatever you say. But she'll be disappointed.'

'Don't worry. I'll explain to her.'

'So when will you be going?'

125

'Why do you need to know? You don't have to worry about us. We can take the tram to the station.'

## 4

'Anna, it's past seven, time to go to bed.'

'Mum said I could go to bed later today. That I'm to look after you.'

'You've looked after me quite enough for one day.'

'Don't you want me to tell you something?'

'No, not today, I've got work to do, we've talked quite a lot anyway.'

'And you're not going to bed yet?'

'You know I go to bed much later.'

'Wouldn't you like to help me with my bath?'

'Not today.'

'I thought if we're on our own, the two of us . . . we . . . we'd have some fun.'

'What did you have in mind?'

'I don't know. Wouldn't you like to test me?'

'On what?'

'Dogs. Or rivers. We did rivers at school.'

'All right. If you'll go to bed like a good girl I'll hear you on rivers. And now off to the bathroom.'

'Dad!'

She's lying in bed in her pink pyjamas with a patch of a dog sewn on for decoration. Poor child, she'd been looking forward to the two of us being together, to enjoying my company, whereas I am counting the minutes to be rid of her, to cover her eyes with the blanket of sleep.

'Dad, sit here by me and test me.'

'All right. What's the longest river you know?'

'You can't ask questions like that!'

'What questions can I ask then?'

'Which river flows through Prague.'

'Okay, which river?'

'The Vltava!'

'Correct. And do you know what river the Vltava runs into?'

'We haven't had that at school.'

'But do you know?'

'The Elbe.'

'There you are, you do know. What else do you know about rivers?'

'That there are fish in them, and sand. And people bathe in them. Dad, why don't people bathe naked?'

I have exactly forty minutes left. Normally she goes to sleep at once, but sometimes when she's excited she will lie awake for a full hour. And today she's excited by being here with just me, by looking after me, by having me to herself.

'Anyway, I know why!'

'What do you know?'

'They wear swimsuits so they shouldn't fall in love with each other. The girls told me.'

'What did they tell you?'

'I couldn't tell you that.'

'Well, go to sleep then.'

'Dad, what would you do if you saw a naked lady?'

'Where?'

'In the river, for instance.'

'I don't know. If I were on the bank I'd look away, and if I were in the river too I'd just swim on.'

'Bet you'd swim to her.'

'I'd have thought you girls might talk about something a little more intelligent.'

'Dad, you aren't going already?'

'I've got to do some work.'

'Dad, it's a long time since you last told me about guinea-pigs.'

127

'Not today.'

'Just for a little while.'

'No!'

'A tiny little while . . .'

'Do you want a slap?'

'Will you leave the door open?'

'No!' God, why am I so harsh with her. After all, it's not her fault. She's enjoying being here with me. And I am fond of her. Sometimes when I'm worn out or unhappy she senses it and comes to me to tell me something she thinks might cheer me up.

'Mum always leaves the door open. And the light on in the hall.'

'All right. I'll leave the door open.'

And suppose Camilla comes back or Anna wakes up? I'll have to lock the front door. But it will be awkward to lock the door the moment I ask her to step inside. Maybe she won't come in. All she said was she'd try and free herself.

'Dad, I'm afraid on my own.'

'But you're not alone.'

'I am, here in this room. Dad, I'd like to have a dog.'

'We won't discuss it now.'

'Do you think Margit's sharing Mum's room?'

'I've no idea. Probably.'

'Dad, I'd like to share your room with you. I'll come and sleep with you since Mum isn't here.'

'You'd never go to sleep if I have the light on.'

'I don't mind the light, Dad. I'll cover my eyes.'

'Now not another word or I'll shut the door!'

Quiet. I've got to leave in twenty minutes. Suppose she doesn't fall asleep by then?

'Dad, I'm feeling sad. I'd like Mum to come back this evening. That would be great, wouldn't it?'

'All right, I'm shutting your door now . . . Or wait a

128

moment – did Mum say anything to you about returning this evening?'

'No, I was just imagining it – how nice it would be.'

I'm sitting motionless in my room, I haven't even switched on the light, I'm listening to the tick of the old wall clock and to the sounds from the nursery. The thought of what I am about to do overwhelms me. A quiet moan from next door, maybe we'd better go to some wine-cellar, Camilla would never forgive me for bringing the other woman to this flat, for doing it right here. And suppose she refuses, suppose she starts shouting and Anna wakes up, comes running in in her pyjamas, she could have a trauma for the rest of her life from what she sees? I'll lock her in.

I'll lock the front door and I'll lock the door of her room, and I'll lock up my conscience, and then . . . what will happen then?

5

She's still sitting in the car, I'm climbing the stairs on my own, I open my own front door like a conspirator (suppose someone is watching from one of the neighbouring houses and sees her), Anna is sleeping, curled up into a ball, I'm locking you in, my little daughter, and now I'm creeping down again.

'So that's your house?'

'It isn't my house, it belonged to that old woman who died. If she hadn't died I'd never have met you.'

'And this is your room.'

'It's our only room.'

'Not a very pretty room, I don't think. An awful lot of things in it but nothing human.'

'What do you mean, human?'

'I don't know. Some rooms, the moment you enter you

know who lives in them. The person's age, whether he's dead keen on something, like stuffed birds or old coffee grinders. Or if he's got a sense of humour. But here you can't tell anything. Who's this?'

'Darwin.'

'Who's he?'

'You don't know who Darwin was?'

'No. Maybe some relation of yours or maybe somebody famous, but it isn't a pretty picture for a wall.'

Finally she sits down. She turns her slate-coloured eyes towards the ceiling and waits.

I've got her here. She's sitting in my room in her colourful short dress which doesn't conceal much, in the shoes I gave her, her long shiny hair black against the blue chairback. I could kneel down before her and start kissing her but the right moment hasn't arrived yet, so I first get some wine and sandwiches. (Dad, what have you got there in that bag? Nothing, this isn't for you!)

She's still sitting there just as I left her, her eyes fixed on the ceiling. Maybe the ceiling, at least, has some character. But she's probably not taking it in at all, she isn't taking anything in, she's asleep with her eyes open.

'What's the matter with you?'

'I'm frightfully tired. Igor didn't leave till this morning, I feel as if I haven't slept for a week. He doesn't seem to need any sleep at all, during the day he's filming, he's making some film about ancient churches, he clambers up to all those high spots, I get giddy even looking up from the ground. But if you saw him you'd think he almost wasn't there, if you looked at his trousers you wouldn't believe anybody could get into them.'

Trousers flung over a chair in some room, some hotel room, and you in another man's arms, I'm beginning to feel jealous, even though I really shouldn't care whether she fell asleep in her husband's arms last night or someone else's.

'Do you love him?'

'I used to love him terribly. Each time he comes I lose my head completely.'

'Now you don't love him any more?'

'I don't know. Now he's gone I don't think about him.'

She is drinking wine. Under her carefully painted eyes she really does have rings or even wrinkles. In a moment I'll embrace her and nothing else will matter. I'll be like her. All that matters is the moment, and at this moment she's here with me, she's so close I need only reach out to touch her.

'Couldn't you put on some music? It's so terribly quiet here.'

'What kind of music?'

'Some record or other.'

'I haven't got a record player – only the radio, and if I turned it on Anna might wake up.'

'Who's Anna?'

'My daughter.'

'I didn't know you had a daughter, I thought you were hiding some other girl here, that you'd invited a lot of girls while your wife's away. But why shouldn't you have a daughter, you could even have quite a grown-up one.'

'This one's seven. I also have another. The other is younger.'

'So you have a little girl – my something would have also been nearly seven.'

'Your something?'

'I'm saying my something because I don't know what it would have been. Maybe also a little girl. I was sixteen at the time, Thomas was still in his second year, we couldn't keep it. But now and again it occurs to me that he might be a year old or that he might now go to school. Pity you can't turn some music on. I'm feeling cold from this silence. All day long I was somewhere where there was music. At home, too, I have music on all the time, but if Tom's about it drives him round the bend, seeing he's a musician. He believes that music should be an experience. When I'm at his place he unscrews something from the radio so it won't work. But now I'm not often at his place because he's always away somewhere with his group. I don't even know where. At one time he used to send me a postcard from every stand, always the same: Just arrived, they've got a House of Culture here and the beer's lousy and no girls about. Performing tonight, I'm thinking of you and kissing you, my little owl. Now he doesn't write to me any more. He probably tells me where he's going but I forget it at once because I'm no good at geography.'

She looks tired. She's drinking although she clearly doesn't feel like it. And maybe she'll make love with me even though she doesn't feel like it. After all, for love-making she's got her husband and Igor and those clowns at the theatre and some Italians, and God knows who else, she doesn't need me, she certainly doesn't need me for that.

'What else would you like me to tell you?'

As if in return for those few sandwiches and the wine she had a duty to entertain me. Or maybe she's trying to delay me. That's why she's telling me about her husband and about her unborn child.

'I'll tell you how I met Igor.'

She's trying to put off the moment she doesn't want and isn't longing for. She can't be longing for it if she's been making love all night with someone else. She knows that while she's talking, while she's talking about other men, she's stopping me from speaking. She's stopping me getting closer to her.

'That was at least four years ago, I was in the mountains with some girls. Tom came along too but he could stay only a couple of days. Am I boring you?'

'No, why would you be boring me?'

'The way you're looking at me. You look as if you wanted to gobble me up.'

'I'm attracted by you. That's why I'm looking at you like this. Because I'm attracted by you. Tell me, are there a lot of these men – men you love?'

'You do ask some strange questions. Do you think I count them?'

For an instant her face stands motionless before mine and I have a close-up view of her slate-grey and incredibly familiar eyes. 'My dear, my lovely one, I love you, you're so beautiful, so sweet, so marvellous, I love you.'

Her eyes are closed, she's lying almost inert at my side, she lets me caress her without a single word or a single movement that might betray some feeling. At last she opens her eyes: 'You want to make love to me?'

'For heaven's sake, don't ask such silly questions. Can't you see how I want you?'

She sits up and with a few movements strips off her dress and two small items of underwear.

She is petite, she has an almost childish body and small unattractive breasts. She's once more lying in the place that has for so many years been reserved for my wife, and her carefully made-up face with eye shadow on her lids and eyebrows looks unreal, as if attached to a white and un-made-up body.

All of a sudden I don't feel any passion, not one hint of desire, but rather a sense of unease at the thought that the door might abruptly open, that suddenly there might be a ring at the door, that my daughter might wake up and call out: Dad! I am fearful that I might not be up to competing with all those men, with all those lovers she has undoubtedly had, from whom she's come to me, embraced and kissed all over and satiated with love. I am feeling nothing now except anxiety, I am cold (in this room it's always cold, with Camilla we make love under the blanket). And I feel the strangeness, the hostility of that cold, white, improper body which is getting ready to test me, to compare me, to transform me into one of those swift and fleeting incidents, whereas I am losing everything and giving everything, for the first time in my life I am committing a betrayal by crossing the boundary into another life, and, already naked, I tiptoe to the door and turn the key and I shiver with cold, I wonder my teeth aren't chattering as I lie down with her.

I've been hungering for her so much, if only she would utter a single tender word, if she gave just one little hint that she cared for me, but surely she does care for me if she's here, I'm sure she doesn't do anything she doesn't want to do, anything she wouldn't enjoy doing. Except that to her all this means nothing, maybe she is doing it from gratitude, maybe she just wants to repay me for those few lunches and those blue Italian shoes which are now standing by the couch. I am straying over her body with cold moist fingers which suddenly are unable to perceive the warmth of her body and are turning inward themselves, probing their own mortality.

'Make love to me then! Make love to me, what are you waiting for?'

And I know now that I can't, that I won't be able to do it, that I can't manage it now, perhaps because it is this room or because she is so much of a stranger, because I don't love her enough, or maybe because I want her too much and am afraid that I won't measure up in her eyes.

But now, as she is humiliating me by inviting me to do what anyone else in my place would have done long ago, I feel a wave of impotent rage rising in me: I want to humiliate her too. For her unparticipating and haughty strangeness and for being prepared to give herself to me without love, like a whore – that's all.

'Well, don't lie there like a stone. Can't you at least move a little, for heaven's sake?'

'You think I should move a little? But maybe I don't know how. Maybe you should teach me.'

There is scorn in her extinguished eyes, if indeed there's anything in them at all.

I squeeze her, I shake her till she groans. Not from ecstasy but with pain. Eventually she pushes me away: 'Leave me alone now, leave me alone.'

I am lying here, moist with perspiration, I am not looking at her. I'd like to say to her: I'm sorry. And explain that what happened, or rather did not happen, had been her fault. That I still loved her, that I was longing for her, that she shouldn't leave now, that I needed her, that I'd go with her wherever she wanted to and that I'd stay with her and make love to her all night long just like those men of hers, even if I had to die afterwards.

She's dressed already, she's pulling out a little mirror from her handbag and tidying her hair. 'Aren't you dressing?' asks a stranger's voice.

'You want to leave already?'

'I'm terribly tired. I haven't slept for several nights.'

'All right, I'll drive you home.'

This is the end, I can't face up to seeing her again. Maybe it's just as well I haven't been unfaithful to my wife. I can still claim that I haven't been unfaithful to her. But do I still have a wife after tonight?

6

Camilla returned by the fast train instead of the express. (She was rocked about for an extra hour in the overcrowded, stuffy carriage in order to save sixteen crowns, while I was spending money on a strange girl.) I spot her a long way off, in spite of the crowd pouring out of the carriages.

She's dragging a huge bag, filled no doubt with cabbages, carrots, lettuce and cauliflower from grandmother's garden, with grandmother's eggs and home-cured bacon. She is inconspicuous, unattractive in her cheap easy-wash dress and down-at-heel scuffed shoes, my wife is returning to me, even though I don't deserve it, in a moment I'll be driving her to the flat that is our home however much I tried to foul it. (Late last night I cleaned up carefully, I swept the floor, poured the remaining wine down the lavatory and put the bottle in the dustbin of the villa next door.) I love you for coming back to me, I should kneel down here in this disgusting filth of the railway station and ask your forgiveness. 'Look, there's Mum,' and Anna rushes off to meet her.

I am back home, what was it like, how are your people, thank you, they were asking about you, they were sorry you didn't come along; and for dinner there is home-cured bacon and cabbage, the flat once more is ours, the things around are lifeless and cannot testify, everything is in order, everything will be in order again, all's well that ends well. 'How about going for a walk?'

'Outside, you mean?'

'Why not?'

'We haven't had a walk for a long time.'

'Exactly.'

We walk down the narrow pavement along the garden walls, a little way on the suburban meadows start, and then some fields, we are walking towards them: it's a quiet and calming spot. I take her hand, her so familiar palm.

'Imagine, some young man tried to pick me up on the train. A motor mechanic, but he talked to me about music and the theatre, and he subscribes to a literary weekly. He guessed my age at twenty-six.'

'That's how one usually guesses it.'

'And he gave me his address.'

'And did you give him yours?'

'No, I didn't.'

We walk on in silence, we're leaving the light of the last street lamps behind us. She presses against me but only because she's afraid. 'Shouldn't we get back?'

'I want to say something to you.'

'About her?'

'No. I wanted to say that it was a good idea you leaving, it gave me time to think everything out.'

'You didn't even see her?'

'You know perfectly well you left me with Anna. But I didn't want to see her, I wanted to think about the two of us.' I realize with horror that I almost believe what I'm saying, that I have almost forgotten yesterday and last night, so much do I want to forget.

'And what's the result of your thinking?'

'That I love you.'

She is silent. She walks alongside me, not saying anything, I don't know what she is thinking, whether she believes me, whether she's glad or unhappy. But I have a need to talk. To talk away last night's humiliation and talk her into again giving me her favour and love. 'She was a very ordinary girl, I don't understand what attracted me about her. I behaved like a fool, I was even incapable of working properly.'

'Why are you talking about her like this? Has she left you?'

'But there was nothing between us! I just thought everything out. I need you, the children and a home. I love you all.'

'That's a good thing.'

'What's a good thing?'

'That you love us like this.'

It sounds sarcastic but perhaps only to my ears because I know the scale of my lies. I take her by the waist and kiss

137

her, it's ages since we last kissed like this out of doors, at least several years.

'So long as you're not mistaken. So long as you don't mistake me for some other woman.'

'No, I only love you. I could never love anyone else.'

'You always exaggerate. You exaggerate in everything.'

'What do you mean?'

'You don't know moderation in anything, David. I've often wanted to say this to you, you don't do anything in moderation.'

Silence. In the distance, down an invisible road, move the headlights of cars.

'When I first met you I liked it: your being obsessed by having to achieve something. But nowadays I often feel that it would be better if you were more normal. If you also cared about other things.'

'What else should I care about?'

'I can't make you see that if you don't feel it yourself. You can only ever think of one thing at a time. You're living with us but sometimes you act as if we weren't there.'

'That's because I have such a lot of work.'

'No, it's not because of that.'

She's probably right. It never occurred to me that she saw me like a person possessed. And it never occurred to me that this might make her unhappy. 'All that's going to change when we leave, you'll see. Over there we'll be living unhustled and calmly. And Saturdays we'll go to the seaside – like that time, remember? And we'll make trips to Scotland and to the Lake District, they have little steamers there, too, and we'll feel happy in the quiet among the lakes and the hills.'

Promises and promises, I'm holding her round the waist, we are walking back home down the familiar street and I talk and talk and all the time I know that with each

138

sentence I'm moving further away from the truth, from what happened and from what may happen yet. And later in the evening, when I'm finally in bed, when we're lying side by side, when she's sleeping with her head on my shoulder, I wish, for the first time in my life I wish, that I didn't exist, that I could escape from my fate, so I needn't carry on with any activity or any lie or any humiliation, so I needn't ever again utter a single sentence, excuse, request, a single promise or declaration of love. I wish there was never another funeral, I wish I could be sufficient to myself, be on my own, but I need her, I particularly need her now, that's where she's unfair to me, I do need love, at least someone's love, someone's affection.

It's all so shameful. Can I ever escape from it?

# CHAPTER SEVEN

## 1

It is night, it is the first phase of sleep, interrupted suddenly by a foreign high-pitched note.

I run into the kitchen and pick up the receiver. At the other end first there is silence, then finally I hear her voice.

'This is Iva. Have I woken you up?'

'Never mind. What's the time?'

'I don't know, somewhere around midnight. We had a show this evening. Then we had some drinks but it didn't amount to much, so I thought I'd give you a ring.'

'Nice of you to think of me.'

'You're probably cross with me – not getting in touch at all?'

'No, it was just that I was very busy.' How is it possible that she should ring me after that embarrassing and disastrous evening?

'Tom is very busy too. Everybody's very busy. Except me. Tom's gone off somewhere to Moravia. Do you know if a place called Police is in Moravia?'

'It isn't. What are you doing right now?'

'You think we could be doing something right now?'

'No idea. What's the time? Hang on, I'll switch the light on. It's half past twelve. Do you feel like going for a drive somewhere?'

'Going for a drive? You're thinking of a pleasure trip at this hour?'

'It doesn't matter. I'd just like to see you. Even if I had to get back fairly soon.'

'And you'd come all the way out here to see me?'

'Yes, but I'd rather not come upstairs. Wait for me at the

entrance. In half an hour. No, I'll be there in twenty-five minutes. Will you wait by the entrance?'

## 2

'So I'm in your car again.'

'You're in my car again. It felt strange these past few days when you weren't there beside me.'

'Seems I belong here now, in this car.'

'Yes, you belong here now.'

'You won't take anyone in your car except me?'

'I won't take anyone else.'

'I felt furious at the idea that you might be driving some other girls instead of me.'

'I didn't drive any other girl. I never drive any girls at all.'

'And where are we going now?'

'Nowhere in particular. We'll get back again soon.'

'And this is where we're going to stop?'

'This is where we're going for a little walk. Or don't you want to?'

'We're going for a walk in the fields?'

'It isn't a field, it's a meadow.'

'There won't be snakes there? I'm terrified of snakes.'

'There are no snakes on the path.'

'And won't it be wet in the meadow?'

'I don't know. I hope not. But I've got a blanket. Shall I take it along?'

'How should I know if you'll need a blanket? But we won't go far. It's quite dark here. And there are bound to be lots of snakes everywhere.'

'We won't go far. Just a few steps. And hold on to me.'

'Well, I've certainly never walked on a path like this in the middle of the night. Is this the sort of place you take all your girls to?'

'I don't take any girls anywhere. Don't you think it's nice here? This is far enough. I'll spread out the blanket.'

'Make sure there are no snakes here. Or ants. Feel if there are any with your hand. I can't bear them biting me in the behind.'

'It's perfectly soft grass. Can't you smell it?'

'I can't tell, I can't smell anything when I'm cold. Hurry up with that blanket or I'll freeze to death.'

'Come closer to me, darling, your face is so cold. You phoned – I thought you'd never phone. That we wouldn't see each other again. But now I'm here with you. Do you love me too?'

'I don't know if I love you too. But anyway I'm here with you now.'

'Maybe this isn't happening at all, maybe I'm only dreaming.'

'You think I'm just a dream?'

'No – because I can feel you.'

'Shall I take my clothes off? Wait a minute! But you'll have to make me warm.'

'My darling. My love.'

'Now you can feel me even more?'

'Now I can feel you all over.'

'I can feel you too. I can feel you close. Very close. Very, very close.'

'My sweet. You're my delight, such delight. I could die now.'

'You'd die in this meadow? Why don't you say something? You've really died!'

'I love you, I love you very much.'

'You mustn't die. How would I get back home?'

'You've been waiting for me?'

'But I told you I'd be waiting for you today.'

'You told me? Well, I completely forgot. I've got a terrible memory. I was swotting up history all night. Did you know that in 1657 a certain Jindřich Khintzer Přibyslavský, of whom no other details are known to us, wrote a *Comedy of Our Lord's Resurrection*? What would you like to do?'

'Don't worry, I haven't got much time either. I've got a lecture to give in half an hour from now. I just wanted to see you. Where were you off to?'

'Nowhere in particular. I don't know myself. Just strolling round the city, window-shopping. I'll probably have a look at the antique shop in Celetná. Sometimes they have beautiful little madonnas with the baby Jesus. Did you know that another play that's come down to us from that period is the Rakovnice Christmas Play? Its author is thought to be the Jesuit Jan Libertin. It depicts an argument between the shepherds and the kings about who Jesus was actually born for – for the kings or for the shepherds. I'd also like to have a look at Darex, they said they were expecting some little velvet dresses.'

'You want to buy a dress?'

'You're crazy, I haven't even got – wait a minute, let me count it – I've got exactly nine crowns eighty. That's got to last me till the end of the month. No, I just want to have a look at them. A lot of girls go to the shops just to look at things.'

'I'll come along and have a look with you.'

'You'll be bored to tears. You have more serious interests. And you have a lecture. Look, a chimney sweep. I'll be lucky.'

'I'm lucky already.'

'You're lucky already?'

'I'm walking along the street with you and I'm happy.'

'You're walking along the street and you're happy that you have a lecture quite soon.'

'I'll ring and say I can't manage it today.'

'Why don't you ring from this box and I'll have a look at these dresses while you do.'

'Looked at them all now?'

'No, I'm still looking. This red one here, don't you think it's terrific?'

'I'm no judge. Perhaps it is. How much would such a dress cost?'

'I've no idea. I don't even ask.'

'Hang on then, I'll ask. Would you like to try it on?'

'Think I could try it on? Isn't that silly if I'm not going to buy it anyway?'

'Go on, try it on; they don't know you're not going to buy it anyway.'

'Okay, I'll try it on. Wait for me here.'

I've never bought a dress for my wife. She's always bought all her things herself.

She never wanted anything from me. When we were courting she didn't even want a scarf and she certainly wouldn't have accepted a dress. Maybe this girl won't accept it either. It might make her feel I was buying her. But I'm not buying her, I only want to give her a little pleasure. Except that this is probably what all men say when they are buying women.

'Well, here I am, but I really shouldn't have tried it on at all. But I wanted you to see me in it. I'm taking it off straight away.'

'Well, do you like it? Do you want to have it?'

'You're out of your mind. Why do you ask?'

'Yes, miss, we'll have this one.'

'No, you're out of your mind. Six hundred. It's not

worth that much. Just a piece of velvet.'

'Why isn't it worth it if you like it?'

'You're out of your mind!'

'Will madam wear the dress straight away?'

'I don't know . . . Hold on . . . Come along to the fitting room for a minute. Look here, I'm going to take it off. Here it is. Go and take it back. It's a lot of money. Don't be a fool. I really can't . . .'

'Why can't you? I love you. I'm making you a present of it because I love you.'

'You're sweet. You really are sweet. No one's been that sweet to me before. Wait, I want to kiss you. I love you too. Yes, I love you too.'

4

Midnight. Ten minutes past midnight. Why should she ring, we didn't arrange anything. Why am I constantly thinking of her? I can see her standing there in her slip, kissing me with three mirrors around us; I shall never forget how we were standing in the fitting room with its floral curtain and she was kissing me. I find her touching. I don't know if I find her touching because I am in love with her or whether I am in love with her because I find her touching.

I am losing my sense of judgement. She is an ordinary girl, she'd kiss anyone who bought her a dress like that, and I'm only crazy about her because I've never had a mistress. She's an ordinary girl who might have an affair with anyone, but I don't care, I'm happy with her, I love her the way she is. Maybe because she is the way she is.

The telephone bell.

'I just wanted to tell you I'm wearing the dress you gave me.'

'Where are you calling from?'

'I'm in Tom's flat.'

'You're speaking from Tom's?'

'He's not here, he's off on tour. And I didn't feel like sitting at home. So I put on the dress and thought I'd come over to you. But then I said to myself your wife would probably be angry if I turned up and so I ended up here. I can't stop myself looking at the dress. Would you like to come round and look at it?'

'You think I could come and visit you there?'

'I don't know if you can. How should I know if you can?'

'I don't even know where it is.'

'Where you took us that first day. Opposite the little park. The window next to the baker's. I'll leave the lamp on, one with a kind of blue shade. If you tap on the window I'll come and let you in.'

'And when's your husband coming back?'

'How should I know? Perhaps today. Or in a couple of days. Or three. Or maybe he isn't coming back at all.'

Twelve forty-five. I won't have any sleep again. And one of these days Camilla's bound to wake up and notice that I'm out. And what will happen then? I should be more careful, I won't risk losing my family for the sake of a few hours. As if it was just for the sake of a few hours! A terrible habit, wanting to measure everything, to add up everything.

A bakery and a blue light in a window.

'Don't make any noise. I'll be with you in a moment.'

A key in the front door, five steps, another door, a hall full of posters. A crucifix and a Virgin Mary. African drums.

'What are you looking at? That stuff is all Bert's. All we own here is the bed and this bag and a wedding photograph. Tom hung it up here. Why are you looking like this?'

'Hold on, I've got to get used to it all. There's a lot of strange things here, or just a lot of things.'

'Bert collects ancient drums. This one, he says, is three hundred years old. And here he has a gallery of drummers. This is Ginger Baker. And that's Ringo Starr, if you've heard the names. Want to drink something? Bound to have a bottle somewhere. The place is quite filthy, no one's been here for at least a week. But I'm not going to clean up for them. What were you doing this evening?'

'I was writing.'

'You're forever writing lectures. You must have a trunk full of them. I went to the Golem restaurant with a colleague. Incredibly nice man, does abstract paintings. Invited me up to his place but I said I couldn't, he's bound to think there's something wrong with me.'

'I'm glad you didn't go with him and phoned me instead.'

'I wanted you to see me in this dress. I would have gone out with you in the evening but you're writing those lectures. Do you think it still suits me?'

'You look fantastic in it.'

'Wait, don't be silly, you're crushing it. You can't do that. If you like I'll take it off. There, it's off. How long can you stay? Shall I make up the bed? I'll be sleeping here anyway when you've gone. But I'll just have a look at the mirror. I must say goodbye to the dress.'

The sound of running water. I'm lying on a strange bed. Her husband is asleep somewhere on tour. My mistress is running the water. My wife is asleep at home. I am here. The light is blue and there are masses of drums everywhere. I don't know who Ginger Baker is. She could have gone home with her friend but she didn't because there's something wrong with her. Perhaps she does love me. Seventy days from now I'm leaving. I'll be lecturing in a strange lecture theatre. There's still another me. I'm said to be obsessed with my work. I wanted something different from just lying in a room full of drums, waiting for her. I'm waiting for her. Waiting for her to come to me. Waiting for that one thing, I only want that one thing, I'm now thoroughly obsessed with her. Everything else is fading away and vanishing. It's I who have abandoned and betrayed everything else.

Is it possible that I don't mind, that I have exchanged everything for this single moment? Who am I really? What's left of me? Is this still me? Am I mad? Am I weak or strong? Am I sick? Or is this what I really am?

Silence. Footfalls. I'm straining towards that single moment, towards that first contact. 'Darling, I can feel all of you in my palms, I can feel all of you in every single finger, in every cell, I feel you a million times, I feel you more than I do the whole world. Do you still love me?'

'I love you for saying such pretty things to me.'

'I love you for being able to say these things to you. My love, you're like a ball of wool around my fingers, I'm unwinding you, I'm winding you round myself. This is how I'd like to stay all my life.'

Silence and vertigo and her breath. I don't know anything. I mustn't fall asleep. I mustn't fall asleep because I shall have to leave. I mustn't fall asleep because it's a waste of time to sleep when I can be happy.

And so I lie on a strange bed, with a strange woman by my side, and over my head a wedding photograph from which I'm missing. I'm rolling about in someone else's marriage bed and I am happy, but surely this isn't possible, it can't go on like this, it can't go on without punishment; I shall be punished, yes I shall be punished, for she knows not what she does.

'Do you still love me, my pet?'

'I still love you.'

'And will you still love me tomorrow?'

'How can I tell what tomorrow will bring? You're odd. You're forever thinking about things. Always thinking about what might happen.'

'I'd like you to love me at least until I leave. Just those few weeks.'

'You're going away? Where are you going to?'

'But I've told you.'

'You have? I forget everything. You taking your wife and the girls?'

'For a year.'

'You're going away for a year. You're going to England. What will you do there?'

'Give lectures.'

'You must be terribly clever if they've invited you to lecture to them. So you'll be lecturing and going out with English girls.'

'I'll be back in a year.'

'And you're leaving when?'

'In seventy days, I think.'

'In seventy days. And you'll be back after a year. So why do you talk about it? For all you know I might be dead by then, or you might be dead. I don't know what seventy days means. I can't picture it. Sometimes I can't even picture that the sun will rise in the morning. I look at the sky and say to myself: maybe this night's going to last for ever.'

'Don't you ever look forward to anything that will happen in the future?'

'No, I never look forward to anything because what I look forward to never happens. When I was a little girl I used to look forward to Dad coming home from work. I knew I could look forward to that. But then he stopped coming home, he took up with some girl and only rarely turned up at home. And when he began to come home again I'd stopped looking forward to it. I also used to look forward to Tom. He'd come every evening and whistle under my window. I wasn't allowed out with him, only to stand by the fence. So we'd stand by the fence and he'd call me his little frog or his little owl, and he'd bring me some flower he'd picked from the next-door garden or nicked from a bed in the public park. Then once we made a date because my folks let me go to a girl friend who lived in a villa up near the Castle and was celebrating something or other. I promised to slip away before it was over and he'd wait for me by Charles Bridge. Well, I looked forward to that for at least a couple of days, having a date, you know, and maybe even letting him kiss me.'

'How old were you then?'

'That was a long time ago, I don't know how old I was. But in that villa we had a high old time, we guzzled a lot of wine, there were crowds of people there and also a boy from the twelfth form, terribly tall and handsome, a 500-metre runner or something, and he'd been ogling me all the time and then he sat down by me and kept talking to me. And eventually he offered to show me some interesting picture, and so I went off with him, and he took me upstairs to some little box-room and there he told me I was the prettiest girl he'd ever seen and would I kiss him. I said no, I wouldn't kiss him, and he laughed and said he wouldn't let me go until I'd kissed him, and he really locked the door and he kept talking about this and that and I was getting anxious that it would soon be six and I'd be late and Tom would be furious, and I didn't even know where he lived, so I asked him to let me go, and he said he'd let me go once we'd kissed, and so I said all right, to go ahead and kiss me because I thought he only wanted to give me a peck. But he started to kiss me and then he threw me on the floor and wanted to do it with me. And I kept shouting at him to let me go now that I'd kissed him and he said he loved me, and tore my new blouse and I started biting him and he got up and said very well but he wouldn't let me leave. And by then it was six o'clock and I was terribly afraid that if Tom walked off I'd never see him again. So I said to the boy to go ahead and do what he wanted to do but quickly because I really had to leave. So he tried to do it with me, but it was no good anyway. He couldn't manage to get inside me.'

'Why didn't you scream?'

'I don't know. He probably told me I mustn't scream. Or maybe I screamed and no one heard me because there was a fearful din going on downstairs. So he let me go, it was seven by then, and I raced there like a lunatic and Tom was no longer there and I thought I'd never see him again and I wanted to kill myself. So I took Dad's safety razor and cut my hand, but when I saw the blood I started vomiting and I'm told I screamed all night long but I don't remember it myself because they carted me off to hospital and by the time I remember again what happened Tom was bringing me tulips and *Mysterious Palms*. Have you read it?'

'No I haven't, but I have it on my shelves.'

'It's the most beautiful book I ever read. I loved Charlotte and I cried at the way it ended even though I knew it had to end that way.'

'Oh my darling.'

'What are you saying?'

'That I love you.'

'Wait, not like that, something might happen.'

'I'll have a wash.'

'Run along then, it's on the left.'

This isn't a bathroom but a hole full of drums and masks. Rags lying about everywhere and the handbasin is there only so they can wash before getting into bed with her. But it is a bathroom with a face of its own, a hole with a face that scowls at me, a hole in which I am trapped, I hurry to be back with her, the towel is so dirty I'm revolted by it, on the shelf there's an open razor, someone might acciden- tally touch it, but there's a mirror hanging from a hook: I am naked, come to think of it I've never looked at myself in a mirror when I was naked, I feel this picture getting into me, my own nakedness with a grinning mask in the background while my mistress is waiting for me.

'I'm back with you again. I can feel you, I'm touching you, you're my delight.'

'My seal. My walrus. You're wet and cold and you're swimming away on the sea. Is England across the sea?'

'A small sea.'

'I thought a vast one.'

'I'd love you even if it was beyond a vast one.'

'Better love me now.'

'I'm loving you now.'

'Love me more. Love me faster. Love me harder. That's right, now. That's wonderful . . .'

She screams. And then silence. I'm falling asleep. I mustn't fall asleep. She's falling asleep, her head on my chest. I've got to leave. I've got to get back to my wife. I've got to clear this place for her husband.

You are asleep. One more kiss. My lips are tired. They are painful.

'You're leaving already?'

'It'll soon be daylight.'

'I'd like you to stay with me.'

'You'd like me to stay with you?'

'Just a little longer.'

'You know I can't.'

'Yes, that's why I love you, because you can't stay with me. Because you're off and over the sea. Because you're a sailor. Run along then!'

'I don't want to leave you.'

'Then stay.'

One more kiss on her closed eyes. With her eye shadow off her eyes are naked.

'When you leave turn off that light in the window.'

'It's me. You haven't gone to bed yet?'

'No, I'm still working.'

'You're always working. I'm speaking from a box.'

'Where?'

'Near us. I suddenly felt depressed at being at home on my own. I felt like blubbing because nobody's thinking of me. That you're in bed with your wife and Tom's in bed with some girl heaven knows where. So I came down to this box to ring you and got soaked through on the way. Got soaked through for you, just so I could speak to you. Can you hear the rain on the roof of the box from where you are? And the glass here's smashed and the receiver's all spattered with rain. Can you come here?'

'But where? Surely . . . surely we can't go to your place.'

'We could sit somewhere. I thought maybe you could drive me out somewhere. We haven't been out together like this yet in the middle of the night.'

It is one o'clock, there are lighted candles on the tables, the waiters wear lilac waistcoats and from the loudspeakers comes a soft rendering of something that should be noisy, if it has to be heard at all. Everything around pretends intimacy.

'I can't bear being at home in the evening on my own. Nothing happens. First they all gape at the TV, while they're drinking tea or coffee and munching cheese on toast. Then Mum can't sleep and walks about the flat looking for her sleeping tablets, asking everybody if they've seen them. So Granddad gives her his gall-bladder tablets. Then they go to bed and snore. I can't bear a flat with snoring in it. I can't bear any of them. They're dead people, nothing gives them pleasure, all they do is eat and sleep, and I feel I'm dying too among them. I have to be with someone who loves me. If at least Tom were here, but he isn't coming back till tomorrow. Tell me, do you love me?'

'I do love you. I love you very much.'

'I'm glad you love me very much and I'm glad you brought me here. I like this place.'

I don't see what she can like about it. At the next table there's a black man with a vulgar painted peroxide blonde and at the table on the right two elderly gentlemen are being attentive to two half-naked creatures who could be their grandchildren rather than their children – everyone here looks vulgar, obscene or rather embarrassingly obscene, the old gent on the right has glistening beads of sweat on his bald head, and I wonder what I look like. Does it show that I have a wife and children at home? I am younger, this girl couldn't be my daughter, she could be my wife and maybe they think she is my wife, except that a man wouldn't take his wife to a nightclub at one in the morning. But why should I be so upset about it, everybody here clearly has a wife at home and they don't seem unduly perturbed by it. She too has a husband and she doesn't seem perturbed by the fact, she's looking happy and talks to me about her Tom although she makes love to me. To her adultery is a fact of life. Maybe adultery is a fact of life and I am simply trapped in some ancient prejudice and have failed to notice that the world around me has changed.

'What's the matter with you, Walrus? You're not listening!'

'I'm listening.'

'You're not. You're sorry you came here. You'd rather be at home.'

'I'm glad I am with you.'

'So why are you frowning?'

'I was just wondering what would happen if my wife woke up.'

154

'Just forget it. If she woke up she'd wait.'

'What do you mean?'

'She'd wait for you to come back. Girls act as if they won't wait, as if they'd run off, but then they wait, and they wait even longer if they think you mightn't come back at all. Let me tell you something. When I was in Sicily with Paula we went to a little town where you could see that big mountain of theirs.'

'Mount Etna?'

'Never mind its name, it was so high that even with that heat there was snow on top of it. A pretty little town, all white stone, as if it had been rolled in flour. And the little streets were so narrow you couldn't walk in them, you could only walk in the square. There was the post office, a hotel and some little shops, there were naked children chasing about and the boys used to ride donkeys or motor-bikes and eat melons and the moment I stepped into that square I said to Paula we've got to stop here. But between us we had less than five thousand lire and everyone there was so poor that it seemed hopeless. And then, in the evening, we heard from a boy about some crazy old woman who was waiting for her dead son to come back home.'

She has suddenly come to life, her face which resembles a mask, a perfect beautiful mask, is transformed, the mask is dissolving. She waves her arms about and leans over to me till I can inhale her delicate scent, her slightly artificial scent blended from make-up, creams, powders and human smell. I am happy to be able to look at her face, it's blissful to be with her. I love her irrationally and incomprehensibly, I am trapped by my own emotions which I can no longer control.

'Just imagine, one of that old woman's sons was killed in the war and then they came and picked up her other son! Whether for the army or for prison I don't remember now, anyway he didn't come back.

'But no one ever told her he was dead and so she's been waiting for him these twenty years or however many years it was that the war ended, and she had his room ready for him in that big stone house, which was full of flowers and birds in cages, and for Christmas she'd buy him shirts and ties, there was a whole wardrobe full of the stuff, and she kept looking out for girls for him to marry except that none of the girls would accept, seeing that he was dead. So they took us to that stone house, two fellows who'd picked us up there, and they told the old woman that I'd heard about her son and that I'd be willing to marry him when he got back.'

'And she believed you?'

'I told you she was crazy. If you could have seen her – hair down to her belly, an enormously big belly. They talked to her for a long time and explained that I'd heard about him or even that I'd seen him, in fact that I'd known him either during the war or just after the war, that I'd met him when he was a prisoner of war and that I was in love with him and heaven knows what else the boys told her.'

'And you stayed there?'

'Why shouldn't I have stayed there? Anyway I had to listen to a lot of chatter about that poor son of hers, I didn't understand a lot of what she was saying but I kept saying si, si, and she was happy that at long last a girl was willing to marry that boy of hers, a girl who'd wait for him with her. And she brought me stacks of photographs and I had to look at all his suits and shirts and shoes and duvets and bed-linen and his school reports from some funny school in Sicily. And she wanted me to sit at home all the time, I wasn't to talk to anybody seeing that I was her son's fiancée. But I always explained that I still had some important matters to see to with the authorities or at the post office, and after lunch I'd slip out.'

'How long did you stay with her?'

'I don't remember now. A week. Or maybe just three days. Until I got tired of that pretty little place. You probably don't approve. You don't approve of my acting the fiancée of a dead boy.'

'It seems a little cruel to deceive a crazy old woman.'

'You think it's a little cruel to deceive a crazy unhappy old woman? You think one should only deceive happy young girls?'

'One shouldn't deceive anyone.'

'That's just talk. Everybody deceives sometimes. Everybody deceives someone else some time. What about you? Have you never deceived anyone? If you'd seen her – that old woman was happy when they took me to her, when I explained I'd wait with her for her son to return.'

'And afterwards? When you left?'

'Afterwards? How can I tell what happened afterwards when I was no longer there? What was that strange old woman to me? Maybe some other girl came along and moved in, that woman had plenty of money and we had nothing. So where's the harm in my moving into her ghost-haunted house and eating some of her tomatoes and some macaroni with parmesan?'

Her eyes are suddenly cold. That incident occurred in another world. Not because a crazy old Sicilian woman figures in it but because she figures in it. She is from another world. Her world is outside the chain of reality in which I am used to living. In her world there's room for love-making but not for love. Or maybe for love too, but not for pity or for sympathy, there's no room in it for any other people. Only for herself. And perhaps not even for herself. Her world is empty and yet her world is full. Nothing more will fit into it. Anything is permitted in it. Being unfaithful and deceiving. Deceiving a woman who's gone mad with despair and making love to somebody she will leave the next day. Talking without attaching any meaning to her words. Because nothing has the slightest meaning any longer. I ought to escape from the world she's drawing me into because I shall perish in it. But it's probably too late and I can't do it.

She finished talking and drained her glass. I am the same kind of crazy person to her. She'll forget me, she'll leave me the day she gets tired of me, just as she left that town under Mount Etna. But she isn't tired of me yet. She rang me herself. She's sitting here with me – my girlfriend. My beautiful girlfriend. Maybe I'll overcome that vacuum inside her. I'll step into it and fill it. She's smiling again. The moment of leaving has come. Where shall we go? 'Waiter, our bill, please.'

'You want to leave already?'

'I've got to get up in the morning.'

'Don't get up then.'

'But I must.'

'Don't think about it then.'

It is half past two. It is still raining outside. A damp smell rises from the road surface and the scent of jasmine wafts over from a garden. Suppose my overcoat doesn't dry out by morning and Camilla notices that it is wet?

'Don't be in such a hurry. I don't want to get into the car yet. Let's walk up this little street, there's a park there.'

'But it's raining, my love!'

'Never mind. I like the rain. We met in the rain and that's why it's always raining for us.'

Her body suddenly clings to mine, my wet arms, her bare arms are cold from the rain. 'My dear Walrus, you came along just when I was feeling low. I love you for that. Do you love me too?'

It is half past two in the morning. In the rain I press against some dirty wall, opposite me are the dead dark windows of strangers' habitations. I am getting wet. My coat is getting soaked but I am with her. 'I love you too.'

'Let's go to the park then. We'll make love in the rain.'

## 6

'David, are you all right?'

'What's the matter?'

'It's half past six. Why aren't you up?'

'I overslept? Must have slept very soundly. I got to bed late.'

'You're working too hard. Why can't you let up a bit?'

'I want to finish those lectures. Holidays start soon. I'd like to have at least a week with all of you.'

'That's nice of you, but you shouldn't overdo it.'

She's looking at me oddly. What does she know? Maybe she woke up in the night. I'm dead beat, she can see it in my face. She woke up in the night, she went to the kitchen, the light was on. She called: David! David, where are you? Silence. She looked in all the doors, she looked out the window, the car was gone. Or else this morning, a little while ago, she touched my overcoat. It's wet. Why is your coat wet, David, where have you been? She's never play-acted with me before, she's always asked straight out. But why should she ask at all, it's all too obvious. She's waiting for me to confess. Like that night when she rang the institute.

'I woke during the night, it must have been two o'clock and you hadn't come to bed yet.'

Silence. Did she get out of bed? Or did she go to sleep again immediately? Surely a person feels the absence of another. There is a difference between the silence of a flat in which there is a living being and one which is empty.

I don't feel like telling any more lies. I'm tired. Yes, I was with her. We made love on a wet bench in the park while you were asleep. 'I was writing till about three.'

'You should take it easy. You've got rings under your eyes.'

'I'll go to bed earlier today.'

'Why don't you ring the institute and tell them you're not feeling well, and sleep on a little bit longer.'

She didn't get up after all. She doesn't suspect. I'm glad she doesn't suspect, that I didn't let on. Tonight I'll go to bed at eight. Or the minute I get home. And then? I don't know. I won't go to her like that again in the middle of the night. In a few days the school holidays start, Camilla will be going away, perhaps she will go away, I'll be on my own for a month, and then, who knows what could happen in a month, maybe she'll stop loving me, or she'll go away with her husband, and then I'm leaving, I'm leaving for a year, for that unimaginably long year. How shall I manage without you, my love? Who'll ring me there in the middle of the night?

'Don't forget you have tickets for the cinema, to take the children.'

'Today?'

'Certainly. This is Friday. Margit is looking forward to it enormously. She was talking of nothing else all yesterday evening.'

'That's fine. I'm looking forward to it too.' (What are the tickets for? Which cinema? Never mind, I'll sleep there. I'm looking forward to sleeping at the cinema.)

'David, something's wrong with you.'

'What makes you say that?'

'Look, how you're dressing. Your shirt's buttoned up askew and you've put your pullover on inside out.'

'I'm tired. That's all.'

'No, there's something the matter with you. Something's worrying you.'

'Nothing's worrying me, I'm perfectly happy.'

'You're still seeing that woman.'

160

'Please! When would I be seeing her? You can see the pile of work I have. I'm sitting over it either at the institute or at home.'

'So you're worried that you're running out of time.'

'I'm not worried. For heaven's sake, leave me alone. Why talk about me all the time? I'm not a child.' I'm shouting at her although I have no right to do so. I'm shouting because I have a guilty conscience. Because I don't want to keep telling lies indefinitely. Because I have a headache, because she's in my way.

'You're leaving already? You haven't even said goodbye to the children.'

'Bye, Anna! Bye, guinea-pig!'

'Come home soon, Dad!'

'Daddy, I'm looking forward to the cinema. I'll sit on your lap!'

7

There's a pile of mail on my desk at the office. I don't feel like reading it. Most letters are concerned with superfluous things. Letters are a vain attempt to compensate for lack of contact among humans. I'm putting my head on my desk for a moment, nobody can see me here.

As soon as I shut my eyes I see you. I see your open eyes. I see them wide-open and grey in the twilight, I see your small unattractive breasts. I see you in that room full of drums and masks. I hear you breathing. I hear your voice. I hear the rain smacking into the puddles. I feel it wetting my neck. Why have I never loved anyone like this before?

Because I had no time. Or, on the contrary: because I had oceans of time before me. It always seemed as if something was yet to come, something greater and more important. I thought it would be success in my work, the award of some title, or some important appointment, or that it would be something material: a house, a garden or a new car, and instead it's turned out to be you I've been waiting for. You're created for loving. I must tell you so when I see you, of all the people I know you're the one most made for loving.

The telephone. How's that possible? I must have slept for an hour. Anyway, it won't be her. She's still asleep. Let it ring. It goes on ringing. Probably someone at the institute who knows I'm here.

'This is Marie. David, the Strong Man's been on the phone, the meeting's put off till ten thirty. And some money's come for you, eight hundred. I've signed the receipt for you. Shall I bring it up?'

'That's all right, Marie, I'll pick it up later.'

'And Milan's waiting here. Would you have a minute to spare for him?'

Why's he bothering me in the morning? Of course, it isn't morning, I overslept. And it's Friday, he's leaving for a conference in Karlovy Vary. My deputy is attending in my place, and I promised to read his paper. Except I can't think about any scientific papers, I can't think of anything but her.

'Ask him to come up in an hour. And bring me some coffee, if you'd be so kind.'

'Coffee?'

'Why are you so surprised?'

'You never drink coffee normally.'

'I worked all through the night.'

'How strong do you want it?'

'I've no idea. How can I tell if I never drink it?' That's just how she'd answer, I'm beginning to talk like her. Eight hundred crowns – probably for reviewing. I'll buy her a present. But first I must read that paper. I'm grateful to him for taking my place there. It's bound to be a bore and a lost weekend. What am I to buy her? I'm no good at choosing presents. I'll take her along to the shops and let her choose for herself. The thymus and immunological tolerance. The privileged position of the thymus in the lymphoid system and some of its peculiarities suggest that this organ participates in some way . . . Why should I read this, after all I know what he could have discovered, I know that so far we haven't discovered anything. The telephone.

'It's me.'

'You're awake already?'

'The phone woke me. Tom rang. He was due back today and he's just phoned to say he won't be, they've got a three days' extension. So I thought I should let you know. Do you think they really extended their engagement by three days or that he's found himself a bird? Maybe I'll follow him and if I catch him there with some silly blonde I'll kill the two of them.'

'When he's got you, why should he take up with another woman?'

'You really believe that? It's sweet of you to believe that. I probably won't follow him. I wouldn't find the place anyway. Sure to do something silly like taking the wrong train. So I'll stay here and maybe we can go somewhere together? What are you doing this evening?'

'I've got tickets for the cinema.'

'You're going to the cinema? You never told me you went to the cinema.'

'I'm taking the children.'

'Ah yes, I forgot you have a lot of little girls.'

'Two.'

'You have two little girls. And a wife. But nobody gives a damn about me.'

'I didn't know you'd be free tonight. You said your husband was coming back.'

'Don't get all worked up. Who said I was talking about you? Why are all men so full of themselves they always immediately think you're talking about them?'

If I stand her up she'll obviously go with someone else. Out of spite. She'll get drunk and then she'll take him home with her to that room with the drums and she'll make love to him there. I'm beginning to be jealous. No, I'm not jealous. I only want to be with her. I want to be with her every moment she can be with me. 'You know what, I'll ring my wife and ask her to take the children on her own. I'll tell her I have a meeting or something.' I'll ring Camilla and tell her I've got to go to that conference in Karlovy Vary.

'And you'll come round for me? We could go to the cinema together. At least you'll see a real film. With your little girls you'd only see some nonsense or other.'

'I'll come round this afternoon.'

'Yes, do come, my Walrus. Do you still love me?'

'I still love you.'

'That's good, I'm glad you still love me. I kiss you for that. Can you feel it? I kiss you down there. Know where?'

8

'You've gone off to a conference? And where is it?'

'In Karlovy Vary.'

'And when will you be back?'

'Tomorrow.'

'You'll stay overnight?'

'That's what I want to do. I want to get some sleep at last.'

'What shall I bring? Do you think we'll go out somewhere in the evening? But I haven't got a thing to wear anyway.'

'Never mind, just come in what you're wearing. You're

beautiful in whatever you've got on.'

'All right. Maybe we won't go out anywhere. Wait, I'll take a book with me. The one I told you about. I'll read to you from it. Or you can read to me. And I'll take a night-dress so you don't have to be ashamed of me at night.'

We're driving along again. You're sitting next to me. You're beginning to belong to me. I wish that each time I looked to the right I saw your face. It seems so familiar to me, as if it had been with me from birth.

'Come on, step on it! Why are you driving so slowly?'

'We're going fast enough.'

'And you can't go any faster?'

'I'm tired, I'm a little tired after last night. I only had three hours' sleep.'

'You think the car's tired too because you are tired? No, wait, I can see it now, you have tired eyes. I'll kiss your eyes. But keep going. Keep going, why are you stopping?'

'I can't drive while you're kissing my eyes!'

'I want you to drive even when I'm kissing your eyes.'

'Have you gone out of your mind? We'll be killed!'

'I don't mind. But now I want you to drive fast.'

'All right.'

I see the world in between kisses. I see the road between moments of darkness. I'm rushing towards destruction. But you want me to drive and so I'm driving, even if we do rush towards destruction. There's a delivery van coming the other way, just leave me some light for an extra second. I used to be frightened of death and now I'm letting her kiss my eyes and I'm happy. Maybe death itself is riding with me in my car, sitting in the passenger seat by my side – attractive and bewitching – caressing and kissing me, let me just avoid this car, we're moving to the black spot of non-existence.

'My poor Walrus, you're all trembling and your fore-head's wet. Don't you want me to kiss you any more? I've got an idea. Let's turn into that forest ahead. We'll read and we'll look for mushrooms and we'll make love in the forest.'


9

'Is that you, Camilla?'

'Where are you speaking from?'

'Hello, can you hear me? I hope I didn't wake you.'

'You're calling long-distance?'

'I thought I'd give you a ring as I wasn't even able to say goodbye.'

'Nice of you to ring, David. I was sorry when I got the message at school. They said you had to go.'

'I rang but you were teaching. Did you take the children to the cinema?'

'I did. They just loved it. Especially that cartoon film about a mole. They were sorry you didn't see it.'

'I was sorry too.'

'Is it interesting?'

'Is what . . . Oh yes. No, it isn't. Same as always. Lots of papers. That sort of thing. Most of it stuff one knows anyway.'

'But you had to go?'

'Well, there are lots of friends here, also from abroad. Case of showing my face.'

'You said there wouldn't be anyone from abroad.'

'I said that? I don't remember talking about it even. Anyway, they're here. Some Frenchman and a West German, and also Bridges from London – the eccentric, remember me telling you about him?'

'When will you be back?'

'Tomorrow. Probably towards evening.'

'Can't you make it earlier? I thought we might spend the afternoon . . . it's so lovely here, today, as we came home

166

from the cinema even the children noticed that the lime trees were in bloom.'

'I'll get back as soon as I can. Bye for now. And go to bed now. I'll do the same.'

'David?'

'Yes . . . What is it?'

'David, I'm lonely without you.'

'Come on, I'll be back tomorrow.'

'I don't know, I've got the feeling that you are ringing from a huge distance. Not from Karlovy Vary but from somewhere very far away.'

'Well, that's an illusion.'

'Say something else to me, David.'

'Sweet dreams.'

I return to a dimly lit hall, where four bearded young-sters in silvery waistcoats are imitating the world: Las Vegas or Monte Carlo, I don't know what the real world is like because my world was somewhere else.

I'm returning to her, to my girlfriend, she's enchanting, delicate, indecently beautiful. She's drinking Campari. I walk over to her, fortunately I can't see myself, I only know that I am a liar, an amateur liar, a dilettante delighted with himself for having played his part well. I'm an adulterer obsessed with my vice, I'm a traitor who has abandoned everything he believed in.

Is this really still me walking across the rust-brown car-pet of this strange, plush, wasteful and indolent world, is this still my face that is now undoubtedly smiling at her? And if this isn't me, who am I? Where have I been left behind? And if it is me how long can I survive in this shape?

Or could this be my real essence and everything else was but a mistake, but a delusion: my scientific work, Camilla, my children, the dream of our own home, of the house I was going to build, the dream of longevity that I would discover, all merely an escape from that creature which suddenly emerged in order to make love, to wallow in ecstasy, to experience a sweet tremor at every lover's moan, a creature which can now scarcely believe the creature that preceded it?

I appear strange to myself, but I don't know whether it's because of what I'm doing now or what I used to do before. I don't know who I am and I don't know if this is still me who is now sitting down next to you, watching you sip a reddish drink of whose very existence I was still ignorant yesterday.

'You're scowling again, Walrus. You're scowling again.'

'I was thinking of something.'

'You're always thinking of something. Your head does nothing except think. I bet you've never stood on your head. When Tom's had a drink or two he stands on his head and he can maybe keep it up for hours. Why don't you have something to drink? I'd like you to have a drink. So that, for this once, you won't be so terribly serious. I bet you're even serious when you're in love.'

10

'My little Walrus, I'm beginning to love you, you do such nice things for me, you've taken me along on this outing and given me *spaghetti alla veneziana* for dinner, and apricots in syrup, and you've taken a room with a blue ceiling, a pity you can't see the ceiling right now but it looks like the sky. Come closer to me, I feel you now, don't move, stay like this, oh darling, I feel you terribly close now, don't move, do you know what, there's that book on the bedside table, pick it up, we'll read to each other.'

'Surely we can't read right now!'

'Why shouldn't we? You pick up the book, we'll read at the same time.'

'All right, I've got the book.'

'Open it anywhere and read, and don't move.'

'There's a corner turned down, shall I read from there?'

'Read anything you like, darling. Oh, I feel you so marvellously.'

*'Listen, ours must be a permanent honeymoon, always. Time without end, until one of us dies. It must never be anything else. Either heaven or hell, no comfortable, safe, peaceful purgatory between the two, for us, you and me, to be kept waiting till we become victims of propriety or patience or shame or remorse.'*

I can't go on. I'm reading, my lips are forming words only to convince me that I cannot perceive anything but you, that nothing else exists but you, nothing but your body which is entwining me, which I'm entering. 'Shall I read on?'

'Yes, read on. Oh darling, how I can feel you now. Today I love you. Today I'm in love with you. Do you love me? Tell me, you love me too.'

'I love you, I love you more than anybody else, more than anything in the world. I love you so much that without you nothing would have any meaning left.'

'Tell me, how long will you love me like this?'

'I'll love you so long as there's any breath left in me. So long as I live. Because after that I wouldn't be alive.'

'You say such nice things to me. You do such nice things for me. I love you. Read me more. Read those next few sentences.'

*'So that it isn't really me in whom you believe, on whom you rely, but it is love . . .'*

'That's enough, don't read on. Now only make love to me. Make love to me fast! Make love to me harder! Oh, I want you so much. Stay with me. I love you. Today I love you. How many more days have we got?'

'I don't know. Wait a minute, another sixty-five, I think.'
'Sixty-five? We'll make love for sixty-five days.'

11

'Is that you, David?'
'It's me.'
'Why are you creeping about like that?'
'I thought you might be asleep. Didn't want to wake the children.'
'They waited up for you till half past eight. But when you didn't come I sent them to bed. They were looking forward to seeing you.'
'And I to seeing all of you. Look what I got for them.'
They are atrociously ugly dolls – but what could I buy when we didn't get up till midday and all the shops were closed except for one tobacconist's where I spotted them among the souvenirs? 'Think they'll like them?'
'They'll be pleased you haven't forgotten them.'
That sentence had a certain undertone, I can feel it but I must pretend not to have noticed anything, I must act normally, but how can I act normally when my body is branded by countless marks?
'Was it a long drive?'
'What do you mean?'
'If the drive took you a long time.'
'The usual. Yes, about normal. Two and a half hours. Maybe a little longer. Why do you ask?'
'I thought you set out before lunch.'
'What made you think I set out before lunch?'
'That's what they told me.'
'What they told you? Who could have told you anything like that?' Who could have told her I left before lunch when I wasn't there at all, when no one knows where I have been? Or could she have tracked me down? Could she

have tracked down the hotel where we spent the night? But they couldn't have told her we left before lunch because we didn't leave before lunch.

'I rang you there, David, don't be angry, I'd never ring you just for my sake, but I remembered that Mother has that Karlovy Vary porcelain of which Margit broke the last two cups, and Mother was so unhappy about it, and so I thought that if you had a minute to spare and could just pop round . . .'

'And how did you know whom to ring?'

'I said I wanted that conference of biologists and they just put me through.'

'Who did you speak to?'

'First they gave me some girl secretary who didn't know about you, she assured me you weren't there at all, but I said that you weren't going at first but at the last moment decided to go, and to look for you – and so they put me through to Milan.'

'To Mencl? And what did he tell you?'

'He said in a very funny voice: "You want David?" as if he was rattled by my phoning you.'

'So?'

'He said he'd go and look for you, and a little while later he came back and said you'd just left. That there wasn't anything important happening any more and that you'd set out for home. That was at eleven.'

It never occurred to me that she might phone me, but I was lucky. And why did he do it, why did he cover up for me? Probably out of some normal male solidarity, I ought to be grateful to him, for that lie, for sharing in the conspiracy.

'Where were you all that time?'

Yes, there remained at least seven hours unaccounted for. 'I was there. I hadn't left. They misinformed him, I'd only gone for a walk down the Colonnade.'

'You walked down the Colonnade?'

That was a stupid lie, I never go for a walk without a reason, and she knows that. 'I'd thought of something, a hypothesis, want me to tell you?'

'You know I won't understand it. And you didn't go back to the conference?'

'I did. Of course I did.'

'And he didn't tell you I rang?'

'I didn't speak to him then. He was in another section.' A terrible thought: she's merely testing me. He's bound to have told her: David? But he hasn't been here at all! And she's now trying to fathom the depth of my betrayal, the extent of my lies, discover how deep I've sunk. And I am leading her down into my bottomless pit, I twist and turn in a labyrinth from which I cannot escape.

'And at the end of it?'

'I didn't stay till the very end. After all, I had the car.'

'David!'

Silence. She's looking at me, waiting. But I am too cowardly or too miserable or maybe I've lost all sense of shame and dignity. I look into her eyes and even attempt a smile.

'David, you're lying. I know you're not telling me the truth; you went off, you drove off to see her and now you don't want to tell me.'

Silence.

'So this is all you have to tell me?'

'What about? I've told you everything.'

'David, we used to love each other. I always thought you loved me, you kept telling me you loved me. Tell me, where were you all this afternoon?'

'What do you want me to say?'

'Just tell me, do you love me? Do you still love me, at least a little?'

Silence. I'd like to say at least one kind word to you but I can't. I don't know why I can't. I lie, I keep lying all evening, I've been lying for weeks on end, I wallow in untruths till I've stopped being aware of the filth I stir up – but I still can't do it. I can't say I love you, even though I'd like to take you in my arms and press you to me before you burst into tears.

'Do you remember, that time, when you came back from Romania, how we went on an excursion by train, and then in the evening we were waiting at some station, it was in Čerčany, and you didn't like the waiting room and so you found an empty truck, a cattle-truck, and it smelled of horses, and there you told me incessantly that you loved me, do you remember?'

I am silent.

'You don't remember? And you said we'd build a house for ourselves, you wanted to build a villa with every room a different colour. One blue, one red, one yellow and one white. You asked me which I would choose for myself.'

'Yes, I remember that, but I don't remember which one you chose.'

'The yellow one, of course.'

And now she is crying. She's not sobbing but big tears are running down her face.

'And you said you'd love me as long as you lived, yes, that's what you said then, David, that you would always love me and never leave me.'

'But I'm not leaving you.'

'You've left me already. Do you think I can't feel it? Do you think I'm made of stone? You left me a long time ago. For everything we had going between us – I know I can't want anything in return for that now, but at least don't lie to me.'

'I'm not lying. And do stop crying.'

'You've always had your work – and what did I have? That stupid school where I have to teach what I don't believe. I've lost all my girl friends because I never had time for them, because you'd never make time for yourself. I had nothing except this place here and you, my family.'

'But you still have us.'

'The children, perhaps. I still have the children.'

Silence.

'David, I'm so depressed. I can't see anything ahead of me. I see nothing that I can look forward to. I'm so depressed I'd like to lie somewhere and not be aware of anything. Not have to get up in the morning, not have to wait in the evening for you to come home, if you're coming home, not think about you telling me lies, that the only thing I ever had is falling apart. I want to be dead, David.'

'That's just a mood. It'll pass.'

'That's all you can say to me? That's all?'

Silence.

'Were you with her this afternoon?'

'No!'

'All right, I believe you. I want to believe you.'

'I'm glad you believe me.'

At last I'm in bed. My wife's lying beside me. The mother of my children. She's crying. I can't go to sleep because at midnight, maybe, there'll be a phone call from her. Another sixty-four days. Actually only sixty-three now. Then we shall be leaving and everything will come to an end. Let me have just those two months. 'In two months we'll be off.'

'You think we're going?'

'Certainly. Over there you'll cheer up. It'll be a different life. Aren't you looking forward to it at all?'

'I don't know. At this moment I can't look forward to anything.'

I feel sorry for her. Everything's changed, everything's in ruins. I recall that I used to go to bed and think about my work. I really did think about my mice, but only because I

174

thought about human beings. I thought of my mother's lifeless face, I thought of you and of myself, all in order to postpone as long as possible that moment of eternal lifelessness. And I never admitted to you that I dreamed of the honours I'd be receiving for it. And I dreamed that you'd be sitting in the audience and you'd see me and you'd be proud of me. I pictured the house we'd build, a house in which we'd be happy. I wanted you to be happy, not to have to teach, for us to go to the seaside together, to walk through Hyde Park together, I wanted to show you the world. All that I was hoping for, I really had no other wish, but now I'm lying here, knowing that I can't fall asleep because I'm waiting for a midnight ring and the only thing I'm hoping for now is that she will ring and say to me, I love you.

It isn't I who's lying beside you, I'm no longer the man you met on the little steamer called Horia, I know that, and that's why I can't tell you I love you, that's why there's no point in your asking me to say it.

But maybe I'm just making excuses. I'm simply selfish and weak. I didn't pass the first test, I'm unable to control my own passion. I'm kneeling before you, asking you: Forgive me.

If only something like forgiveness existed, real forgiveness and not just consolation for the weak.

I suppressed that passion within me for too long, I refused to devote at least part of my life to it, at least a fraction of my time. Now it's caught up with me, now it's gripping me in its embrace, now it's crushing me between its millstones, sweeping me along on a conveyor belt no matter how much I try to escape, it's carrying me relentlessly in one direction, into its jaws, I can see the vortex, the crater I'm hurtling towards. I'm hurtling along, I used to love the forest but there are no trees here, I used to love the sky but it isn't there, everything has turned bloody, I'm hurtling along beneath a low red-hot dome and I feel the breath of flames . . .

'David, the telephone!'

'What . . . what's the matter?'

'David, the telephone. It's ringing. I'm afraid. Who'd ring at this hour? Maybe something's happened to our parents.'

I run to the telephone, barefoot, I run over the cold tiles, I slam the door. I whisper into the receiver: 'It's me. But she's awake.'

'I love you.'

'I love you too.'

'Who was that, David?'

'No one, wrong number. Who'd ring at this hour?'

'I was so afraid. Did he say who he was?'

'No, he didn't. Just said, "Sorry, wrong number." '

[ 3 ]

# CHAPTER EIGHT

1

A beetle was crawling over his bare chest and above his head the swaying tops of the pines alternately revealed and obscured the sky and the now no longer warming evening sun. Directly opposite him somebody, maybe fifty or a hundred years ago, had cut two huge heads out of the sandstone cliff. When she'd caught sight of it from the road she'd said: Come on, let's have a look at those heads. They'd clambered up a steep footpath among the rocks until they'd reached this spot which was screened from the road and from all other sides as well, and from where the two heads could be seen through a gap in the under-growth. And as he lay there by her side he realized that, for the first time in his life, he was becoming aware of a lot of things around him, that he was relating to them, that they were taking root in his memory.

She opened her eyes for a moment: 'Where are we?'

'In the forest.'

'Ah yes, we drove to the forest. You showed me those stone figures. You came here yesterday to carve them out of the rock for me, so you could show them to me today.'

'As a matter of fact, nobody nowadays would carve any-thing out of a rock any more. Out of somebody else's rock, and for no payment,' he said. 'Nowadays no one would even carve a wooden totem, or even a heart into a window shutter.'

'But you did all this,' she said. 'And you didn't do it for nothing either.'

'Today nobody wants to be a woodcarver or a sculptor without actually doing it professionally. I suppose there used to be lots of people in the old days who longed to create something but didn't have the opportunity. They were peasants. So they just picked up a chisel and . . .' He realized that she'd fallen asleep again.

I should be doing something, he told himself from habit, I should be doing something instead of holding forth like a pub bore about how much life has changed. On the blanket lay the note-pad he always carried with him but which he didn't look at now even when she was asleep. Instead he watched the branches of the pines. He absorbed them into his memory. He absorbed this spot to make sure it would always stay within him, with its stone faces and with her face which, among all those shades of green, now seemed, with its artificial eye shadow, just as lifeless and artificial as those faces in the rock.

He looked at her, at this increasingly familiar face which seemed to have been with him since time immemorial, and although at that moment, by daylight, it was by no means beautiful and, in sleep, looked rather dead, he bent over it and kissed it.

'What's the matter?'

'Nothing. I love you.'

'Yes,' she breathed. 'And you took me along on an outing. Carted your little family to their summer destination and then took me on an outing. Think I should get dressed again?'

'That's up to you.'

'I love the sun. I could lie here like this all day and night if the sun shone at night. Do you think it ever shines at night?'

'Yes, beyond the Arctic Circle.'

'Now that's where you should take me, beyond the Circle. That's why I love Italy so much, because the sun's burning there nearly all the time. And everything's warm from the sun. The grass and the people and the walls and the sand. I love the hot sand.'

'And do you love me?' he asked.

'Yes. For taking me on this outing, for carving those figures out of the rock, for being so sweet and looking after me and for being fat and ugly like a walrus.'

Perhaps she really likes me because she's here with me and not with someone else, because she's always with me, even though she's probably with me because I look after her. I take her out for meals and drive her about and I buy her pretty things, but maybe this is real love and I'm doing her an injustice, I know nothing about her, I can't get through to her, she's surrounded by a screen of meaning-less words, incidents and questions behind which she's possibly covering up the emptiness of her soul, I only know her outer shell but I make love to her without bother-ing about her soul, about her sufferings or her sorrows.

She reached out for her clothes. 'I'd better get dressed, it's getting late and you'll probably want to go and eat somewhere.'

'That's right,' and he realized that he'd stay with her all evening and perhaps all night or at least part of the night. He embraced her. She let him kiss her, then she sat down a little way away and put on her clothes. 'I think I must go to Italy again soon,' she said all of a sudden. 'I really need some sunshine and the sea and some little sweetshops and coloured beach umbrellas and seashells.'

'Soon – how soon is soon?'

'How can I tell? In a week or a fortnight. However long it takes to get my passport.'

'But you need an invitation,' he said with growing alarm.

'What do you think – I've got invitations from at least twenty fellows.'

'I thought we barely had six weeks left.'

'What six weeks are you talking about? What are you

counting all the time?'

'I'm off in six weeks.'

'Okay, so you're off. Why should I worry because you're off in six weeks?'

'I thought,' he swallowed hard, 'that we might spend as much time together as we can during that time.'

'That time,' she repeated mockingly, 'do you expect me to sit around in Prague just because you're off in six weeks?' She was dressed now, she took a mirror and a comb from her handbag and combed her hair.

'You said yourself you wanted to be with me the whole time.'

'I said that? So what? I probably felt like that at the time I said it. But you were telling me then you loved me so much you couldn't live without me, and such rot. So why are you off if you love me so much? Why doesn't it occur to you to take me along somewhere? You're taking that silly family of yours that otherwise you couldn't care less about. You're going to take them to the seaside on Saturdays and your wife will be running around the shops from early morning, buying herself new shoes while I'm sitting here on my behind. Well, you have another think coming!'

'Where do you think I could take you?'

'I don't mind where. Take me to Italy, beyond the Arctic Circle or to your England.'

'I can't take you anywhere, I couldn't get a passport in time, nor the money.'

'You wouldn't get a passport!' she laughed. 'You told me you were practically leaving and you still haven't got a passport or the money? And how are you going to keep that famous family of yours?'

'I'll receive a salary the moment I get there and start working.'

'I can get the money. I can rustle up five chaps who'll sell you as much foreign money as you want.'

He didn't say anything.

She put down her comb and mirror and looked at him coolly and expectantly.

But surely I can't take her along and just leave everything here. What would I say at the institute? Or to Camilla? They wouldn't even give me a visa. To walk with her through Hyde Park, to stroll through the little streets of Soho, to take a boat out on Loch Lomond – that would be too much, that would be as if she were my wife. But isn't she like my wife already?

'There you are,' she said, 'and you thought I'd sit here on my behind all through the summer, waiting for you to ring me so you can have fun with me before you bundle up that fat wife of yours and sail off with her? Why don't you go after her to the country and make love to her those forty-nine days which you've calculated so accurately?'

2

The young man stood smoking in the passage outside the Musical Theatre: his large shapeless head sitting, almost neckless, on broad shoulders. He wore a leather jacket and yellow linen trousers, and on the hand which held his cigarette a ring gleamed. He was the type of person who aroused distrust in David, or even unease. He glanced about him. She was standing in front of a shop window, looking at gramophone records without showing any real interest. If she weren't watching him he'd probably abandon his intention and beat a retreat – she'd evidently suspected just that and had therefore come along with him. Now she was smiling at him, even at that distance he could feel the smile to which he'd surrendered. 'I was told you might get me some hard currency,' he addressed the man.

Instead of an answer the man produced a cigarette case,

snapped it open and offered it to him. 'How much?' he asked.

'About eight hundred sterling. Can you get me that amount?'

'At a hundred and twenty-five.'

'But surely this . . .' A woman was approaching them slowly and he fell silent.

'I'm not pressing you,' the man said.

'Look here, one miserable night in the cheapest boarding house costs three pounds. That would be four hundred crowns just for bed and breakfast.'

'I'm not pressing you,' the man repeated. 'Now that they have opened the frontiers a little I've got so many buyers you'd be wasting your time haggling.'

'I'm not haggling,' he protested. 'I just don't want to be ripped off. I mean, that's at least three times the official rate of exchange.'

'Why don't you buy them at the official rate then?' the man suggested, turned his back and slowly walked away.

She was still standing in front of the shop window, gazing rigidly at the plate glass before her. Probably watching her own reflection. If he returned without the money she'd probably be furious with him and in the end he'd buy it anyway. Maybe at a worse rate. And what difference did it really make whether he paid eight thousand or ten thousand, during the past two months he'd spent all the money they'd saved up for their as yet non-existent house, so what difference did it make whether he was left with one door or two, they wouldn't open anywhere anyway. Besides, who would the house be for, who would live in it now?

He caught up with the young man. 'All right,' he said. 'I had no idea it would cost that much. I haven't got enough Czech money on me.'

'How much then?'

'Sixty,' he said quickly. 'I think I've got enough for sixty.'

'Follow me then.' They climbed a dirty staircase. A photographic studio on the right, some chemical enterprise's accountancy department on the left. They climbed all the way to the attic.

She was still waiting in the passage. 'Got it?' she asked.

'I've got it. Fifty-five pounds. I'm to collect the rest tomorrow.'

'I've no idea how much that is anyway. And you're all sweaty. Did you run up the stairs?'

'No,' he attempted a smile. So we'll be off in a few days. I still don't quite know why. High time I told Camilla I'm leaving. I'm off with my mistress on a tour of Europe. We'll cross the Channel so we can make love with a view of the Thames.

'You don't seem happy.' She took him by the hand. 'Aren't you looking forward to our trip?'

They stepped out of the passageway; outside there was blinding sunlight. 'Are you coming round to me tonight?' he asked.

'I don't know, I should devote myself a little to Tom now, seeing I'm off with you on such a long trip. I'll ring you.'

He experienced a jealous fear that she was slipping away from him. 'Do you love me at least?' he asked.

'You know I do. I love you for taking me on such a long trip.' She stopped in the middle of the pavement, stood on tiptoe and kissed him.

3

The phone still doesn't ring. For the past few days I've continually waited for telephone calls. I can hear them even in my dreams. She rings and tells me she loves me, strangers' voices ring and threaten me. And I myself dial non-existent numbers in the hope of getting through, to call you to come to me, I rotate the dial, the numbers dissolve before my eyes and I keep making mistakes. I can't get through to you because I can't find an inner equilibrium. I know that in these dreams my own unease attacks me, the fear that you're slipping away from me, that I haven't got you, that you're leaving me. I find myself in a solitude from which I can no longer make people hear my shouting.

And I had a wife, and two young daughters to whom I was devoted. I had my work, which gave me satisfaction. I believed that all my life I'd manage to remain a decent individual unsullied by deceit. I wanted to be good to the people I loved. Not hurt anyone. Build a house where we'd be happy. I hoped we'd all stay together in this world, which isn't an easy one to live in. And now I'm impatiently waiting for the telephone only to swamp my wife with another pile of lies.

In four days' time I'm off, in four days' time she'll be sitting next to me and we'll drive off so far away that no one will be able to reach me by phone nor I reach anybody.

I'll be driving so far away that I won't even be able to reach myself.

I'm still trying now and then to reach myself, I bang at darkened windows, at opaque panes. No one responds.

Why are you doing all this? Silence. Do you realize you're deceiving yourself? No answer. Do you know that she doesn't love you, that you're carrying her with you like a weight round your neck, dug deep into your brain, and that one of these days you'll stagger and fall, and die?

Silence. No one is answering me. I no longer exist, I have fallen apart, I cannot get through to myself.

I love her and I know that she doesn't love me. I long to hear her say that word again and again, only because I know how meaningless it sounds from her lips. Love must surpass a person in time and space, but she cannot reach any space other than that in which she is dwelling, and she doesn't comprehend the future any more than she remembers yesterday. She only knows how to make love; maybe she makes love so totally simply because she dwells only in the present moment.

The phone at last: 'You waiting for Litomyšl?'

'Yes, I am. What's happening?'

'There's no answer.'

'That's impossible, bound to be someone at home now that it's evening.'

'Want me to try again?'

'Please do.'

They're probably all sitting out in the garden. Camilla, grandmother, grandfather, the children, I've always found that circus irritating, that circus calling itself the family, all that chatter about relations, about the furniture, about an uncle's illness or a great-nephew's graduation – but now I'm nostalgic for it. Why doesn't someone answer the phone? Maybe Camilla has taken the children on an outing. She's showing them flowers and catching beetles and snails. I'm getting ready for an outing myself. Why is it just this trip that strikes me as the peak of betrayal? Surely it makes no difference where people betray one another, whether it is in a wood near Prague or on the banks of the Thames. I probably feel the way I do because going abroad has always been such a precious thing to us. We were living in a cage and dreaming of slipping through the bars one day. I promised her a trip to England even before we were married. Instead I'm taking another woman.

I know she's a stranger and doesn't love me. That's why I want her all the time. That's why I'm doing everything she asks me to do. Some day she'll say to me: Get up on the roof and jump! I'll be lying on the pavement and everything will be over. But I lack the strength to stop it. I am a weakling, I never suspected I was such a weakling.

The telephone rings. 'You're waiting for Litomyšl? I've got your call now. Go ahead.'

# CHAPTER NINE

1

A big sign announced Heidelberg. Above the board hung dark storm clouds. It occurred to him that he might exit from the autobahn and look at the town with its ancient university, and spend the night there before the storm broke, but he didn't, he continued to rush ahead to the next frontier. He always hurried whenever he was travelling, because he wanted to achieve something and he knew that his time was severely limited, and that he must economize on every minute. He denied himself pleasure and superfluous information. Except that this whole journey was superfluous, he'd never yet made such a trip without an objective, a trip which was its own objective, a trip that could come to an end wherever and whenever he chose. He was aware of it, and the thought of the total absence of any objective to this trip subconsciously terrified him, and so he rushed on in order, at least in his movements, to remain the person he used to be.

'Aren't you hungry, darling?' She was sitting close to him, so that he felt her touching him with her hip and bare arm. The names on the signs obviously meant nothing to her; if indeed she was registering them at all, she probably registered them merely as conglomerations of letters and colours, all she was taking in was the drive, the speed, and because he was driving fast she was content. From a bag she produced a roll and a package with Hungarian salami (they'd bought it all in the last town before the frontier, they'd also purchased a carton of juice and several tins of apricots and canned meat, as well as a packet of dry rusks between which they had hidden eighty black-market pounds sterling, paid for in blood, and they had then flung that package, half-opened, on the back seat), she broke off a piece of the roll, put a slice of salami on it and slipped it into his mouth.

He wasn't hungry, he was tired. He'd been driving for ten hours and he'd been driving virtually non-stop.

'Where are we actually?' she asked.

'Near Heidelberg, now we're passing Mannheim and we'll soon have to turn off for Saarbrucken.'

'I mean: in what country?' She put her question more precisely.

'In Germany, of course, still in Germany,' he said in amazement.

'That's fine. I was afraid we might have crossed a frontier and I'd missed it. How far is it from here to Italy?'

'You've got the map in front of you. See for yourself.'

'I don't like maps. They're always full of symbols and meridians and all kinds of numbers, I don't understand maps.'

'Between us and Italy there's Switzerland.'

'Do you think we might drive across Switzerland?'

'We haven't got the visas.'

'Perhaps they wouldn't notice. Last time I was in Italy Mario drove me right up to the frontier and then we passed through some other frontier. It was at night. The customs officials just saluted and didn't even stop us.'

'You probably were in an Italian car.'

'I don't know. It was a pretty little yellow sports car with a folding roof.'

'Well, then it was an Italian car.'

'Okay, I just wanted to show you Italy. I'd love to show you the most beautiful country in the world. One day I'll take you there. We'll drive down to Venice and Florence, and I'll show you the Raphael frescoes.'

She was sitting next to him, talking. Outside it had

started to rain. He perceived her conversation much as he perceived the rain – as a thick grey curtain which he had to break through in order to see daylight.

'Oh darling,' she noticed it. 'Look, it's raining again for us, it's raining beautifully, the cars look like a herd of wet hippopotamuses. They look just like you.'

He took her hand and she pressed even closer up against him. 'They're turning on their lights and if I close my eyes I see them like a rainbow.'

She was now totally with him in the enclosed moving space amidst the rain, in the middle of a strange country, she was inescapably linked with him at least for this moment.

'Drive on,' she put her arm round his shoulders. 'Drive fast, darling, I feel like I'm on a boat, on a gondola.'

He accelerated. Geysers of water splashed up from the wheels of the cars; in the grey mist of the rain he overtook a string of slowly advancing vehicles, he hurtled ahead like a crazy ship down the wet carriageway of an unfamiliar road.

'Can I open the window a little?' He felt the impact of the damp wind and a spray of droplets splashed across his face. For an instant she put her head out and opened her mouth. Then she turned her wet face to him. 'I love you for driving like a lunatic. Because you are not afraid like those people creeping along in front of us.' Then she said, 'Are we still in Germany?'

'We are.'

'And how much longer will we be in Germany?'

'An hour. Or perhaps just forty minutes.'

'Then stop somewhere and look out for somewhere to sleep.'

'You feeling like sleeping already?'

'No. But I've never made love in Germany before.'

2

The little hotel stood on a steep slope, entirely covered with vines – a little hotel in a quiet little town not far from the Rhine, there were no cars moving down the street and in the square there were only three neon lights, one of which belonged to the place where they had put up.

He carried his bag and her little case up to their room: a perfect aseptic refuge smelling of disinfectant and detergents. He looked at the wide double bed with its white linen – this room was a continuation of their car: a strictly circumscribed space, a reserved cell for the two of them, for two living creatures who had severed themselves from the rest of the world.

I'll be here with her until morning, and in the morning I'll wake up by her side and then we'll get into the car again and race on, even though we have no destination beyond reaching a similar cell, and thus it will continue for ten whole days. And at that moment he felt neither longing nor passion but only fatigue or even unease, a horror of emptiness, and he wished he weren't here, he wished he could wake up at home in his own room and could wait for her to phone, so he could spend some time with her in that little room with the blue lamp in the window, a place from which he could depart at any time, from which he had to depart. Maybe I'm just tired, he thought dejectedly. When I'm tired everything seems hopeless to me.

She was waiting for him in the little dining room full of antlers, aquariums, plates and little jugs and Tyrolean alpine scenes on ancient faded canvases.

'I'd have ordered some food for you but I haven't a clue what they've got on this menu.'

He ordered dinner and she ate with her inimitable off-hand lethargy, while inside him an unexpected and crushing malaise was growing, about that evening, about the matrimonial night and about the next day.

'What shall we do now?' she asked when she had finally finished her coffee. 'Do you think they've got some kind of club in this place, or at least a cinema?'

'It's nearly ten o'clock, it's too late for a cinema.'

'But surely we aren't going to bed just yet, not when we've been sitting all day long. How about having something to drink somewhere?'

He wanted to object that he was too tired, but suddenly there emerged before his eyes the pale vision of that room upstairs, of that meticulously clean matrimonial bed, and so he nodded assent.

They walked over the still damp paving stones across the deserted square; from the only tavern came the noise of drunken voices – and that wasn't the kind of place they were looking for. They climbed up a narrow medieval street; behind the windows in the thick walls glowed the coloured light of television sets. At the end of the street, against the sky, stood the silhouette of a massive church. He noticed that the door was half open and that the light was on inside.

'Shall we look inside?' He caught the muted sounds of an organ.

They sat in the back pew. The church was completely empty, except for some invisible person playing a modern fugue. He leaned his head on the ledge. Over the side altar hung a carved Gothic Christ, above him smiled a chubby angel's face. An ancient memory came back to him and for an instant he floated away to those days: huge waves of sound were enveloping him and he was waiting to hear his mother's voice.

She had frozen into immobility. She was so unbelievably quiet and motionless that she must have fallen asleep; so he sat there motionless, not to disturb her. Then he felt something wet on the bare skin of his neck.

'What's the matter? You're crying?' But he said it so softly, if indeed he uttered the words at all, that she couldn't hear him.

Later, when eventually they were lying side by side and he touched her with his hand she drew away. 'Not yet. We've got heaps of time. Tell me something instead.'

'My dear girl, we've driven nearly eight hundred kilometres. Whenever I shut my eyes I can see red rings flickering before me.'

'Why do people build churches?' she asked.

He tried to kiss her.

'Why do they build churches?' she repeated.

He turned away, he was now lying on his back, his left hand touching her belly. 'Are you asking seriously?'

'What does seriously mean?'

'So they should have a place where they can come together.' His mother was standing by his side, making sure he was praying. He was praying but he felt a strange emptiness in the words he was uttering. 'And turn their minds to God.'

'What does turning to God mean? Do you ever turn to him?'

'People have always yearned for something higher. They've wanted to escape from a world of cruelty, lies, hatred and death. When they stepped into such a place they felt that they were getting closer to a realm where truth, love and eternal life reign.'

'I don't understand,' she said. 'What is eternal life? Why do they have to build churches for it? And why is there always a Christ on a Cross? Why do they need a Christ on the Cross for whatever you say they want?'

'You're asking seriously?'

'Yes. Why don't you want to answer me?'

'Because it is believed that Christ is God. It is an image of God crucified.'

194

'Christ is God? I didn't know Christ was God.'

'You didn't know?'

'How should I know? Nobody ever told me. Do you think anyone ever talked to me about God? When I was a little girl my granny wanted me to pray for my little brother who had polio, and for Mum and Dad to stay in good health. I thought then that God was something like a doctor, that he wore a white overall and spectacles, and could make people well. And Christ, the Christ child, came to us at Christmas so long as we were still all together. I thought Jesus Christ was some little child who was born in a stable.'

'You never read anything about it or were told anything at school?'

'I didn't take religious instruction. Mother wanted me to be an actress and she was afraid they wouldn't accept me for college if I'd done religion at school.'

'All right, it doesn't really matter.'

'So will you please tell me how God came to be born in a stable?'

'You want to know now?'

'No one's ever talked to me about such things.'

'What do people talk to you about then?'

'I don't know, I don't remember what they talk to me about. Tom only understands music, Bert goes to church because he's a Pole, but he doesn't want to talk about it to me. He thinks I wouldn't understand. He thinks I'm totally beyond salvation.'

'No one's totally beyond salvation,' he objected. 'That's the very core of Christian belief.'

'Well, are you going to tell me how it was with that Jesus?'

'Very well,' he said wearily. 'I probably don't know it all myself. Jesus Christ is thought to have come from Galilee.'

'From where?'

'From ancient Palestine,' he said quickly, 'on the same sea on which Italy also lies. That was at the time when the Jews had lost their freedom and their country was occupied by the Romans. And the Jews were waiting for a saviour.'

'Where do the Jews come in?'

'For heaven's sake,' he sighed, 'he was a Jew, wasn't he? Jesus was a Jew.'

'I thought he was God. You said he was God.'

'It is believed that in him God took on human shape. In quite a lot of religions God takes on human shape. And if someone becomes a human he's got to do it totally, complete with skin colour and with being born a Greek or a Jew.'

'So why did they crucify him in the end?'

'He took the human destiny upon himself. In this regard Christianity differs from other religions that its God took the human destiny upon himself to the bitter end. Until death. Until that frightful agony that he was dying and everything would be over for him.'

'And he didn't die? Surely a person dies when he's crucified.'

'Yes, as a human being. But not as God. God cannot die. At least that's what the faith maintains.'

'So if he didn't die what's he doing all the time? Maybe he's lying somewhere in the Gulf of Venice, rocking himself on the waves all day long. And I'd also like to know if he loved anyone while he was like a human being, that Jesus.'

'How do you mean?' he asked in amazement.

'I don't mean anything in particular,' she said. 'It just occurred to me to ask if he loved anybody, that God-Jesus.'

'He loved humanity. And his mother.'

'So he loved his mother. I didn't know he had a mother.'

'Everybody's got a mother.' And he realized that this

196

logic had a flaw where God was concerned. There was no point in explaining or arguing that everything was different anyway from what people believe and from what they are taught, if only because everything is different from what people believe and what they are taught. 'It's only a legend,' he said. 'Quite possibly Jesus didn't live at all. Or, more likely, he did live and was a teacher, an interpreter of the Scriptures, who dreamed of the kingdom of love, and for that he was crucified.'

'I don't think you can have someone living if he can't die.'

'But he did die. Once somebody finds himself in the human dimension he is bound to die.'

And suddenly he realized, clearly and inescapably, that there is no way out and that all the effort he and entire teams of scientists are investing must ultimately end up in the void. They had been carried away by breaking man down into millions of particles, by dissecting him cell by cell, by prolonging the life of those cells into infinity, and believing that thereby they could prolong human life as a whole. Except that human life unfolds in the dimension of human time. And time is immutable and uncapturable. What then is left to me, he asked himself half-asleep. What is the point of my work? What will remain of it beyond mountains of paper covered with writing and a few hundred mice killed? How am I going to fill the days that are still left to me? And he opened his eyes into the dimensionless void that was awaiting him. But there, in front of him, already on the bank of the river of the underworld, he caught sight of her.

'My love,' he whispered, 'tell me, do you still love me?'

'Yes, I love you for telling me so prettily about Jesus.'

He woke up in the middle of the night – in the silence of the locked room he was becoming aware of some disturbing noises.

'What's the matter?' he whispered. 'What's wrong? You're crying.'

The sobs were now acquiring a clear character, filling the entire invisible space of the room.

'What's wrong?' he asked. 'What is it?'

She sobbed as if she hadn't heard him.

He touched her face but she pushed his hand away.

So he waited, feeling uneasy at those inexplicable and unending tears. As if quite suddenly and inadvertently he'd touched upon some hidden and malignant disease in her body.

Eventually her crying abated a little.

'What's the trouble,' he asked. 'Did you have a bad dream?'

'I'm feeling sad,' she said in a voice transformed by her crying. 'I'm feeling terribly sad. I'm so lonely!'

'But I am here with you.'

'You're lonely too and you don't love me. You'll never stay with me. No one will stay with me. And I don't want,' she whispered, 'I don't want to be always so alone.'

3

'Look,' she cried, 'here's a little Italian restaurant!'

'Would you like to have dinner here?' She was festooned with small packages. For the past two days she'd been dragging him around through the little streets between Regent Street, Piccadilly and Carnaby Street. She'd bought, or rather allowed him to give her, a pair of high boots covered from top to bottom with golden studs (Oh, my Walrus, these are exactly the kind of boots I've always dreamed about), a belt similarly studded, a handbag and a multitude of little make-up bottles over each of which she'd uttered shrieks of delight.

They stepped inside. It was a cheap place, a few red-covered tables and rush-bottomed chairs, on the walls photographs of Mount Vesuvius and the Forum, and posters inviting tourists to Rome, Venice and Milan.

A short swarthy man with a thin moustache, in a shiny suit (probably the proprietor) chose a table for them (they were all empty).

'At last something human in this dreadful city,' she sighed. It annoyed him.

He was tired and bored with the hundreds of pairs of boots she had examined, handled and turned over, deafened by the unceasing din of hidden loudspeakers and blinded by the fireworks of colours, by all those dazzling rags, scarves, squares and souvenirs.

She probably had no idea of how he was suffering, of the sacrifices he was making for her; most of the time she was unaware of his company.

She ordered *minestra di cappelletti alla romagnola, ostriche alla veneziana a cinghiale* in *agro dolce alla romana*, and a bottle of Cabernet di Treviso, and for him, because he declined to choose for himself, calves' liver *alla veneziana* (so you should have at least something in the style of Venice in this dreadful city) and fried mushrooms.

From the ever-present loudspeaker, evidently in her honour, came the sickly-sweet music of mandolins.

'It's just like there,' she said, 'see how marvellous it is? In a moment I'll feel that when I step outside there'll be the Grand Canal flowing past the door, and I'll begin to feel happy.'

He knew what was coming next. She'd be talking about Italy, all those meaningless little stories, those eternal effusions which not so long ago he'd found touching, but now he had a horror of them because they were only the continuation of the vacuous day that had just ended.

But there was no escape, he was trapped, he was tied to her, he was hopelessly linked to her emptiness.

She reached out for the parcels which he'd put on an empty chair. 'You think I could have a peep at them before they bring our dinner?' she asked. She undid the string, carefully unwrapped the paper and lifted the lid of a box. The stench of leather was wafted over to him, he felt almost sick.

'They're beautiful. Do you like them too? Shouldn't I put them on?'

'I'd have thought it was a little too warm for high boots.'

'Yes,' she admitted. She replaced them in the box. There was a rustle of paper. She was undoing another package.

'For heaven's sake,' he couldn't control himself, 'do you live only for those shops?'

She glanced up at him in surprise. 'You don't like me looking at the presents you gave me? I thought you'd be pleased to see how happy they make me. But you think this isn't refined enough.' She sat up in a well-mannered way. 'Has it occurred to you that I don't even know why I am alive? That's because nobody ever talked to me about it. So how should I know what I'm living for?'

'Surely everybody reflects on it some time,' he said, but immediately regretted not having kept quiet.

'Tom says I never think at all. Thinking exhausts me.'

The short swarthy man placed a tureen with soup in front of them. Slowly she stirred the yellowish liquid. 'You live for your work. To invent something so fantastic everyone will fall on their behinds and stupid ugly girls with glasses will wait for you outside your institute so you can sign their albums. But I can't invent anything, and besides it wouldn't amuse me. I'd much rather just drift.'

'And you enjoy that?'

'I probably do, if that's how I live,' she said. 'Or maybe I don't but I don't know anything else. But I expect I quite enjoy it so long as somebody loves me.'

'And when nobody loves you any more?'

'How can I tell what will be? Maybe I'll be dead by the time no one loves me any more. Tom once had another girl, or perhaps he didn't even have her, she only pursued him and he was quite bowled over by her. I told him I'd do something to myself if he didn't leave her alone, and just then I was due to go to Italy for the first time, Paula had been there before, and she said to me: Don't be a fool, you'll be so happy there you won't even think of him. And so I went off with her, I wanted to see Venice and everything before I killed myself, and as a matter of fact I was happy there and I realized that there were heaps of fellows who wanted to love me, and that did me good.'

She fell silent and turned her attention to the soup.

I wonder, does she feel anything when she tells these stories? She speaks of death and love as casually as about a wine label. Does she experience genuine feelings and real sorrow or despair when she talks about them, or are these just words to her, words she inserts between herself and me to drive the silence away?

She was still eating and he was unable himself to start a conversation about anything, so he kept silent and felt a rising distaste, a depressing emptiness oozing from those garish posters on the walls and from the music he was listening to, from her eyes, from the life he was leading at that moment.

Maybe she was quite happy, maybe a lot of people would be happy in his place, but he felt unable to be so himself. 'When I was a boy,' he said, to drive away the silence and also because he'd never really told her anything about himself, 'my mother used to sing Italian songs, or perhaps they were arias from operas. And she sang them in Italian. But then she stopped during the war because the Italians were our enemies.'

'The Italians were our enemies?'

'Yes,' he said, 'in fact I can remember the Italian soldiers and especially their officers. They had comical uniforms, at least they seemed comical to me then. Golden cords all over the place.' And as always when his memories touched on the war, long-past images came before his eyes, tanks with the grey-green uniforms of German troops, and aircraft in close formation in the sky like flocks of monstrously overgrown birds. 'Immediately before the end of the war they brought my father a whole transport of their wounded.'

'Why are you telling me this?' she interrupted him. 'I don't want to hear about the war now.'

So he fell silent and she attempted a smile, her practised smile which communicated nothing and signified nothing but further reinforced his sense of depressing emptiness.

4

They were staying on the first floor of a small hotel in Camden Town. Their room with its sulphur-coloured and torn wallpaper and its threadbare and revoltingly spotted runner in the same colour was long and narrow, so incredibly long that, if fog entered it, the two beds at opposite ends of the room would be out of sight of each other. Under their only window, a simple, unwashed window, six streams of noisy vehicles moved almost continuously.

He hated the down-at-heel room which was unsuitable for sleeping and even more unsuitable for love-making, and which aroused in him a sense of emptiness and shipwreck. But this was perhaps only his own feeling and she felt quite happy there and therefore was not looking for anywhere else.

She was a little drunk when they got back (they had sat in that Italian restaurant till nearly midnight – a number of young Italians had come in and one of them had talked to her for a while from the next table while he, full of bitter jealousy, had been waiting for the moment when they'd both get up and make a date). The moment she stepped through the door she flung off her clothes and ran some water into the hand-basin. 'I think I'm going to put those high boots on after all,' she said. 'I don't suppose they'll mind if I wear them to climb into their frightful sheets.'

He was now also lying on the bed, the one by the door, without looking at her. He'd never thought that doing nothing could be so exhausting. Perhaps it was his own fault – he could never let up. He was unable to move through life at an easy pace and without a precise purpose. He would take a holiday so he could work his way through books he hadn't found time for during the year. He would take a swim in order to refresh himself for more efficient work during the rest of the day. He'd take a walk in the woods in order to sort out his ideas undisturbed. Camilla realized this and showed understanding for his needs. She could walk by his side silently, not disturbing him when he was thinking, she was even ready to listen to him, to listen to his complicated theories, his boring papers about always the same experiments and register that male mouse number so and so much lived a whole three months longer than its blood brother, she was able to put questions to him which convinced him that she was sharing his world. Camilla belonged to him, whereas this woman belonged to another, barely comprehensible, world, one which had for a while fascinated him but which now terrified him by its terrible and absolutely non-participating and indolent emptiness. I wish I were back home, not having to listen to her, at least for a single day not having to see her or listen to her, being on my own and getting back to my work.

'Look,' she exclaimed, 'aren't they beautiful?' She stood before him naked, drops of water glistening on her shoulders and breasts. She was holding her boots on her two palms, in such a way that they supported her breasts.

203

He glanced up at her and turned away again.

'You don't like them?' she asked.

'I don't know. I'm just not in the mood for your boots now.'

'So you're not in the mood?' She sat down next to him on the edge of the bed. 'Why aren't you in the mood? Beginning to bore you, am I? Are you bored because I don't know what I'm living for?'

'Why don't you let me be? One doesn't always have to be in the mood.'

'I don't like it if someone who's with me isn't in the mood,' she declared. 'I don't find it amusing to watch you acting bored.'

'Don't watch me then.'

'You've been acting bored all day, do you suppose it amuses me to see you acting bored? Do you think I couldn't act bored too? You think you're a lot of fun?'

'For heaven's sake, go to bed and be quiet!'

'I'll be quiet when I feel like it! Do you think it's fun trudging around from dawn to dusk with a fat bored walrus when the world all round's full of handsome young men?'

'Why don't you let them pick you up then and go off with them?'

'I may do just that when I feel like it. Or did you think I wouldn't do just that when I felt like it? But first of all you're going to make love to me!' She got up and walked to the other end of the room.

Six more days. I can hold out for six days. We'll drive on somewhere, it's tolerable when we're driving. She loves riding in a car and I can see some new scenery. I enjoy new scenery. And when I get back it'll all be over. Maybe it's a good thing I came here with her, at least I know now what she's like. I'd never have come to know her if I hadn't taken her on such a long trip.

'I've put those boots on,' she spoke up. 'Don't you want to see what they look like on me?'

He didn't even move.

'Darling,' she said from the distance, 'I didn't mean it like that. You bought me these beautiful boots, I didn't mean it like that.'

He turned his head. She was lying naked on the white sheet and on her feet she wore her high boots. The golden studs gleamed dully in the poor light.

'They look good on you,' he said.

'Aren't you coming to me?'

He made no answer. He was lying down again, a long way from her, so far away that he could look about himself without seeing her.

'Come on, my Walrus, surely you won't keep me waiting. Surely you don't want me to go on my knees. Come here,' she said, 'come to me, darling. I want you. I love you. I want you now. Come!'

And he got up, he really got up, wriggled out of his clothes and walked barefoot down the sulphur-yellow runner, with the chilling humiliation in him that he was going to her in spite of what she'd said to him a little while ago. She was now lying before him, shamelessly, obscenely half-undressed, like an illustration in a men-only magazine.

'Come,' she whispered, 'come to me, darling.' And she reached out her arms for him.

5

It was a bright day, with a mild breeze. People were lying on the grass and by the Serpentine prettily dressed children were feeding the swans. The air smelled of moist earth, exotic flowers and exhaust fumes, and from the distance came the incessant rumble of cars.

'Shall we lie down here?' she asked.

'You want to lie down here?'

'Why not? You can tell me about Jesus or King David. Or we could just lie in the sun and sleep.'

At the appointed place, as for the past one or two hundred years, groups of people were crowding round the speakers. He admired the custom, he was enthusiastic over anything that lasted, virtually unchanged, over the centuries: *The Times*, parliament, the uniforms of the Yeomen of the Guard at the Tower, the street names, the bowler-hatted gentlemen in the City. ('The monarchy is the most ancient secular institution in the United Kingdom. Its continuity has been broken only once in over a thousand years; and in spite of interruptions in the direct line of succession the heredity principle upon which it was founded has never been abandoned.')

She watched the various speakers without interest – she doesn't understand what they're saying, he realized, so he tried to translate for her the speech of a huge half-naked and incredibly tattooed muscular type, and he only stopped when he realized that the speech was without beginning or end, and without head or foot: after all, who'd make a sensible or intelligent speech in this place, who'd waste his time lecturing a pack of curious tourists at Speakers' Corner?

He felt a sudden sense of disappointment, as though some promised famous star had failed to turn up or had lost her voice. He pushed into the biggest group, where a handsome young Indian was delivering a fiery speech to an audience that listened to him in silence.

She was standing by his side, any kind of interest had drained from her features, she was asleep on her feet. Then she noticed that he was observing her, attempted a smile and asked him like an obedient child: 'What's he talking about?'

206

'Nothing,' he said quickly, 'come along, you wouldn't be interested.'

'Where are we going now?' she asked.

'Would you like to look at a gallery?'

'All right, let's look at some pictures.'

On a patch of grass in front of the gallery half-sat and half-lay a group of barefooted long-haired young men and women in jeans and tattered shirts, their food laid out on a large spread-out Union Jack: sandwiches and yoghurts in colourful containers. She stopped and looked at them longingly.

She belongs to them, no matter what I do, she belongs to them and not to me, she wants to sit barefoot on the grass and prattle about Venice, about lovers, about Ringo Starr, she wants to lie on the sand on the beach and sleep, so she can go dancing in the evening and prattle about Venice, about lovers, and about Ringo Starr, and about how she lay in the sand on the beach, and look for a new lover. He felt bitter resignation at the fact that he was no longer at an age when he could sit down barefoot and in ragged clothes on a patch of grass. 'Do you want to sit down too?' he asked.

'No, I'm going to look at pictures.' They walked inside.

He didn't really know why he was taking her there, he wasn't particularly fond of galleries himself. It was hot inside, a multitude of canvases, a lot of incessantly recurring subjects, unfamiliar names, too many people and an almost unbreathable humid air. There was no point in drifting past those coloured canvases, she was right, it would have been more sensible to lie on some lawn and stare into the void, drink wine or eat a melon. There was no difference between eating a melon and looking at a sunset by Turner or some monstrosity by Francis Bacon – in certain circumstances both activities were merely a killing of time and of boredom.

Nevertheless he didn't give up his intention of filling her time more usefully and so led her in the direction of Piccadilly Circus – it was getting dark by the time they got there (on the way she'd stopped at an amusement arcade, coming to life in front of various machines and with the fixed, excited gaze of an addicted gambler had lost something under a pound). Large hand-painted posters announced the latest theatrical hits and between the posters glowed coloured neon lights.

'Would you like to go to the theatre?' he suggested. 'To some musical?'

'Do you think we'd get tickets?'

He tried in vain to obtain tickets. Besides he didn't really want to sit in a theatre, he didn't want anything except to be back home with his work.

As they were walking along he suddenly noticed a small illuminated sign over an entrance. The name of the street was right. The lamps were on by the entrance, a group of men in dark suits were standing in the foyer inside and a liveried doorman was opening the doors of cars drawing up. So this is the place: he felt excited and unexpectedly moved.

'What's the matter?' she asked. 'What is this place?'

'It's a concert hall. A very ancient and famous one.'

'But I don't want to go to a concert!'

He didn't hear her. 'My mother was to have sung here. But she had to cancel her recital because I was about to be born. When I was a little boy I made up my mind that I'd bring her here some day but she died before I ever got here myself.'

'Why are you telling me all this?' she asked. 'What do I care that you promised your mother to bring her here?' As if she'd been waiting all day for just this moment. For the moment when he'd reveal to her the spot where he was vulnerable. 'That's why you've dragged me through the streets all evening so you could show me this building? I can't bear concerts,' she declared, 'I can't bear the people who perform in them. Tom used to drag me to concerts but then he gave it up. He knows I can't bear them – those fuddy-duddies in tail-coats and white dickies and those ageing ladies squeezed into corsets and long golden robes, who open their mouths like at the dentist, so that everybody can see they've had singing lessons from Signora Puccini.'

'What are you getting so excited about? No one's forcing you to go to a concert.'

'So what? What will we be doing all evening?'

'What do you expect? We'll have something to eat and then we go back home.'

'So what you're planning is that we'll have something to eat and then you'll drag me back to that revolting dirty brothel?'

'What would you like to do then?'

'I'd like to go somewhere amusing. I'm sick and tired of acting like your stupid wife whom no doubt you drag through stinking galleries from morning till night.'

'Stop it. Don't shout like that in the street.'

'You're an intolerable bore. Why don't you at least take your tie off? Why do you keep acting as if you were eighty?' With unfailing instinct (maybe she was just following people of her own age) she found a disco round a few corners.

In a passageway with black wallpaper, under red and green light bulbs, stood some young people in jeans and girls in short skirts. They climbed a few stairs, he opened a door into a vestibule and instantly found himself in the middle of a furious electronic din. Through a wide archway he could see into the hall, where dozens of dancers were jerkily appearing and disappearing under the continuous flicker of magnesium flashes. Garish and monstrous psychedelic patterns were projected on the walls. He stopped short in the doorway, deafened and blinded, then he rebelled: 'I'm not going in here.'

'But I am!'

'No,' he caught her wrist. 'We are not going in here. I don't like this place.'

'Do you think I don't know why you don't want to come in here?' She tore herself free. 'You want to save a few lousy shillings. You've been dragging me to the park and to the gallery because entrance is free there.'

'That's a vile thing to say.'

'You think you're holding me in your hand, that without you I can't move a step because you've got all the money. Except that I could find a thousand men here to take me to a cheap dump like yours. You're disgusting,' she hissed. 'Revolting. You've stuck yourself to me. I can't stand you. I hate you for tagging along with me like a shadow. I can't bear to look at you even.'

'Don't be a fool. Stop being silly and come along!' He tried to drag her away.

'Don't you touch me. Don't touch me again. I can't bear you touching me. You're like a hippopotamus. A hippopotamus in a tailored jacket and a tie. A tie all dribbled over! Go away! Piss off! I don't want to see you again!'

'All right, you stay here. How much shall I leave you? How much will you need?'

'I don't need anything,' she screamed. 'Any boy, if I as much as wink at him, will pay for whatever I need and will take me wherever I want!'

He thrust a five-pound note into her handbag and she disappeared through the door of the disco.

For a moment he stopped in the black passageway. All around him drifted colourful shirts and skirts and blouses, long-haired girls who resembled her, even if they spoke English. Now and again the din oozed out through the opened door. He'd have to wait there until midnight, maybe even longer, but there would be no point in that either. She'd leave with somebody else and most probably would pass him by without noticing him.

This was the end, he realized. And he felt self-pity, an almost childish self-pity, that she had wronged him.

6

He returned to the hotel. The shelves and the table were piled high with her belongings: brushes, little bottles, tiny make-up brushes, powder and cosmetics, and on the bed, carefully folded, lay her nightdress.

He sat on his bed. As he shut his eyes he saw her slight figure in that dark passageway. Magnesium flashes were going on and off. He saw two stone heads in the middle of a forest and her head on an old worn blanket. She was standing before him in a white slip in the fitting room with the floral curtain and kissing him, kissing him while the music was playing, the music was playing incessantly: in the wine cellar and in the disco and in her theatre and in the room with the drums and in the church and in the shops, it was on everywhere till his head felt like bursting. She was leaning over him, whispering: I love you, you're so good to me, no one's ever been so good to me. He didn't understand her: why had she left him when he'd always been so good to her, when he'd sacrificed everything for her, when he'd given up his time, his work, everything he had lived for in the past, when he'd surrendered himself solely in order to win her, to fill her time for her, to fill her total all-devouring emptiness?

It was his own fault. He'd been too afraid of losing her. But he'd lose her precisely because he'd lost himself. He wasn't anybody any more. Only a supplicant for her favour. Like so many others. He couldn't really interest her.

But perhaps he was seeing it all too much from his own point of view. From her point of view he probably seemed different. Except: what point of view? Her point of view didn't know any meaning to life nor obsession with a goal, her point of view didn't know any future, and hence no ambition, it didn't know any past, and hence no obligations that might stem from it, it didn't know loyalty, and hence also no disloyalty, from her point of view he shouldn't have given up anything. From her point of view he was merely a dry old stick, a boring elderly (though possibly kind) sugar-daddy who was trying in vain to hide his boredom, to hide his unhappiness at not being able to do what he was used to doing.

To her it was a matter of indifference that he was giving anything up, there was no need for him to do that, all she wanted was that, while he was with her, he shouldn't long for anything else, that he should be able to lie in the grass in Hyde Park and be happy simply lying there; that he should be able to bury himself in the sand on some beach and not think of anything other than that there was a blue layer of air above him; that he should be able to drink, to get drunk to the point of carefree oblivion and enjoy losing his sense of duty, of the world and of time. That he should enter a disco and forget that it is possible also to move outside this deafening space. So that, at the moment he caught sight of her, the rest of the world and the people in it should change into shadow-play figures which he could let flash past in his conversation but not in his mind. That he shouldn't think of having to leave for anywhere. That he shouldn't think of the next day. That he shouldn't even think of the next day coming, let alone that he would have to live through it or act during it. None of these things was he able to do. Even when he'd decided to come here with her he'd never for an instant freed himself from pangs of conscience and a sense of wrong.

He had left his world but he hadn't managed to enter hers. He found himself in the void.

He turned back his sheets and undressed. He no longer belonged to her life, he should get used to the thought that she didn't belong to his.

He washed. Her toothbrush stood next to his in their single glass. He took hers out and laid it on the shelf.

He went to bed. Outside, in a continuous, only rarely broken stream (interrupted by the traffic lights at a crossroads), the herds of cars were still noisily rushing past.

There was nothing for him to think about if he didn't want to think of her. He was utterly alone in his little hotel in Camden Town (in the next room a bed was creaking under a strange body), he had been abandoned by everything he ever had, by all his relationships, all his goals, all his ideas; he was just lying there with the sensation that it was only his body that was lying there, a body from which the spirit had departed. Maybe they would find him tomorrow: his body, or if she came back after all she'd find it here and call the manager who'd then have it removed somewhere where they could perform an autopsy.

He was lying there, time was obviously passing even if he was unaware of its passage in its usual dimension, it was probably midnight or even later, he was no longer thinking of her, he was thinking of nothing, but somewhere in his subconscious mind he was waiting, his whole being was focused on the moment when, after all, the door would open and she'd come in, when she'd come in after all, at least to collect her things, when she'd appear and thus, if only for a brief instant, lend meaning to his existence, to his endurance here in this little hotel in Camden Town with its sulphur-yellow wallpaper.

But the emptiness which lay spread out in him and before him was gradually changing its shape, turning into a watery surface over which a mist was rising in swathes.

He stared into that mist, fixedly and persistently, until he could make out a shore beyond the water. In the early morning mist he made out a sleeping island with two army-type tents. He saw the fine glittering droplets on the taut canvas. At last his mind had found something to catch hold of, a vision of home, of a long-past home from which he had so needlessly gone away. And just then his two daughters came rushing up to him joyously and flung themselves on his bed, the older one climbing astride his chest while Margit clambered up on his knee. And they were both so light that he didn't feel their weight at all. Then Camilla appeared in the doorway (That's nice of you to have made a little time for them) in some very old clothes.

What on earth are those things you're wearing?

Have you forgotten them? These are what I was wearing in Romania that time. I put them on in your honour.

In my honour?

In your honour, in honour of your homecoming.

Yes, I've come back home. Where have I come back from? I can't remember where I've been. Do please tell me where I've come back from.

Camilla is smiling and the children are smiling, the way people smile when they are talking to a gravely sick person, lying to him about his prospects.

And suddenly he realized the truth. He had died. He was dead and they knew he was dead but they wouldn't tell him, that was why they were smiling, why Anna was so light that he didn't feel her, why Margit was rocking on his knee without his being aware of her, that was why Camilla was beginning to dissolve, to fade away, oh please stay, don't leave me, I want to touch you, I can't make it, I can't even move, there's nothing left of her now, not a shadow, not even those clothes, I killed myself, I remember now, I put an end to my life, but I don't know where – it wasn't at home, it was somewhere far away.

It is almost one o'clock, the room is still stuffy (she hasn't come back yet, but I'm really not thinking about her now, I'm thinking about my wife, I'm thinking of home), and he felt a need to do something to dispel his depression.

He pulled a sheet of notepaper from his briefcase (during his whole time abroad he'd sent his wife only one single postcard) and began to write.

He found the activity calmed him. He still had a wife, he had children. One day he'd forget, he'd have to forget, the other woman, this crazy, impossible love affair, but they would endure, they would remain with him and he with them, after all they belonged together – that's what he'd always believed: that people who once opted for a common destiny belonged together for the rest of their lives; and I did what I did from a confusion of my senses, from some sudden sickness. And he wrote as if nothing of all this had happened (he always, provided he wrote a letter at all, only gave a brief account of his health, accommodation and the most important aspects of his surroundings), he wrote about the paintings at the gallery, the speakers in Hyde Park, the fact that he'd suddenly found himself in front of the place where his mother was to have sung. Then he remembered that he hadn't come here for a holiday but on official business and also in order to find a place for them to live in Epping or even in Hampstead, but that it would be best for her to choose the place for herself. And he pictured her reading his letter (send it express the next morning, otherwise I'll be home before the letter) with Anna looking over her shoulder, and he experienced a sudden sense of relief and the need to write her something tender, and so he wrote: 'I'm constantly thinking of you, you are the only person in the world with whom I am at ease, the only person I love, and will continue to love, and only when I'm away do I realize how much I miss you. I'd like to be with you now and hold you in my arms and tell you that you're the only woman for me.'

He signed it and hid the letter in his briefcase. He was almost calm. He'd returned to his wife, he'd returned to his own world. Tomorrow he'd arrange whatever he could, seeing that he was over here, and the following day he'd return home (assuming she turned up before then he'd take her back with him – but that was all).

He lay down again and picked up a magazine he'd bought at a news stand in Piccadilly Circus the day before. IF WE EXTERMINATE OUR INSECTS WE SHALL ALSO EXTERMINATE OUR BIRDS, and fell instantly asleep.

He didn't know what the time was but it could have been two o'clock or even later when out of his sleep he heard her voice. She was talking to someone outside the door. More accurately, with her perfect pronunciation (she was, after all, an actress) she spoke just five of the fifteen words she knew: I thank you very, very much. And a male voice with a foreign and ridiculously sibilant pronunciation burbled something in reply.

He sat up quickly and smoothed his hair – then he reached for his magazine again.

She came in. 'Oh darling,' she said, 'you've been waiting up. I knew you'd be waiting up for me.' She was drunk.

'I was afraid you wouldn't find your way,' he said, stunned by the manner in which she'd addressed him.

'And I found it all right, see?' she said quickly. 'These English are so obliging, although actually he wasn't English, being nearly black. He danced with me quite terribly and then he took me to supper to a fantastic club, where the waiters wore green tailcoats like the water-sprites at the Lantern. The place was full of rich people and across one whole wall they had a picture of some queen, and we had oysters and then an enormous steak and with it some strange vegetables and then doughnuts covered in chocolate, and we downed a lot of Scotch, he had a red silk shirt with gold buttons and check trousers and beautiful teeth and he kept telling me: You are so nice (again perfect pronunciation) and I love you, and he wanted me to come with him to his hotel but I didn't go with him because I thought you'd be waiting for me and I was anxious to tell you everything and I've brought you this, they were selling it at the place where we danced.' And she handed him a record with an enormous number of coloured figures and bizarre heads on its sleeve. 'It cost two pounds, it's the latest Beatles, I wanted to buy it for myself too but I thought you'd be angry if I spent so much, I suppose I can always come and listen to it at your place.'

'You know I haven't got a record player.'

'Never mind,' she was talking rapidly, 'so we'll play it somewhere else, like at our theatre, tell me, are you pleased with the record I bought you?'

She was standing by the hand-basin, closely inspecting her face in the grimy mirror. 'I'm glad I'm back with you, my Walrus. I could have gone off with that darkie in the red shirt but I didn't because I wanted to be back with you.'

He closed his eyes. Her words were caressing him as if her fingers were already on him, as if she were already touching him with her whole body. Maybe she loves me after all, but do I love her? Do I still love her or do I hate her? How long can I keep up this game?

He heard the material of her dress rustling on the chair. He was still not looking at her.

'Why don't you say anything?' she asked. 'Aren't you pleased I'm here again? I thought you'd be pleased to see me back, that I didn't go with that darkie!' She sat down on his bed.

'Why did you do it?'

'Why did I do what?' she asked with astonishment. 'Did I do anything?'

'The scene you made there.'

'I just wanted to go dancing,' she explained, 'and so I went. There's nothing wrong in wanting to go dancing, is there?'

He didn't reply. He only answered her in his mind. You hurt me. You spoke to me like you would to a lout. You shook me off like someone who was molesting you. For an instant you revealed your real feelings towards me. Now I don't want you. Leave me alone. Go and find someone else for this kind of game.

'Come now, my little Walrus, come now,' she was talking to him as if to a child, 'don't glower like this or I'll begin to be afraid. Tell me you're not angry and that you're pleased I've come back.' He felt her fingers touching his skin, enveloping his body in widening circles, he felt her arms pulling him to her, pulling him into the world from which he had just been trying to escape, a world in which nothing exists except what exists at this particular moment, where everything is forgotten that happened a mere hour ago, and where what is happening now will be forgotten an hour hence.

'Come on now,' she was whispering, 'bet you're glad I'm with you again.'

And she re-emerged from the darkness into which she had, for him, submerged, she came back to him for this one more night, maybe the final night. She was here with him, totally with him, she was totally his for this one night, for this moment, and he felt an ecstasy rising in him as his hope returned: she has come back, she is with me, perhaps she loves me.

'I'm glad you're with me,' and he embraced her.

'Darling,' she said, 'don't think about it any more. I belong to you, now I belong to you. Don't you want me to belong to you?'

'Yes, I want you to belong to me. To be with me.'

218

'And I am with you, close to you, my little Walrus,' she whispered, 'and I love you. I love you for bringing me here, where everything's so nice, that you're so good to me and that you've waited up for me. Tell me, do you love me too?'

He was holding her in his arms. She was with him, he hadn't been left on his own although he had already assigned this night to loneliness. Nothing mattered except that he was holding her in his arms, that he could love her.

'I love you too.'

'Tell me, do you love me a lot?'

'Yes, I love you a lot. I love you more and more. More than a week ago. More than yesterday. I love you as much as it's possible to love anyone.'

He could hear her breathing getting faster. 'It's marvellous being with you,' she whispered. 'It's marvellous that you love me so much. Nobody's ever loved me so much. I've a terrible need for someone to love me so much. I couldn't live without somebody loving me as much as you love me.'

What she's telling me is: I couldn't live without you. Maybe she really will love me some day, that row last night was unimportant to her, maybe I even caused it by my intransigence, but she's come back, she wants to be with me. 'My dear, my love, I wouldn't want to be without you any more, I couldn't live without you. I love you more than I ever thought I could love anyone.'

'Oh, you love me so much you couldn't live without me, I know you love me a lot, my darling, I belong to you, it's so marvellous with you, it's more marvellous with you than anything in the world. Stay with me always. Stay inside me always. Let it never end. Stay mine forever. Stay! I can't bear it, I can't bear it today, it's so good. I'm dying. Today I'm dying. Ah, love me. Love me all the time. Don't stop loving me, ever. Now you belong to me.

Now I belong to you. I'm yours entirely. Oh, how I love you. I'll stay with you. I'm happy with you. Darling, my Walrus, I'm so happy now!'

She fell asleep locked in his embrace. He got up. It was three in the morning, he felt a dull pressure in his head and he was shivering in spite of the stuffiness.

And what happens now? I just can't go on with her kind of living and loving. It doesn't worry her but it's destroying me. I must tell her that we should break if off, that we must break it off now before we begin to hate each other.

Anyway, we'll be going back in four or five days, and then I'll only have two weeks left before I leave again, before I remove myself from her, and this will be the end of it, this could be the end of it. Over a year we'll forget each other, over a year she's sure to forget me.

But do I want her to forget me? Don't I want her, even after that year, to ring me at midnight and to wait for me in that crazy room with the drums?

He found a glass container with sleeping tablets in his case, he swallowed one and went back to her. She was sound asleep. He touched her arm with his palm.

I'm thinking again about what will be in a year, I'm thinking of meeting her again before we've even parted, she'd laugh at me.

Don't sleep, my dear, come to me, tell me you love me, that you'll ring me again, that you'll be waiting, repeat the words you said a little while ago, say: I'll stay with you, I want to hear it again, I want to hear your assurances even if I know they're worthless.

Suddenly there arose before him, unexpectedly but clearly, the image of the long-haired American woman with LOVE ME on her chest (he was thankful for the vision, at last a different image, at last one that did not fill him with longing or sorrow), it was that evening, he realized, that fateful evening, if only I'd stayed there, if only I'd talked a little longer about those hundred-year-old Beatles and about her horse, my life could have taken a different turn.

He felt nostalgic for the days when he had a family and children and peace of mind, when he could talk of immortality and dream of his discoveries.

A man can't have everything, he can't cope with two passions, one consumes the other and eventually destroys a person, I wish I could sit at my desk now and reflect on what I have in fact always reflected on. What actually was my field? IF WE EXTERMINATE OUR INSECTS WE ALSO EXTERMINATE OUR BIRDS, I used to love the quiet of the evening, the glow of the table lamp, the scrape of my pen, I'm wandering between cliffs of calculations, around me tower gigantic cauliflowers of papillomas and mountains of thymuses, I'm looking for the way ahead, I'm beginning to guess the direction, I'm trembling with anticipation, I'm wishing the nights would not end, I'm hoping I won't be overcome by fatigue, I'm hoping my brain will magnify, and just then the telephone rings. I run to the kitchen, I'm barefoot, I'm cold, the tiled floor is icy.

Is that you, my Walrus? So you're back? I've been waiting for you for a whole year. Do you still love me?

I love you, my dear. I'm coming over. Are you still in the same place? Wait, don't go. I'm driving over. If you didn't exist, if I hadn't met you, I'd have never known that unique, vertiginous, blissful, sweet . . .

It was quite late when he woke up, road noise outside was at its peak. He saw her sitting by the table, half-dressed, reading the letter he'd written to his wife the day before.

'That letter's not for you!' he said. 'Where did you find it?'

'So it wasn't for me? But you wrote it, didn't you?'

'I didn't write it to you,' he said. 'I don't understand how you could rummage in my briefcase.'

'I thought straight away that you must have written it,' she said. 'Only you can write such nonsense: Only now that I'm far away do I realize how much I'd like to be with you now and how much I love you. I simply couldn't live without you. Your wife must have a lot of fun with you!' She tore the letter up into small pieces and dropped them in the waste-paper basket. 'But sometimes it's bound to get boring,' she said, 'if someone loves you so he couldn't bear to live without you.'

He hated her: her hair in a mess, her face bloated with sleep, a stranger, and vicious, he hated her so that he felt like hitting her, knocking her off her chair and hitting her, kicking her, silencing her somehow so she couldn't mock him any more.

'Listen,' he said at breakfast (she was facing him across the table, perfect again: made-up, her hair done, in an orange dress with large purple patches and fiery sun-wheels from Carnaby Street, so that the two young Indians who were eating their breakfast at the next table couldn't take their eyes off her), 'that was rude of you to read that letter of mine. But it really doesn't matter now. At least I don't have to tell you now.' He hesitated for a moment. What would happen next? What would he do without her?

'What don't you have to tell me now?'

'When we get back,' he said, 'we'll put an end to it.'

'Put an end to what?'

'We won't go out together any more.'

'We've been going out together? You had the impression that I was going out with you? I'd say we did rather different things together than going out.'

'Let's not argue,' he said quickly. 'I hope you understand me. We have another five days here. Provided you want to stay. But let's not argue those last five days.'

'I'll argue whenever I feel like it,' she declared. 'For all I know I'll argue right through those five days if that's how I feel.'

'Just as you like.'

'And I'll go on arguing even afterwards, for all I know, I'll argue with you for a whole year if I feel like it.'

'Oh no,' he said triumphantly, 'you won't. Because I shall be leaving. In a few days I'll be leaving for England again!'

'So you think you'll be going back to England?'

'You know I will,' and he felt a sudden stab of fear. 'You know I'm going to England for a whole year.'

'Maybe you won't, maybe I won't let you!' She stopped abruptly as if considering an idea. 'Maybe I'll kill you if I feel like it!' And she smiled at the two young Indians at the next table.

# CHAPTER TEN

1

At last he was pulling up in the familiar place outside their house. He looked up at the windows (Camilla had said she'd stay as long as possible, he wished she would, at least he'd have a day to recover, a day on his own), but the window was open and he suddenly saw the movement of a fair head.

'Dad! Dad's home!'

He got out of the car. Children's footsteps racing down the stairs. (How many years since I last saw her?)

'Dad, what have you brought back for us?'

'Daddy, Anna gobbled up all the peaches and then drank some milk and then she had the shits!'

'Don't be rude, you!'

'Where's Mum?'

'Mum's in the garden. I'll get her. What have you brought back for us?'

'She's telling tales, I never drank any milk.'

And there's my wife now, my unattractive wife, she ought to eat less, groom herself a little, why does she wear such a crumpled dress, I must kiss her, I must embrace her – she is my wife.

'David, you aren't looking well at all. You've got terribly thin!'

'It was tiring.'

'Why did you go by car? What was the idea of taking the car?'

'It was much cheaper that way.'

'You always say it's only worth driving if there's more than one in the car.'

'Yes, but not when you go abroad. I took a spare can of petrol with me – saving hard currency.'

'But it must have been a terrible journey. The distance! You've got rings under your eyes.'

She is speaking with a stranger's voice. She speaks differently. No, she speaks the same as always, it's I who hear her differently. I must caress her. 'But you're looking well. You've got a good tan.'

'We only got back the day before yesterday. It was nice out there. Why didn't you write more?'

'I wrote a few times.'

'All we had was two postcards. Were you able to fix up everything?'

'Oh yes.' I had actually been to the department. I'd found hardly anybody there – as was to be expected at the beginning of August. One ugly bony secretary who'd never heard of me, it took me half an hour to persuade her to reveal to me where I might get hold of Ford, and one exceedingly boring but friendly assistant who insisted on showing me the laboratories and proving to me how everyone was looking forward to my coming, and so I spent two whole hours there while she was sitting in a bar opposite the museum, drinking gin which I'd ordered for her, and all I could think about was that she might get tired of waiting for me and that she'd be sure to be joined by some Italian or Brazilian or other young man who'd take her away somewhere. I was afraid of that although we had actually broken up, although I had informed her that this was the end and that these were our last days together, our final three days, but I was still afraid someone might take her away and deprive me even of those final three days with her.

'So you found somewhere for us to live?'

'No, you'll be able to choose for yourself. Things aren't as they are here. It's easy to find accommodation. Or a whole house. But I told you that in my letter.'

'No letter arrived. Probably still on the way.'

'Daddy, come upstairs. I'll help you with your case.'

'No, little one.'

'I'm not little any more.'

'All right then. You take these two packages. You can unwrap them upstairs.' And I'm standing in our only room, pulling the presents from my case: a book about dogs for Anna and a little pig that dances (Oh, Daddy, isn't that great, it dances on its own!) and a sweater for Camilla. (Aren't you buying anything for your wife? I'll get her something but I don't know what. A sweater perhaps. Hold on, I'll help you choose one, I love choosing sweaters. I'll choose a sweater for your wife. Look, how about this one, it's very striking.

Too much so.

You think it's too striking for your wife?

I'd say so, and not only for my wife.

That's what's worn nowadays, you dummy. You'd buy her something for a funeral. She's a girl too, after all. Or isn't your wife a girl too?)

'You must be out of your mind, David, how on earth can I wear this thing?'

'That's what people are wearing these days. All the girls over there were wearing this kind of thing.'

'But I'm no girl, David. I've got two children.'

'What difference does it make, you having two children?'

'Nice of you to want to see me in something like this, just as if I were twenty, but people would laugh at me.'

'Dad, translate the name of this dog for me.'

'Daddy, are you going to tell us about guinea-pigs tonight?'

'Of course I will, little one.'

'I'm not little any more.'

'Why do you keep calling her little one?'

'Why shouldn't I?'

'You never used to call her that.'

'Daddy, the little pig won't dance any more!'

'Hang on, I'll have a look at it.'

'Are you hungry, David? What would you like to eat?'

'Dad, when are you going to tell us what it was like over there?'

'There's some chicken left over from lunch. Shall I heat it up for you? And where did you actually stay?'

'In a small hotel in Camden Town.'

'Where's that?'

'How can I describe it to you? When we're there I'll show it to you.' (I'll show you the room where we made love, where we hated each other and loved each other again, I'll show you that fat proprietress in her wig and frightful violet dress, she'll glare at you from her powdered face, at the way you've changed, at the way you've got fat and old in the few days since she saw us.)

'And you spent the whole ten days there?'

'Where else would I go?'

'I was just thinking: whatever took you so long there? You said you'd return sooner.'

'There was a lot of work to be done. In fact they would have liked me to stay. Just wait till I tell you. But I would have got back sooner if I hadn't waited for Ford to return from his holiday.'

'I thought he'd invited you and that's why you went there. Why wasn't he waiting for you?'

She's suspecting something again, but maybe this is the end now of this eternal quiet and desperate interrogation. I'm sorry to be deceiving you. And you're suspecting it and want to know the truth and at the same time you're afraid of it like a sick person. I am your cancer. 'We hadn't fixed up anything definite. Anyway, his assistant was there. He wanted me to . . .'

'Dad, come and tell us about it all, we've had our bath!'

He sat down in the middle of the room. From the wall Donald Duck and a host of dog photographs smiled down on him. They used not to be there. She probably brought them back from her grandmother.

'Listen then. There's a magnificent palace there. A royal palace, and in that palace live real kings and queens.' And I am waiting in the crowd in front of the palace and I see you, one step ahead of me, your dark hair blowing into my face. In that crowd you are the only familiar being and I am happy to have you.

'So what about that palace, Dad?'

I can't tell them about anything real. Everything is connected with her. I have to improvise. But I can't think of anything because I want to think of her. 'Every day at noon soldiers on horseback parade in front of the palace, in magnificent red uniforms and helmets which are at least 400 years old.'

'They haven't gone bad yet?'

'What hasn't gone bad yet?'

'Those helmets, if they're so old.'

'But helmets don't . . .'

'She's stupid, Dad, I'll explain it to her later. Helmets don't . . .'

She's lying by the sea, in a completely new swimsuit of picture-postcard blue, there on the greyish-yellow sand, it's a deserted stretch of coastline and tall grass is pushing through the sand and seagulls are flying overhead.

Do you think I could lie here in the nude?

'Come on, Dad, tell us more!'

'And other soldiers, on foot, they march around each other like on a music-box, about-turning and lifting their feet up ridiculously. In the end they change places.'

She's undressing and now she's almost blending into

228

the sand, only her dark hair looks like some seaweed washed up by the sea. Where are you going?

Just walking a little on the beach.

Stay with me. I want you to be with me. Can you hear the surf? I love the roar of the sea.

She's holding me, she's pressing me to herself. She's writhing in my embrace and although the waves are splashing behind me I hear her moaning.

Only two more days. From the moment I told her it was all over she'd suddenly seemed to begin to care for me. She keeps calling me and doesn't let me move away a single step. Just as if she were really beginning to love me.

'And what then?'

'You be quiet now. It's late. You'll see it all for yourselves.'

'But you haven't told us anything!'

'Let Dad be now, he's tired out!'

It seemed unaccustomed and almost strange to be lying next to his wife, but he tried not to think about it (rather like her when she'd lain next to so many different men), fortunately he was so overcome with fatigue that his awareness was blurred, or else he was overcome by a newly discovered and dulling indifference that he no longer felt anything, that nothing mattered to him, that he could even make love to his wife, though he was scarcely aware of what he was doing.

'David, what's the matter with you?'

'I don't know what you mean.'

'This isn't you, David. What was that you were whispering to me?'

'I don't know – I was telling you I loved you, that's what I was saying.'

'You said things you've never said to me before.'

'But I love you. I missed you – not seeing you for so long.'

'I know that, but it just isn't you, David, or else you think that I'm not me.'

'Who are you then?'

'I don't know who you think I am. Probably the girl you wanted to see that sweater on.'

'But that was for you.'

'David, were you really in England all that time?'

'Where else would I have been?' He got out of bed. Bare feet smacked against the floor. His passport was in his breast pocket. 'You can see for yourself. Official confirmation that I was there all the time.'

'Leave it, surely you don't think I want to check up on you.'

'Go on, look at the stamps.'

'No, I believe you. I'm sorry, David, I'm dreadful. But sometimes I feel that I'm already – well, that there's nothing about me now to make anyone still love me.'

Silence.

'Well, tell me, what is there about me?'

'You belong to me. You're my best girl.'

'You still believe that?'

I am so weary. Of those words, of love-making, of the lies, of the quarrels, of pretending, I am all alone as though in the middle of the ocean. I am alone because I shan't see her again even though she is in the same city as myself. 'Yes, I do.'

'That's nice of you, David, I missed you too.'

My wife is lying curled up in my arms, sleeping. That's just how the other one slept that last night on the seat of the car. That was in France but I'm not sure where. I don't know and I can't remember the names of the Départements, besides it makes no difference, it was about five hours' drive from the coast, we'd driven through a thunderstorm, a thunderstorm so bad that most cars vanished from the roads, but we drove on and when it was getting dark we turned into a minor road and drove along the shore of a lake, the steam was rising from the dark surface, as if the water was boiling, and then along a sandy track, the sand was sodden with water and yielded softly under the car's wheels and along both sides were parched shrubs. We stopped there and I had to move a lot of parcels from the back seat and the still unfinished carton of juice, and put it all on the sand under the car and then I folded down the seats and made two uncomfortable beds. Meanwhile it had become dark, there was still summer lightning in the distance, and a short way from us there must have been a railway line because a train thundered past, but otherwise there was absolute quiet. I could hear the raindrops drumming against the roof and the seagulls screeching in the air, and at that moment I realized that I could never return: return to my work or to my wife, I realized that my efforts to go abroad were in vain, that my life's meaning no longer lay in my going abroad and achieving something. The meaning of my life lay in holding her in my arms, in being able to listen to her breath and to be allowed to repeat to her: I love you. And because my life's real meaning, at least as I had always understood it, could not lie in anything of the sort, my life had no real meaning, just this instant of bliss torn from emptiness.

It was getting on for midnight, and although he was tired to the point of insensibility he had still not fallen asleep. He was waiting for the telephone to ring after all, to disturb his meaningless existence once more and to return to his life the quality of a pointlessness enclosed within itself.

2

The flat is full of clutter. Grocery cartons, suitcases and crates of books.

'For heaven's sake, why are you taking all those pots and pans?'

'You don't think we'll need them?'

'I've no idea but we aren't going there for the rest of our lives.'

'A year's like a lifetime – at least where pots and pans are concerned.'

'And all those clothes! And wouldn't two or three pairs of shoes be enough?'

'And suppose we want to go to the theatre? And in the winter the girls will want to go skating. And something for the rain. It'll rain a lot there, won't it?'

'All right, I won't say any more.'

'Shall I take the big teapot or the one that was grandmother's?'

'Whichever you like.'

'No need to snap, I'm only asking.'

'I couldn't care less about teapots. I don't give a damn about pots and pans, shoes or teapots!' I'll have a lot of pots and pans, shoes and shirts with me but nobody I really love. What am I going away for? To what purpose? I haven't even been able to finish my lectures. I've barely done one-third. I'll be wasting all my time over there writing them. The whole journey's pointless now. I'm going only because at one time I wanted to go. Because in my earlier life I'd said yes, I want to go.

She sat down amidst all the clutter and started crying. She's crying because I shouted at her. Because she doesn't want to go either, she's going because of me and I shout at her. She's going because of me and I don't want to go. 'Leave it for now, you're tired. Come to bed.'

Last night I dreamed that I was dialling her number from a telephone box. The box stood in the noisiest street, huge blue and white lorries were ceaselessly thundering past and I couldn't hear any voice at the other end. And then I dreamed a totally incomprehensible dream. I was a prison warder, I don't know when, whether during the war or now, I saw the camp quite clearly in my dream: a lot of wooden huts in the mountains, I had a uniform, riding boots and a dog. They brought me a prisoner whom I was to interrogate. He stood facing me and smiled, and then he spat in my face (I'd seen that scene in some film long ago), I began to beat him and he just laughed at me, and I beat him and he spat in my face, and I beat him and kicked him and then I let my dog loose on him and watched it sinking its teeth in his throat, and I hated him, I hated him so much in my dream that I don't understand where all that hatred comes from inside me. Who is it I want to kill in my subconscious? Her, myself, the one now sleeping by my side, or only my conscience? Or maybe the memory of her who mocks me?

That last night, when she was clinging to me on the uncomfortable bed made of the car seats, when we slept for a while and woke up again and made love and fell asleep again, while the soft drops of rain were falling on the roof and the seagulls were still screeching in the air, she suddenly whispered to me: You saw the lake? Come on, drive over to it. Drive into it!

You want to swim?

No, drive into it in the car. Let's drive together along the bottom of the lake.

You've gone mad!

No. I just want to drive with you along the bottom of the lake.

Then silence. I thought she was sleeping and maybe I had dozed off, the rain was soporific and then suddenly she whispered: Come on, darling, let's drive there. Come on, I want to drive there with you. We'll make love there before the water engulfs us.

You're crazy.

I want to go there.

Stop it!

It's also like a dream, that night in the car on a deserted track among the fields, between a railway line and an unknown lake under the rain. Silencing her with kisses. Restraining her with a shattered body. Between moans she whispers: I want to go there. I don't want to stay here. Drive on. Drive on darling!

So I got up in the middle of the night, barefoot, squelching in the soaked sand, and I flung the parcels back into the car and the by now sodden carton of fruit juice and tipped the seats up again and at that moment I noticed the dawn rising above the infinite sea of haze-covered fields.

The quiet of the night was suddenly torn by the telephone. A dreamily distant voice: 'Is that you? You haven't gone off yet?'

'Where are you calling from?'

'I'm at Tom's. But he isn't here, he's playing somewhere in Benešov again. He'll be there for at least a month. I just wanted to know if you'd left yet.'

'I haven't left yet, I'm coming over, my dear, I'll be with you in no time.'

3

'So you've come?'

'I'm with you, my dearest.'

'You haven't forgotten me yet? No, don't touch me, you're no longer here. We've said goodbye. I can't let anyone touch me who isn't here any more.'

'But I haven't left yet.'

'But you are leaving, you've practically gone. I've got used to your being away. You're practically a strange man. Doctor . . . except that I can never remember your name. Doctor Walrus. Guess who wrote me a letter, doctor? See, doctor: Igor. He's coming some time next week. You won't be here then any longer. You'll be a total stranger then.'

'Don't say that. I'll never be a stranger. And you'll never be a stranger to me.'

'Don't upset yourself, doctor.'

'I beg you.'

'Don't beg, doctor.'

Silence. I look at her. She's sitting there in a colourful, almost translucent, little dress from Carnaby Street, swinging her bare legs. It's not even a week since we last saw each other. Exactly six days. It was such a long time that I thought I couldn't survive it. I'm floating on a sea with no lighthouses in sight. Only a faint hope that there is a shore on the far side. That I am coming back and that you'll be here. That I'll come back after a year and you'll be here, even if you won't know me. I'm floating on an ocean and maybe I won't see you again. But this time I've come back. And I'm here with you.

'How are you getting on, doctor? Everything packed yet?'

'We're in the middle of packing. And don't call me that.'

'I forgot. You're a professor.'

'I beg you . . .'

'Don't beg, professor!'

She got to her feet. 'Care for some coffee, professor?'

'My dearest love,' he said. 'I've come because I couldn't bear being without you any longer. I'd have come even if you hadn't rung.'

'So you would have come even if I hadn't rung, professor? And how is your wife? Your fat and contented wife? Got her pots and pans together? And her grater? Tell her not to forget her grater.'

'Don't talk about her, why do you have to talk about her?'

'Surely she belongs to you. Or do you think she doesn't?

She belongs to you so much that you're taking her along with all those pots and pans and the grater. I can't stand her. I hate your wife and the way she can be packed into a suitcase like the bed-linen!'

'She isn't looking forward to it at all,' he said needlessly.

'And I hate you, the way you're packing up your family and your books and your grater. Do you think I don't know that you'll stay there?'

'But I . . . I promise you . . .'

'Keep your stupid promises. You're always promising and begging. Why have you come over at all? Why have you come to remind yourself? I'd stopped thinking of you.'

'But you phoned.'

'I wanted to know if you'd left. If you'd pushed off with that little family of yours.'

'My love, it's not my fault I have to leave. I'd much rather stay here with you. I'd like to be with you always, because I love you.' He tried to stroke her hair.

'Don't touch me.' She pushed his hand away. 'Silly talk, it's not your fault, and you'd like to be with me always because you love me. You love me so much you're hurrying to catch your train. Give over! I don't give a damn for your silly talk about loving me and coming back. Turn around! Turn around at once!'

He turned around and heard the quick grating of a zip and the rustle of underwear.

She was lying there, the blanket pulled up to her chin. 'Well, come along then,' she said, 'what are you waiting for? What have you come here for? In a little while you'll have to go back to your stupid fat wife and you're sitting here holding forth about how you love me.'

'Don't go away, darling, my Walrus, stay with me a little longer, I want you with me, I just had to phone you today. While you're still here. Stay with me. Who am I going to ring now when I'm lonely at night? Who's going to drop orchids through my letter box? Who's going to drive me around at night? Do you know when I began to love you? That first night in the car, when you were sitting next to me, puffing like a seal and not kissing me. Anyone else would have tried to kiss me but you were afraid. Drive me somewhere. I'd like to go for a drive with you tomorrow and eat out. You've always fed me and said such nice things to me.'

'But my love, I'll be coming back to you.'

'I don't want you to come back. I want you to stay with me. I want you to stay here with me always. Oh darling, hold me closer. Now I can feel you holding me. I want you always to hold me like this. When I'm with you I know I'm safe. I know you love me, I'm at ease with you. You do nothing but buy nice things for me and I love you for that, I'll be yours for that, I'll stay with you, I'll make love to you, we'll make love together till we go crazy. You'll be coming to me at night or else I'll be going to you whenever you want me to, because I love you, I'll come whenever you call me. Stay here, don't go away, darling, stay with me, don't leave me alone here, you know I belong to you, I've never belonged to anybody the way I belong to you. That's why I rang you, I rang you myself, even though we'd said goodbye to each other.'

'Very well, But what will happen if I stay here, how are we going to live? Surely we can't go on living as we have done in the past?'

'I don't know. I don't know anything. I just want you to stay. To be nice to me. I need you to be nice to me.'

The light of dawn is creeping through the window. I lack the strength to depart and I know I cannot stay. Whatever I do will be wrong.

'Oh darling, you're staying, you'll stay here, I know it, I can feel it, come closer, I want you, I'm yours, it's driving me crazy the way I'm happy with you, I'm entirely yours, I've never been yours as much as now.'

And once more I experience the bliss to which I have sacrificed everything, to which I am sacrificing everything, I love her, I love you, my dearest, I'll stay with you.

5

Camilla is sitting in the kitchen, drinking tea out of an enamel mug (the china is all packed in crates). Her eyes are bloodshot and she is pale. God knows how long she has been up.

'David, you were out all night.'

It's half past six in the morning, it's useless to pretend.

'She phoned me during the night.'

'She?'

'She was feeling sick and she rang me. She's here alone. I took her to hospital.'

'Why should she ring you in particular?'

'She doesn't know anyone else with a car.'

'What hospital did you take her to?'

She doesn't know her name anyway. 'The Bulovka.'

'And why didn't you wake me?'

'I didn't want to wake you, I thought I'd get back before morning.'

'In which case you wouldn't even have told me you'd driven her there.'

'Why shouldn't I have told you? I'd have told you in the morning, but I didn't want to wake you.'

'And what was the matter with her?'

'I don't know yet. Perhaps her appendix. They'll have to examine her.'

'They've kept her in?'

'Yes.'

'Which department?'

He became alert. 'Surgical, I suppose. Yes, I think it was Surgical.'

'You don't even know which department you took her to?'

'It was Surgical,' he said.

'Which ward?'

'That I don't remember,' he said wearily. 'I don't remember the number.'

She went to the telephone. 'But it was Surgical?' she asked.

'What are you trying to do? You don't even know her name!'

'That doesn't matter,' she said; 'I don't expect they have a lot of girls brought in at night with appendicitis. Anyway, you'll tell me her name; surely you'll want to know how she is doing?' She turned over the pages of the directory and then dialled a number. 'Surgical, please.'

Quite possibly they did have a girl brought in at night with appendicitis. It's a big hospital. But there wasn't any point in it anyway.

'Put it down. I didn't take her there. I was at her place.'

She hung up. 'So you lied to me.'

He said nothing.

'I know you've been lying to me,' she said. 'I could feel it. You had an affair with her! You had an affair with her all this time!'

'I had an affair with her.'

'You're in love with her.'

'Yes, if you must know. I can't explain how it happened.'

'And you didn't have enough decency or courage . . .' Her voice gave out.

'I thought it would blow over. That once we'd left I'd be cured of it. I didn't want to torment you.'

'You think you didn't torment me?'

'I know I did, but I didn't want it to be worse than it had to be.'

'Than it had to be?' she repeated in amazement. 'And what happens now? Do you think I'll come with you to a foreign country when you're not in love with me any more?'

'I'm not going.'

'You're not? And you let me pack everything.'

'I changed my mind during the night.'

'When you were with her?'

'Yes. I can't leave her here alone.'

'And what about your work? I'd always thought your work came before anything else. Or at least before all of us.'

'I've probably changed.'

'She's changed you,' she corrected him. 'That whore's changed you.'

'Don't talk about her like that.'

'She is a whore,' she declared savagely. 'Chasing after a married man with two children. Don't try to tell me she didn't want anything out of it!'

'What's the use?'

'So what are you going to do now? Are you going to move in with her when you can't leave her alone?'

'But she's got a husband.'

'So where does that leave you? Or do you expect me to look after you while you're having an affair with her?'

'No. I don't expect anything. I don't want to leave you. Give me at least a little time to think things over.'

'But I don't want you,' she said fiercely. 'I don't want you here.'

And everything has started to slip, everything is collapsing, everything is vanishing: my children, my wife, too late to hang on to them. That's what I have done. What have I done? And why?

'I'll try to keep out of your sight as best I can.'

'My God,' she sobbed, 'what a bastard you are! A cynical one, too. What has that whore made of you? And all those cases ready packed. All that wasted effort.'

'You know perfectly well that I have nowhere to go.'

'You can go to your father. He's on his own anyway.'

'And what do we tell the girls?'

'You should have thought of that before. All I know is that I don't want you here.'

Sobs. At last she got to her feet. By the sideboard stood an open packing case, all ready for transporting the crockery. The day before she had laboriously wrapped every single plate and every single cup in newspaper and then placed them into wood shavings. Now she took the first plate (it was a wine-red plate with a broad gilt border, one from a set she'd had as a wedding present), shook it free of the paper and then smashed it on the floor. The fragments flew in all directions.

He looked into her face, into that familiar face, and it hurt him to see her despair, the weakness which made her turn against inanimate objects instead of against him, he felt regret over what he had done, at causing her such a humiliating and possibly enduring pain. 'Stop it,' he shouted at her as she prepared to smash another plate. 'You'll wake the children.'

6

It was only half past five. He parked his car outside the department: might just look in even though I have nothing to do there (my lectures for this year are cancelled, after all

I've left for England), maybe I'll find someone I know, although I have no real friends here, I never had time to make any, and now I have more time than I know what to do with.

He walked round the building but he didn't go in; at half past five he wouldn't find anyone there anyway. At a small supermarket on the corner he bought a couple of rolls, some processed cheese and a jar of apricots in syrup in case he managed to find her after all.

She had disappeared. Probably gone away without letting him know, before he was able to tell her that he'd decided to stay.

He got back into the car. I could stop off at Father's but it isn't really the place for me. The city was full of long-haired girls. He kept seeing her everywhere. My love, he called out to her, at last I've found you. I've been looking for you these past three days.

You're still here? You haven't left yet?

I wasn't due to leave till tomorrow. But I'm not going.

You're not going? So what will you do?

I'll stay here. I can't live without you.

You don't want to live without me?

The thought of that year seemed like death. Like darkness without end.

So you're staying for me, you're giving up everything for me.

I sent them a telegram. I spent half a day concocting a letter, making a kind of apology. I invented a disease and a tragedy in the family. But even so I lost face.

Never mind, I'll love you without a face. I'll make you a new face.

It wasn't easy for me. All my life I'd been hoping for something like this, to be able to work under such conditions and with such people. But I wouldn't have been able to do any work if I couldn't see you.

So why didn't you take me with you?

You would have gone with me? But you've got your husband here.

But over there, silly, I'd have you instead!

Good heavens, I never thought of that.

He stopped outside her block. In the letter-box with the white horse he saw the envelope he'd dropped in two days before. ('Get in touch. Phone me or write, I've got to talk to you.')

She'd gone away. Why shouldn't she have gone away? We'd said goodbye. As far as she knows I've gone abroad. She knows I've left her. But I haven't left her, I've stayed here – I'm the one who's been left. I've got no one but her.

Why shouldn't she come with me? During the day she could walk around the shops or sit in some wine bar or sleep, she'd enjoy that, that would be enough for her, such a life, and I'd be earning enough for her to buy anything she fancied. Maybe she'll ring tonight. But there's a lot of time till midnight. I'll drive over and have a look at the other flat. If she came with me that year might still be saved. But she won't come with me, she's got her husband here and her classes, and she'd get bored over there after a couple of weeks. She'd come back again and I'd be left there alone. But what am I going to do here? My post at the institute's been filled for a year. I haven't got my work any more, nor my family, I haven't got anything or anybody.

So in fact you're unemployed! You're unemployed because of me. At least you'll be able to drive me around a lot. We'll be going on outings all the time. Soon it will be September. September starts tomorrow. I love September, it's a beautiful month.

He stopped by the little park, opposite the house with the bakery. The aroma of warm bread hung on the air but the window of the little flat was shut (in this heat she would surely keep it open), and on the window ledge inside stood a vase with a wilted bunch of carnations (who put it there, who brought her those flowers and when?).

He entered the building, rang her bell and waited, he rang again, then he put his ear to the door and clearly caught the sound of water quietly dripping.

He had nowhere to go, he could stop here, sit in the car and wait; this was as good a place as any, but he was too restless, he was unable to persevere in a state of inactivity or to concentrate on any meaningful activity.

A short distance away was that cemetery. The gate was open, they probably didn't lock it even at night. The grave was already overgrown with grass, the headstone was obviously of the cheapest kind. If I hadn't come here that afternoon (is it possible that it happened this spring?), if I'd told a small lie to Camilla then, told her I'd been here, how many lies I might have spared her, and tomorrow I'd be leaving, tomorrow I'd be landing in London, all my life I'd been hoping to do just that, I'd be taking Camilla and the children, I'd be living a different life. Is it possible that a single moment so determined my fate or has it always been within me, the need to opt out of the obvious road of my own life, a longing to sweep away my tranquillity, to live through an experience even if it were to destroy me?

Oh yes, they could still leave, perhaps they could still leave: he found an inflatable mattress in the wardrobe, blew it up and spread some blankets on it. Then he took the telephone off its shelf and put it next to his mattress.

He lay motionless on this not too comfortable bed, waiting for a call that did not come.

7

Women were coming out of the baker's (only half past five on day three of his stay in England) and the ground-floor window was open. He went rigid. Of course it could be just her husband or the fellow who owned the flat, but he was unable to control his impatience. He leaped out of the car, only five steps up luckily, not even enough to make him puffed.

She was wearing only a slip. 'It's you? I thought you'd left long ago. Hang on, I'll get dressed.'

The single room was full of cigarette smoke and on the little table stood two empty wine glasses.

'Have you got your husband here?'

'No, Igor was here. Stopped for half a day. He's off to Italy to make a film. I'd like to go with him, you've no idea how gladly I'd go with him!' She was standing by the open wardrobe. 'I'll take this dress, the one you bought for me. The one from England.'

She went to the bathroom but she left the door open.

'Where were you all this time?' he asked.

'In Benešov or whatever the place is. From time to time I've got to join Tom, seeing that he's my husband.'

She came back, wearing the colourful rags from Carnaby Street. 'Would you like some wine? Igor brought me such a big bottle.' From the cupboard she produced a demijohn sitting in a raffia base. 'Except you probably won't want to drink if you've got the car here.' She poured some for herself. 'I went off to see him because he was blubbing into the telephone about how frightfully bored he was. If he was any good and drank less he could have a little car too and could come and collect me. It's no distance really. Except he hasn't even got the bus fare.'

He looked at her and said nothing. She was beautiful and cold and a stranger. She displayed not a trace of pleasure at seeing him.

'It's a frightfully boring place, Benešov,' she continued, 'and sitting all day long in that dump. Our window gave on to the town square, but there's nothing in the square, only buses. I didn't get up till midday but even so I couldn't stand it. I'd have come back the following day but I said to myself if I left he'd only pick up some girl, what else can you do in a dump like that? Why are you still here?'

'I stayed here, I didn't go.'

'You didn't go? They wouldn't let you leave?'

'No, they would have let me leave all right.' Suddenly, as he was about to utter the real reason, he hesitated. 'Surely you wanted me to stay here?'

'I wanted you to stay here? Wait a minute, what are you saying?'

'You didn't want me to leave,' he said with growing horror, 'you wanted me to stay with you. That last night we were together you said you wanted me to come and see you or else you'd come and see me – if only I didn't leave.'

'I said that? That I'd come to see you?'

'You don't remember?'

'I probably did say it if you remember it. I probably felt like that, one says that sort of thing.'

'Are you saying you didn't mean it?'

'But surely you didn't stay because of that! When they were giving you a post and a pile of money and when heaps of kids were waiting for your lectures?'

He was silent.

'So why did you stay here? You're not going to tell me that you threw all that away so you could come and make love to me.'

'I thought you loved me.'

'Love, love . . . Did you really think I would love you all my life? That I'd love you because you sacrificed yourself for me and remained here?'

'I did it for my own sake. I love you.'

'You're unbearably devoted. I loved you because I knew that you were leaving, that it was all coming to an end.'

246

He said nothing. She was a total stranger, so distant that he couldn't overcome the distance.

'You think you'll be coming to see me all your life? That I'm going to turn my back on everyone else because of you? You expect me to become your second faithful wife?'

'I don't think anything. I don't expect anything.'

'You're a fool. I can't stand you. Why didn't you leave? You'd have forgotten me, we'd have forgotten each other.'

'I couldn't forget you.'

'That's what one says. And what do you think will happen now? Why didn't you leave when all the time you've been telling me fairy tales about you leaving along with that family of yours?'

'I should have left. I wanted to leave, but . . .'

'You're a fool,' she interrupted him. 'Christ, I can't stand you. I hate you!'

He looked at her cold, perfectly made-up face, into her stony eyes, and he found in them not one trace of joy or even understanding. *If she knew that I abandoned not only that trip but my entire life, that I've left everything behind me . . . The worst of it is that I love her, that I still love her, that I want her, God, how I long for her. At least once I'd like to be with her again, she's different when we're together, she forgets the outside world, she's mine, at least one night, at least today, so that what I have done shouldn't be so totally meaningless.* He bent down to her but she pushed him away. 'What's this?' she asked angrily. 'Sit down again. Listen, Walrus, I'll tell you something. It is nice of you to have decided to stay here, that you loved me so much. But it's idiotic, do you understand? Now you run on home again, pack your cases and be off with you. You've got your passport, haven't you? Yes, I know it says in your passport that you can travel. So get packed and go!'

'Too late,' he said.

247

'Then just go home and embrace your dear little wife, take your little girls to the cinema, do something – I don't want you here.'

'All right, I'm off.' He tried to embrace her but again she pushed him away.

'I know what you want. You want to say goodbye. But I've said goodbye to you already. I can't any more. You were nice to me. So be nice now and go. And don't come back.'

'As you wish. If that's your wish you won't see me again.'

'Yes, if it's my wish I won't see you again. And if it's my wish then I shall see you again. You'll do anything I wish. You're so nice you're unbearable. I'm afraid of your love. I get worried by your idiotic devoted love.'

'All right. I won't come again, even if you want me to. I'll never come again. I had a feeling it was pointless but I still thought I had to stay here.'

'You didn't have any feeling and you didn't think anything,' she shouted at him. 'You wanted to make love to me. And you'll come whenever I want you to, you'll always come when I call you.'

'No, I shan't come again. Not now!'

'You'll come because you love me. But I shan't call you because to me you're no longer here. You've gone already. For me you're over there. If you like I'll write you a letter. Even though I hate writing letters. What are you waiting for? Go now, go!' She stepped up to him, placed her hands on his shoulders, stood on tiptoe, kissed him on his forehead and said softly: 'If you love me, go now. Go, I'm asking you to go!'

8

He was lying on the inflatable mattress (Oh, Dad, you slept on this little mattress? I'd like to sleep on it with you), in complete and black emptiness, he was no longer waiting for a midnight call, he wasn't waiting for anything, he didn't even have to spend the night here.

*Oh darling, you say such nice things to me. You do such nice things for me. You're so nice. Nobody's ever been so nice to me. I love you. I love you today.*

Why was she so afraid of his love for her when she always wanted him to love her? She was incapable of bearing the weight of real love. She was able to flit from one person to another, a superficial creature who was bored and deceived herself into grand emotions.

*Oh darling, hold me. Today I feel how you're holding me. I want you to hold me like this always. I know you love me. I'm at ease with you, you do nice things for me and I love you for them, I'll belong to you for them, I'll make love with you, we'll make love together till we go crazy.*

No, that isn't right: she loved me as completely as I loved her. She was sick with a longing for love because in her life she'd only rarely experienced it. No one had ever really loved her, including that boy she married. So why did she reject me?

Because we can't live together. I realize that as well as she does. She is right. We can't live together. We could have carried on as in the past, but could we have really done it? I've lost my family – I'm a different person now. I would be hers exclusively and would want her to be mine exclusively. But she can't belong to anyone exclusively. I couldn't live with her. I couldn't bear it. But can I bear to live without her? And he felt a pain rising in his throat, if he were a woman he'd cry. Yes, I'd cry like you cried in that little hotel in Germany, the night we spent in that little hotel in Germany, I'd cry because I am alone and lonely.

Why did I give up so easily? Why did I let myself be

chased away like a little boy? Why did I promise to go away, to go away for good? Because she was right. But does it matter whether she was right or not when I'm longing for her?

It was half an hour after midnight. There was a time when he would go to bed at just that hour. He'd wash, slip in by Camilla's side and instantly fall asleep.

The rubber mattress was uncomfortable and his head was touching the cooker. I'll think of her just as if nothing had happened, as if we were still having an affair. I'll try to get back my post at the institute, I'll be a normal person again. You'll ring and I'll come. Even in the middle of the night. I'll come to you, I'll take you in my arms, my dearest, so you won't be lonely.

No, none of this will happen. I'll do nothing but work. I haven't lost that much time. I can still manage to do what I want to do. You don't even know what I do. But everyone else does, the whole world does and acknowledges it. I am sitting in the Great Hall of the Stockholm Academy and I am thinking of you. I get on a plane, I escape from the newspapermen, I'm coming to you. It is night, of course, it is raining. A chimney sweep is climbing up a ladder. This is me. I got a prize! Do you know about it?

Oh darling, you're a chimney sweep. We'll have good luck.

Suddenly the telephone burst into frightening ringing a few inches away. Half asleep he groped for the receiver in the dark.

'Is that you?' He recognized her voice. It's her. She's ringing me. He held the receiver in trembling fingers and said nothing.

'I'm feeling sad,' he heard her voice saying, 'I've got the radio on but . . .'

He gently pushed her away, he detached her from himself. As if it were infinitely heavy, he held the receiver over its rest for a moment, then dropped it. He was shaking all over.

The telephone rang again. In a moment it would wake Camilla or the children. Although this didn't matter now. But I can't talk to her. I can't drive out to her. There's no sense in it. He ripped the cord out of the wall.

Silence engulfed him. Let her ring, let her call out for me for a change. There's no point in our talking, she knows that herself, she knows it as well as I do. She just wants to torture me. Maybe she'll begin to love me when she sees I don't want her any more.

But no, this isn't a game, and you can't start it all over again whenever you feel like it. I don't want to restart it. He remained lying where he was, even though he was longing to be with her. He was lying there, even though in his mind he was tapping at her window.

You saw that lake, didn't you? Drive into it. Drive into it in the car. We'll drive along the bottom of the lake together. I want to drive along the bottom of the lake with you.

You're crying? Why are you crying? Be sensible. We've got to get back home.

I'm feeling so sad. Nobody loves me. Nobody ever loved me. I don't want to be alone. I don't want to remain so alone.

We are driving over the dam, the mists are rising over the surface of the water.

Stop!

No, we're off now.

Stop! I want you to stop. I don't want to drive any further. I don't want to go back home. I want to stay here!

But I must get back. We can't stay here. Be sensible.

I don't want to be sensible. I don't have to get back.

You've got to get back too. You've got your home there. You've got your husband there.

You're telling me this?

I'm sorry.

You're disgusting, oh how all of you are disgusting. Let me get out and you can drive on.

No, we're going together. I'll let your seat-back down, my dearest, and you can go to sleep.

I don't want to drive on. I've nowhere to go. Let me go, you brute! You bully! Let me go!

You're crying. Why are you crying? You're not alone now, I am with you.

Suddenly, while they were travelling at speed, she opened the door and with one single jump, a magnificent swimmer's dive, she rose up into the mists which were billowing around them and all he heard was a splash and through a tear in the mist he saw her sinking into the translucent, glass-like transparent water, sinking towards the bottom amidst jellyfish, sea horses, dazzling red coral and winking fireflies, a stream of rainbow-coloured bubbles rising from her mouth as she sank ever faster to an as yet invisible bottom.

He awoke, filled with a sense of unease. It was not even two o'clock. He'd only slept for a short time.

Hurriedly he put on his clothes.

In the distance he could see that the light was still on in her window, the blue lampshade behind the yellow blind. He felt a sense of relief, he'd yielded to the mood of a dream, he'd raced over here needlessly, he could have simply phoned. He stopped under the window and wondered if he should tap on the pane.

From inside came the muted sound of music, this wasn't at all a proper time for visits, but nevertheless he stood on tiptoe and knocked on the glass.

The music stopped, he heard a male voice announcing something or other in English or German, he couldn't make out which. He knocked again, all was quiet inside, maybe she'd fallen asleep, with the light and the music on, that wasn't anything unusual, or else she was offended, hardly surprising, and wouldn't open the window for him seeing he'd hung up on her in mid-sentence.

He stepped back from the window and tried the front door handle. The door was open, five steps up, a dark musty corridor, he stopped at her door and rang the bell.

I don't care.

What don't you care about?

Whether I live or die. I'm not afraid of death.

He rang again.

Drive faster, darling.

I can't drive when you're kissing my eyes. Have you gone crazy? We'll be killed.

I don't care. You saw that lake, didn't you? Drive into it. We'll drive along the bottom of the lake together. I don't want to go on. Let me go! You brute! You bully!

This is nonsense, he said to himself. One says that kind of thing. She didn't have the slightest reason. After all, she drove me away. She wanted me to go away. I wanted to stay with her.

He rang, now almost continuously.

But it didn't matter who had driven whom away, what mattered was that the thing was at an end.

Someone on the landing opened a door. 'What's going on?' yelled a sleepy voice. 'Have you gone mad? Want me to call the police?'

He was again standing outside the house. She's sulking. She's laughing at me while I'm making a scene. This is exactly her style, after all she's an actress, there's no reason why I should raise the alarm.

I can't just tell people that I had a dream in which I saw her drowning, but neither can I just walk away. Suppose she's swallowed some tablets and every minute counts?

I'm sure she hasn't swallowed any tablets, I never saw a single bottle of tablets at her place. And why should she do it, anyway? She had no reason. If anything, I'd have the reason.

Suddenly a memory floated up. He was standing at a door, ringing the bell, while a key was in the lock inside.

Maybe she's got somebody with her and that's why she doesn't want to let me in.

Except that she probably wouldn't mind at all and would calmly let me in to demonstrate to me how quickly she could find a replacement. She might also have gone out and left the light and the radio switched on, especially if she was upset. But if she was upset she might also do herself some harm. Why should she, though, surely I wasn't worth it to her. Was I really not worth it to her? I don't know, I just don't know, I didn't understand her.

He stood helplessly in front of the house. He might try and break the window, but what grounds did he have for that? And at that moment he remembered that third person whom he'd never thought of, whom subconsciously he'd never taken into account. She'd said: in Benešov. Now, at night, I can do that distance in no time at all, in ninety minutes I'll be back here with a key.

He tore down the empty highway. I'm out of my mind. Maybe she's got somebody there after all, and here I am bringing her husband home to her. A rejected and jealous lover bringing back a totally unjealous husband. And perhaps she isn't in at all, and then I'll look even more foolish. Or she's lying there, having done something to herself, and in that case I should have broken the window instead of wasting time on this journey.

She's not lying there, she hasn't done anything to herself, she had no reason. And suppose I drove her to it? I wrecked her world just as much as she wrecked mine. In her world there was room for a lot of words and feelings which were not to be taken too seriously. Suppose I destroyed her by taking for real what shouldn't have been taken for real?

But was I all that real? Surely I disclaimed her all that time.

I was good to her and at times maybe even generous – I felt that I'd bind her to me that way. I tried to win her, to buy her and her love with lunches and dinners and wine and shoes, with clothes, lipsticks and powder and crazy driving and my complaisance. I bought her by being good to her because that was the only way I had of winning her. And because I wanted her more and more I stepped up my kindness to the point of self-sacrifice and sometimes I had the ennobling feeling that I was really being self-sacrificing and unselfish. And all the time I continued lying, denying her, because I didn't want to admit her into my life permanently, I wanted to make love to her but not to live with her.

She must have realized it; at that little hotel in Germany, she started to cry in the middle of the night, she realized that I didn't love her, that I only wanted her like all the others, and that my words and deeds were just a way of getting her.

And subsequently she couldn't believe that I'd decided to stay here because of her, she must have thought that I was merely trying to drag her to the shore of another lake, where I would once more leave her. So maybe it really was more than she was able to bear. And a cold anxiety settled on his forehead and he could no longer dispel it.

9

He was on his way back to Prague as fast as his engine would make it. The young man by his side was dozing. When he'd tracked him down at his hotel (in his excitement he'd been unable to recall his name and then, when he'd finally got to his room, it had taken some time to wake him up) the man had been unable to grasp what he actually wanted from him. He'd been drinking all evening (as indeed he did any other evening) and he hadn't quite shaken off his stupor. In the end he'd let himself be put in the car, where he'd fallen asleep again.

Now he opened his eyes and said, 'So you're David. Iva talks about you sometimes. She said you'd been good to her. That's very nice of you. She needs that, she's like a small child and she needs people to be good to her. If she were any different,' he continued with a suddenly awakened communicativeness, as if he'd frequently reflected on this subject lately, 'I'd probably be annoyed that she accepts those pretty things from you. But she's like a child and I know that if she accepts them from you it doesn't mean anything.'

'Quite so,' he said quickly. 'Have you known one another long?'

'Seven years. She's always had more friends among the boys but I know I can trust her. If ever she tries to tell me a lie I see it in her eyes at once.'

'Yes,' he said, taken aback, 'she really is like a child.'

'Sometimes we don't see each other for maybe as much as a month, I'm away on tour and in the summer she sometimes goes abroad. This year we wanted to bum around Bohemia but then she got an invitation from some girl friend in England, so she went there. She loves foreign parts. I don't know if I got you right but if you think she's done something to herself, and if you think so merely because she first rang you and then she didn't open the door for you, then you've alarmed yourself needlessly, she's simply asleep.' He closed his eyes again. 'I'm sure you've gone to this trouble needlessly, she wouldn't do anything to herself. I've known her since she was a little girl and every time we quarrelled or I refused to do just what she wanted she'd threaten to do something to herself but she never actually did. Except once,' he remembered, 'she tried to cut herself then, maybe you've noticed it on her wrist, but then someone really did her wrong. Some swine did her wrong. But now, what reason would she have? She's asleep, you'll see. You've no idea how soundly she sleeps.'

'Yes,' and he drove round the cemetery and his head-lights picked out the tops of the trees in the little park, and he pulled up in front of the baker's. In the window the lamp with the blue shade was still on.

'It's terribly decent of you to have gone to all this trouble in the middle of the night,' the young man was evidently expecting him to drive off now because, after all, what business could he have now that he, her husband, was back?

'I'd like to go up with you, just to reassure myself that nothing . . .' he quickly suggested. 'I'll wait outside your flat if you like.'

'But of course – after all she phoned you.' For a while he fumbled in his pocket and then for a long time, an incredibly long time, he tried to insert the key in the lock. At last the door opened, the young man stepped in first and David followed him into the hall.

He had some familiarity with the stuffy smell of that room (the smell of the leather drumskins, of dust and of unaired walls), but his nose registered yet another barely perceptible, but to him very familiar, smell, and he froze with horror.

There was a yell from the room, he was already in the doorway, and first of all he caught sight of the young man, his back against the wardrobe, his face as white as a sheet, and only then did he see her. She was lying on the couch (the couch they had made love on together, where they

had made love to the point of madness and unconscious-
ness) in the same little dress she'd put on in his presence
that afternoon, she was lying there motionless – sound and
dreamlessly asleep with her eyes perfectly made up.
Mascara outlining her eyes (they'd bought a tube of that
black mascara together in Carnaby Street), her eyebrows
meticulously drawn and coloured, and her eyes wide
open, and only then he glanced at the floor to see what his
nostrils had already informed him of, a large, unevenly
spread dark patch which hadn't dried yet, which hadn't
yet soaked entirely into the well-worn carpet.

'My little owl, my little owl!' the young man was screaming, 'what have you done, what have you done to me!'
Then he turned to him. 'Surely you're a doctor or something of the kind, she said you were a doctor!'

So he stepped around the puddle of blood and even
though he knew that it was in vain he touched her white
and unexpectedly naked forehead with his palm.

Her left hand, he now noticed, dangled lifelessly over
the edge of the couch and was hideously marked by a long,
almost black gash. On the blood-spattered chair lay a razor.

He stepped back from her again.

Her grey-blue eyes, her slate-coloured eyes seemed to be
gazing up at him without, even now, demanding anything. Her mouth was distorted into a painful grimace and
her nose projected from her suddenly sunken face. He
gazed at her, his glance clung to that face and slowly he
recognized her, the high white forehead, the eyes, the
whole face – now that she had become rigid in death he
suddenly recognized the features, the likeness. As though
his mother was lying before him, dead for a second time.

'Don't just stand there!' (How long had the young man
been shouting at him?) 'Isn't there anything you can do?'

At last he pulled himself together. And so he bent over
her and again closed her eyes.

## 10

The police had left, the doctor had come and gone, the corpse was covered with a dirty sheet. Perhaps he should do something about the young man who was sitting on a chair, sobbing, but what could he do after what he'd just done and (so far still secretly) caused?

He passed through the small crowd that had collected outside the house; immediately behind his car stood a yellow baker's van from which bread was being unloaded. He didn't really want to leave, it seemed to him that he couldn't leave, that he still had to do something, to confess, even though there wasn't anything to confess to. He went across to the little park which was deserted at this early hour. On the grass hung the first threads of gossamer. A beautiful warm sunny autumn day was dawning, a day virtually made for the two of them to drive out of the city, to beetle down the road through the Vltava valley between yellow hillsides and reddish rocks.

He sank down on a bench, his energy exhausted. If only he could sleep now, soundly and dreamlessly, distance himself from his own life and know that he would never have to return to it.

And suddenly he saw her, walking on the shore in the dazzling light, this wasn't the lake shore but the shore at Dover, that final day when they were walking down to the ship together and she laughed because they suddenly got splashed by a wave: my Walrus, now I love you, you're a real wet walrus, she was walking up towards him, running up to him: beautiful, desirable, loved, the only creature he'd ever loved passionately, the only one he believed he really loved as much as he was able to, the only way he knew how to, their final day together, he might have still kept her back, and just then he saw a magnificent and horrific wave – like a painted wave – rushing up from the sea, and he screamed in terror, but she didn't hear him, she couldn't hear him, she was running, unsuspecting, towards him because she still loved him, at that moment she still loved him and wanted to be with him, and he realized that he must either run towards her and perish together with her, or he must turn aside, throw himself immediately towards the rocks, and that was what he did and with a few frantic leaps he got up on a rocky cliff and just then he heard the thundering roar of the wave, and when he turned his head she was gone, there was only the deserted shore, the sand, the bare shingle. A black hearse now pulled up by the baker's and three men in black got out, three ravens, they opened the door of the vehicle, pulled out a coffin and then with the coffin climbed the five steps of the house.

He got up from the bench and placed himself immediately under her window, which was now open, and from inside he clearly heard a heavy object being pushed and a strange unconcerned voice said, 'Get hold of her lower end.'

For a moment he found himself in his white-tiled world, filled with the dying bodies of dogs and unconscious mice, whose stomach cavities he'd open with sterile scissors, in the world of structural formulae, torsion balances and centrifuges, in a world where blood was separated from bodies and bodies separated from life and from death, in a world that had its own language, where different laws and different logic applied, and which permitted him to extend his hands against death itself. But death had struck at him, it had come to him out of that real, separate world, where there was still uncomprehended and unquantified life, love-making, jealousy and sorrow, where unexpected and desperate hopelessness might still occur, it had come to him to remind him that this other, real, illogical, passionately irrational and irrationally passionate world continued to exist and refused to let itself be squeezed into that world of his, casting doubt on all his endeavours.

From inside came the heavy sound of the wooden lid being closed, then he heard footsteps approaching, as if making straight for him, as if marching directly towards him. He was frightened, he tore himself away from the wall and fled to his car.

If only he had just one place to go. One thing to do. And it occurred to him that he must get some flowers or perhaps a wreath. I'll have a wreath made for her of roses – that is if roses can be made into a wreath.

He drove to the florist, to his now regular florist, and as he caught sight of the familiar, plain bespectacled face (her hair had grown a little longer) behind the counter he felt a sense of relief.

'Can I order a wreath from you?'

'A wreath?' she seemed surprised. 'Oh yes, we'll have one made for you. When is it to be for?'

He didn't really know when the funeral would be, if indeed he would discover its time and date at all.

'Within three days.'

'That's fine.' She produced a note-pad from a drawer. 'I'll write out the order for you.'

'I would like roses.'

'That's fine, I'll make the order out for roses. What text would you like?'

Oh yes, a text, he realized, since I'm ordering a wreath, a real wreath for a real funeral, and a wreath must have a ribbon with a text: REST IN PEACE or I WILL NEVER FORGET! or FORGIVE ME, I KNEW NOT WHAT I DID. And suddenly he felt that it was an unnecessary and improper gesture to send a wreath with a ribbon or even without a ribbon. What right had he even now to remind her of him?

'I'm sorry, perhaps I'd better think it over a little,

perhaps I'll take ordinary flowers instead. I'll just take a bunch of roses.' And he pointed to the vase with roses.

'Again the whole lot?' she asked and he was pleased that she remembered him.

'Yes please.'

She took the roses from the vase, a big bunch of yellow and white and deep red roses.

'But you said in three days' time,' she reminded him. 'I could have fresh ones sent to you.'

'Yes, you're right.' Suddenly he remembered something. An unrealized idea of long ago. 'But wrap these up for me anyway.'

He watched her making up the bouquet. He hoped nobody would come in, what would he do with such a huge bunch of roses?

He took them from her, paid for them, and handed the flowers back to her. 'These are for you.' He looked at her plain, slightly spotted face with her rather red snub nose.

She blushed and shook her head. 'I can't accept this from you.'

'But you can.'

She hesitated for a moment. 'You've lost someone?' she asked quietly. 'Someone you were fond of?' She took the bouquet from him and put it down on the counter. She glanced towards the door and quickly emerged from behind the counter. She was short, now that she was standing just in front of him. She raised herself on tiptoe, with a movement he was familiar with, and quickly kissed him on the forehead.

And at that moment, as her lips touched him, he felt a single gigantic rock of pain detaching itself within him, another instant and it would start slipping and bury him underneath: to return, to return, but to where and to whom, somewhere into childhood, to his mother who didn't even love him and to beg her: stay with me just a

262

little longer, to beg for a single caress, and he felt himself shaken apart by a feverish spasm of grief, he felt long-forgotten tears rising up in him and he turned and walked out of the shop as fast as he could, even though he had nowhere to go.

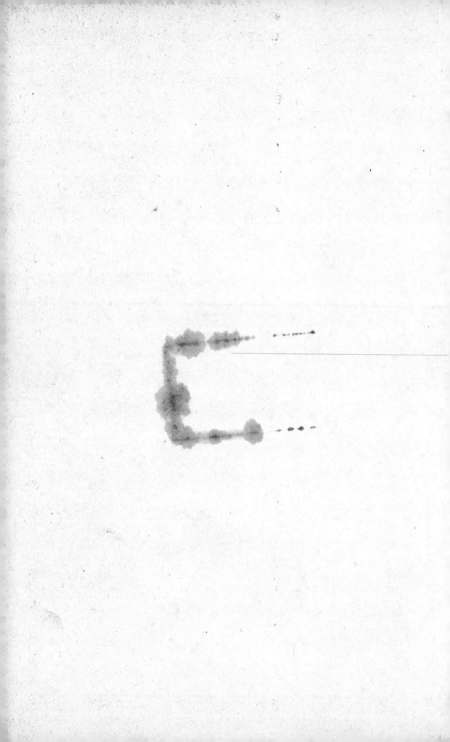